The Last Judgement

STEVEN VEERAPEN

CONTENTS

THE LAST JUDGEMENT

PROLOGUE

Rome, 1572

The pope was dead. So, as far as Marcello Agosti was concerned, was God. Religion, unfortunately, was not. He stared down at the sketched maps and diagrams strewn across the table in front of him and then glanced at his own right hand. The fingers were bent, curled inwards, all grace lost. Hideous, he thought, cruel. The left was a little better, but not by much. He tilted his head back and closed his eyes, inhaling the scent of good wine and the slow drift of smoke from dozens of candles. It was pleasant. One sense ravaged, the other at its peak.

'These will do,' said his companion.

'Yes,' said Agosti, opening his eyes. The word came out tightly. He knew he could have done better had his hands not begun to decay. Silence fell between them awhile. Eventually, a soft knock came from somewhere towards the rear of the house. They exchanged glances before his friend stood and left the room. Agosti waited, letting his eyes wander over the dimly lit tapestries that lined the walls. Then they fell on the turret clock that weighted down the maps: an Italian copy of a French design – another thing of artistry, of beauty. Again, that little clutch at his heart. Not for the first time he wondered if what they were planning was right. It was not that he did not believe in God. Oh, he believed that a creator did exist, at some point in the distant past, and gave mankind His gifts and curses. But the benevolent father was either long dead or had departed to make mischief amongst some more distant spheres. In the meantime, the Roman Church had become a curse on the land. It was the same with all the manmade Churches, and their agents were the most bloodthirsty and viperous men on earth. If in doubt, one had only to look at the bloated bishops and their hidden bastards, or the fire-breathing, women-hating Lutherans trading in fear of eternal damnation. All were merchants of terror, free to burn and maim as long as people were afraid.

Now, with the end of his usefulness, with the end of the

century approaching, with France riven, England riven, Scotland … he could feel the collapse of the whole edifice of religion. Art, science, reason – all would spring from the rubble of superstition.

Still, he nursed the slightest of doubts about speeding it along. Better he should cover that up.

As though in challenge, his friend entered the room, a cowled monk at his back. Agosti raised his eyebrows in question. 'It is here. Downstairs.'

'Do you gentlemen know how to use it?'

'We do,' said his friend. Agosti said nothing, disgusted. A man of faith, supposedly, selling death.

'It is dangerous,' persisted the monk, pulling back his hood. He was young, no more than twenty-one. A halo of red-gold hair stuck up in delicate tufts.

'That is our affair.'

'For some extra payment, I can teach you how it works. You must have a care how you handle it, how you touch it. Don't open the box before you mean to use it. It has very great power. Who's it for?' Interest glittered. 'Some rich men? You're owed money from them?'

'We aim,' said Agosti, 'to put a stop to a bloody butcher before he can take up his trade.' He bared his teeth in a grin, ignoring both the startled and then the warning looks on his friend's face. The monk had noticed nothing.

'It will put an end to him, then, I promise you,' he blabbered. 'Butchers are greedy, cheating fellows, I've heard the abbot say so – sell you dog meat as soon as good beef. I'm sure he deserves it. I have seen it tested myself.' When neither man answered him, the monk thrust his hands into his pockets and shrugged. 'You owe me, gentlemen. For conveying it all here, too. Don't forget the cost of conveyance through the streets. I had to rent that cart.' Agosti nodded at his friend.

The other man's mouth twitched in a smile. 'Yes, brother,' he said. He turned his back on the monk and fussed with the purse tied to his belt. This time the young man smiled. Then he looked down at the confusion of papers on the desk. 'What … this looks like …' Before he could finish, a small, thin blade was drawn across his throat. His hands jerked upwards. Agosti looked away as his friend, having the wit, swiftly lifted the gurgling man's cowl up and around his head, stemming the spray. It was a skill to be able to do it so cleanly.

'All over my hands,' he said, as he lowered the body to the floor. He bit his lip. 'Their deaths or ours. Theirs or ours.' He glanced up, not quite shame-faced but not proud either. 'If they're allowed to pick a bloodier butcher than ever before … it'll be men like us put to the flame first. It's them or us. I confess I can scarce believe we're doing it. It seems a mad enterprise.'

'Mad? We desire something and we are setting about achieving it. Madness would be desiring something and doing nothing.'

'True. Very true. Strike or be struck.'

'Heh. You don't need to convince me. He had no one waiting outside?'

'No. As you thought, he stole it – he won't have told any of his brothers. Not where he was going either.'

'Hardly matters now,' said Agosti. In return, his friend gave him a hard look. 'Did you enjoy it?'

'What? Did I … this?' He nudged at the corpse with his boot and then, as though instinctively, put a hand to his own throat. 'Of course not.'

'Why shouldn't you, eh? His God enjoys it. Flying through the welkin like Jupiter, coming for us all with his bolts. Striking us all down with infirmity and death.'

'Pfft. Fables, all. As well you know.' He stepped away from the body. 'I … you're in one of your foul humours.' Agosti caught him chancing a look down at his curling hands. 'They cloud judgement. Can't afford that, not in this enterprise. This stuff … I can watch it, make sure it is … put to its use. A weapon no man will see coming, as we were promised. If the monk spoke true, it will work beyond magic.' Agosti gave a choking laugh at the word. 'Beyond the natural sciences. Beyond your art.'

'If he was not a pestilent liar.'

'And if he was – well, then we will have failed and no man

the wiser. I do this alone, Marcello. I've told you. Try nothing.'

Agosti lapsed into silence again, his eyes on the clock. It was true; his friend had arranged safe passage into the city. In truth, only he was expected to be there, and so only he could accomplish the great plot. Still, it would be a sight to see – one last great sight. It would become the stuff of the greatest art the world had ever seen. He had already begun toying with names of the works with which the great artists would immortalise it once free from the corrupting hand of the Church: *rubrum in inferno liberabis*; *mortem a tyrannis*; *infernum iudicium*; *caeleste iudicium*. Yes, it was the right thing to do. The whole Church pushed to its knees. At length, he said, 'did he give it a name, this strange material?'

'No. Not that he told me, anyway.'

'It should have a name. This deed deserves one.'

'Think of one then. Whilst I am set to work. You're changing the subject. You must stay here for however long it takes. The last conclave was …'

'It will not take weeks, this one. Not if the rumours are true. It shall be over more quickly than it took the pious old sin-spout to die.' The image of Pius V hobbled into Agosti's mind, half-crippled, fingering beads as he stumbled through the streets of the eternal city, a crowd of yawning and complaining clergymen and Swiss Guards keeping the crowds away from him. Dead now – rotting down into his basest elements. Agosti's white teeth gleamed at the thought. Pius's last days and hours should have been full of fear, knowing he was to be the last of his line: Agosti himself had made sure the old fool had knowledge of what was coming.

When the red hats are bowed together, the end will come on a fiery breath.

Prophecies did not need to come from charlatans to frighten people. His friend's voice broke into his thoughts, but the smile remained.

'Days, weeks – remain in this lodging, I beg you. A man might be hidden away for a night or two in that place, but no more. Remain here. It's a fine enough place.'

'When not tenanted by dead boys.'

'Marcello.' A warning tone.

'Yes, my friend, I will rot quietly in this fine house. I put my faith in you, a dog amongst the wolves. Take that creature's purse and throw him into the street. Somewhere distant from here. Use his cart if you must, stolen from his abbot's house, I should think. Take the cowl, though, keep it. It will stop them discovering who he is so quickly. It might be useful. And mind the stuff. When you get it into the city be sure it is well hidden. Buried amongst all the plundered art. Perhaps you might hide it amongst the construction stuff of their new-planned fancies.'

'I am no fool.'

'No. If it is indeed powerful enough to serve our turn...' His eyes had wandered back to the sketches. Somehow, he would find his way inside too. If he could not see it – and the nature of the attack would mean he could not safely be in the room to watch death arrive – he could at least be close enough to hear the screams. He could be a part of it – part of a scene beyond artistry.

1

Jack Cole leant on the handle of his broom, admiring the plaza which stretched out before him. He and the others had swept it prior to the arrival of the cardinals, who had flooded across it in a tide of red, led by the late pope's *maestro di camera*. After the great ones had disappeared into the palace, it all had to be swept again. The courtyard was huge – larger than any he had seen in English, French, Dutch, or Scottish palaces – with a polished stone floor decorated in chequered tiles. On each side rose delicately painted sandstone walls punctuated by huge, ornamented porticos.

'Finished?' Jack turned to his neighbour. The plaza was so large that it had to be divided into sections for the servants to sweep. He replied in Italian that he had. The language flowed easily, as new languages always did with him. He and his wife, Amy, had been in Italy now for almost a year, living amongst the English Catholic exiles who flooded the city in search of spiritual comfort. He turned to look behind him, where stood the front entrance to the apostolic palace complex. Silently, he offered up a prayer of thanks. If he had not been amongst the Catholic community who stood at the entrance to the Vatican when the dying Pope Pius had returned from his farewell trip around the Roman pilgrimage sites, he would not have gained his position amongst the lower servants. He could still hear the old man's broken Italian as he cried out, 'Lord, you know I have always been ready to shed my blood for their nation'.

What he was doing now might be considered a betrayal of the dying pontiff's benison.

'What now?' he asked. The other servant, a young Roman called Pietro, just shrugged. The Italians, he thought, were more fond of leisure than work, even the servants. Jack looked up at the darkening sky. Both sun and moon were visible, the latter bathing the plaza in the colour and atmosphere of the ancient world. The religious statues set in recesses became Roman and Greek gods and goddesses. Only the upper edges of the tall buildings were still lined with traces of gold.

A long way from Norfolk, he thought, a long way from York

and France. Though he knew it bordered on sacrilege, the place did somehow feel closer to heaven. That he, a man who had killed at least five men, not all of whom deserved it, should be here amongst the blessed and the sacred … that was surely a sign of forgiveness.

'That Farnese, huh?' said Pietro, breaking into his thoughts. 'What a man he is. He'll get it. You want to bet?' The young Roman looked over Jack's shoulder as he spoke. Cardinal Farnese had been one of the first to arrive – a tall, handsome man of about fifty who had bestowed smiles on all the servants as he swaggered through across the plaza and into the palace complex. As the others had arrived and entered, Farnese's booming voice had greeted each in turn. When Jack had edged towards the entrance to the apartments, he had glimpsed the ebullient cardinal clapping two new arrivals on the shoulder. Farnese, the Holy Father.

'Perhaps,' he said. Somehow, seeing the men who would be pontiff robbed them of the ethereality of the office. One never thought of a pope as having been a priest, or even a cardinal – one imagined they were born into the world as wise, white-bearded old men rather than wooing and clawing their way up to the office.

'So, my man, you want to bet?'

'No. I dunno. Who'll get it, I mean.'

Pietro shrugged again. 'What age are you, huh?' Jack told him. 'Pfft, I'm older than that.' Puffing his chest, he added, 'twenty-five, I am.' This time Jack rolled his eyes; the boy was younger than he was. 'You stick by me, my man. You can make real money if you talk to the right men in this place. It's what I'll do, and you see if I don't walk out of here a rich fellow. Hey, time to get the place lit, huh?' One of their fellow servants on the other side of the plaza had appeared carrying a lit torch and was putting it to one of the sconces that lined the square. Slowly, man by man, unspent torches were lit from the main one as gradually the courtyard in front of the Cappella Paolina erupted into festive light, turning the little church and its attached buildings buttery.

Just as Jack stood back from his sconce, watching as flames

lit a guttering pool around it, a sudden commotion from the direction of the great gatehouse turned him. The other servants followed suit. 'What is this?' asked Pietro, now at his elbow. 'More work. Ugh. Someone is come late.'

'What?' asked Jack. Even the torches did little to really illuminate the square. 'They're all here.' Around fifty cardinals had arrived over the course of the day, the majority Italian, one Polish, a few Germans and a couple of Spaniards.

'You want this one, my man?' Pietro yawned, slouching into his tunic like a retreating tortoise. Jack said nothing. Pietro had studiously avoided dealing with all of the late arriving cardinals; Borromeo, whom everyone had assumed to be the last and latest, he had palmed off on the fellow on his other side.

Jack stepped out into the square, just as two riders clattered in through the principal portico.

A man in black dismounted first, immediately helping an elder, resplendent in red. 'Who is it?' Jack mouthed.

Pietro shrugged. 'Don't know. Find out, though. And tell me.'

Huffily, the two men began striding through the plaza, their heads down. Jack stepped out and into their path.

'Your Grace?' he asked, keeping his head low.

'Granvelle,' snapped the man in black. Jack looked up into the younger priest's rugged, swarthy face, framed by a cloud of dark hair. 'Cardinal. Mechelen. Antwerp. I am Hernandez: Father. You will address to me only please.' The elder put out a hand on his harm, cutting off the curt recitation.

'Might you stable our horses? We have had a long ride.'

'The doors nearly locked on us,' snapped his conclavist in badly accented Italian.

'And we must thank God that did not happen. Please. The others, they are ...' He motioned in the direction of the palace. The old man had a kindly face, but it was deeply flushed, his exhaustion barely held in check.

'Yes, your Grace.'

'Take us, please. Our things will be sent to our chambers?'

Jack looked back towards the horses, laden with saddle packs. They were coated in a thick layer of road muck. 'The grooms will see to it.' He plastered on his best service face: an impassive expression and tilted head. His natural desire in awkward or new situations was to smile broadly, but that wouldn't do; over-smiling suggested sneaking insolence and guile, and encouraged masters to think their servant wasn't taking the work seriously.

'Good, this is good. Take us, please,' the cardinal repeated, still gently.

Jack bowed in assent, gesturing to Pietro to see to the horses. As he led the two prelates through a stone portico leading off the plaza, he could see his lazy friend starting an argument with some other servants over who should do the work. 'I'm here to sweep, to clean, get some groom, I'm no groom!'

Their heels clicked over marble and then crunched into carpet as they crossed through a hall, out a door to the right, and so into the wide, columned hallway, open along the righthand side. It had been pointed out to him earlier, when he was being given the instructions on what he must keep clear, as the loggia of Raphael, the famous painter. Its ceiling was arched and painted with realistic classical figures, and every column along the way was covered in coloured devices. The floor, tiled, had been polished and waxed. Even to walk it felt like stepping across the pages of some fantastical work of antiquity – it forced a reserve into Jack's step. He led his charges down it, pausing only when the sound of chatter drifted from ahead and to his left.

Most arriving cardinals having missed the noonday dinner, the *maestro di casa* of the old papal household had arranged for supper to be served on buffets in the state chambers of the Sala Ducale, which lay off the Raphael hallway. More likely it was a chance for the cardinals to swap greetings and indicate who it was they planned to vote for as the new pontiff. Rather than a great and glorious religious service, the whole thing had a whiff of the racketeering that went on amongst gentleman and yeoman farmers when a local notable was seeking to be made a member of parliament, albeit scented with incense. Dimly, he wondered if the rosy faced old man at his back had any inkling of his thoughts, or whether cardinals considered the thoughts of young servants at all.

Jack led them along a path towards the double doors, where

two Guardsmen in their red-and-gold slashed doublets stood sentinel, plumes quivering on their black satin caps. The festive costumes did not fool him. The stories of the Swiss Guards' military skills had echoed throughout Italy following the battle against the Turk at Lepanto the previous year. He opened his mouth to announce the late arrivals, only for the priest to forestall him, barking out his announcement. The guards, giving military nods in unison, made a show of opening the remaining wooden door.

Jack stepped aside to let them enter. Just before Granvelle did so, he breathed, 'we have no valet with us. No time to secure one. Perhaps you would find us a man.' He lightly clapped Jack's shoulder before moving indoors.

As light spilled out, Jack could see various cardinals milling. Just as the doors were being closed came an outbreak of muttering, above which rose the voice of Pietro's favourite, Farnese. 'G-Granvelle?' Something of the gregarious bonhomie had disappeared from the fellow's tone. Whatever Cardinal Granvelle's arrival meant, it looked like lengthening the odds.

Well, thought Jack, that was that. If the last arrival had only just snuck in as the city was being locked down, he now had the full complement. He would remember the number easily enough if not all the names or faces. Now just to keep his ears and eyes open for what was said and done as the days ticked by.

He wandered back along the Raphael corridor, glancing over to his left. Between the columns on that side the hallway was open to a large rectangular courtyard dotted with potted trees and intertwined with gravel paths: the San Damaso, it was called, and it was in the buildings on the opposite side that he and the other servants would be allowed to take their rest. At the thought of it, a yawn tugged at his jaw and he turned away, maintaining the stately stride the Raphael loggia hall seemed to demand.

When he returned to the plaza, he found that the number of servants had swelled. Like massed soldiers, they stood in rows. He slipped in at the back, next to men he didn't know but who wore the same buff-coloured homespun. 'What are we doing?'

'*Maestro di casa* to speak to us,' mumbled his new neighbour,

10

an older man with a thick moustache. 'When the rest are here.'

Over the next quarter of an hour, a trickle of men traced Jack's path from the Raphael walkway, others appearing from the direction of the Piazza San Pietro. Looking over the crowd, he estimated that there were upwards of a hundred servants to tend the conclave, not including the cardinal's own attendants, each great man being permitted one conclavist, or secretary, and one valet. They were divided, as he had anticipated, by labour: cleaners like himself at the back; ahead of them grooms; and then handlers of bedlinens and clothing; all the way up to the professional gardeners, barbers, cooks, physicians, and household officers.

When all had arrived, the master of the household, Bishop Cirillo, appeared. An attendant of his own placed a wooden coffer on the ground and he stood, looking down his nose at the sea of upturned faces. His beard fanned out over his chest.

'Gentleman,' he said. His voice was high pitched and, despite the box adding to his lack of natural height, he seemed nervous and unsure of himself. 'We value your service in this, the most sacred of all endeavours. As their Graces select our new Holy Father, we must give thanks to God for their wisdom.'

'Hoping he keeps his job,' said the man next to Jack out the corner of his mouth. 'New pope might mean new household and the little sheep shall not want thrown from their pen.' Jack ignored him as the bishop continued what was obviously a rehearsed oration.

'What you serve is the passage of one of the greatest mysteries of the true faith.' He paused for effect. 'The papal election. The conclave of cardinals. It is your job, it is your purpose, to see to the earthly comforts of our great ones. You must keep this sacred place clean, as our guards keep it safe. You must be on hand always. Speak not to the cardinals directly – their minds are on higher things – yet you must be ever ready to provide anything that their Graces' conclavists or valets request, day or night. In the beginning, food will be plentiful. As we progress, it will be less so, in accordance with the strictures laid down, it shall become scarcer. After supper this evening, our holy guests will be confined to their cells not far from the Sistine Chapel, the better to focus their minds on the great burden to which they are called.

'Secrecy. In the past, it is true, that men in service here have bought and sold information taken from this place and carried it to the walls, yes, to the very gates and porticos, even as the conclave is underway. This will not happen. Any found to be trading in the mysteries of the faith will be mewed up in a cell within these walls, and worse when the conclave is finished. Remember, the chronicles of eternity are being written in the villas of this great palace.'

A little murmur ran through the crowd. To Jack, it did not sound frightened or dismayed, but vaguely contemptuous. 'The place has more leaks that a Turk's galley after Lepanto,' sneered his vocal neighbour. 'No doubt the red-robes will make a good amount selling what they know is happening.' Jack turned in annoyance, his mouth open to speak. Something in the man's manner stopped him. A cold, angry bitterness seemed to have him in its grip. He was old, older than most of the serving-men. Odder still, he had one hand folded over another and both appeared to be twisted and infirm. It was an illness Jack had seen in older folk before – the swelling of the finger joints until the hands became fat and crooked. It prevented them from working, for the most part, and made them useless as servants. Uncharitably, the word 'cripple' ran through his mind and he turned away from it and the man.

Cirillo raised his own hands for silence. 'You understand. This is good. You are all to have the honour of resting hard by the papal apartments, that you might be nearer to the cardinals and their men.'

'Rest!' cut in the moustachioed man. 'Rest with our eyes open till they want something. Hard by the papal apartments. On the rat-beshitten floors of the old pope's kitchens.'

'Remember. Keep your eyes, ears, and mouths shut save for to do as you are instructed. The first ballot will take place tomorrow evening at six of the clock, the cardinals then gathered in their wisdom. Go, now, about your business. Dominus vobiscum.' He made the sign of the cross.

Bishop Cirillo took the proffered arm of his attendant and

stepped down from the coffer. He stumbled, and a ripple of laughter moved through the crowd. It looked to Jack like the old bishop was about to cry. Without engaging directly with anyone, he entered the covered hall, the senior servants – his clerk, and the two physicians and apothecary charged with keeping the elderly guests alive – hot on his heels.

'Well, that's us told.' Jack started; he had been expecting his swollen-handed neighbour's voice and instead found himself looking into Pietro's hooded eyes. 'Where are you from, my friend? No, let me guess. Ravenna. You have a sound of the north.'

'England,' said Jack. Without knowing why, he looked over Pietro's shoulder, hoping to see where the strange old man had gone. There was no sign of him.

'Ha! No, really.'

'No. That is really.'

Pietro whistled before speaking. 'England, huh? The heretic witch and the queen in chains.'

'Queen Mary,' said Jack. 'Of Scotland.'

'A very beautiful woman, huh?' Pietro cupped his hands over his chest and grinned. 'So they say, my masters.' He lifted one hand to his face and tapped the side of his nose. 'What's your name? Who are you watching for?'

'Jack. What do you mean?' A nervous grin tightened his cheeks.

'Come on, English – we all watch for someone. Don't make no money from sweeping. Me, I watch for the merchants in Rome. Want to know if they're getting another pope who locks all sin and vice out of this city or not. Pope Pius, God rest him, they say he kept this place like a monastery, not a city. Can't do too much business with a monastery, can you?' Jack frowned, but he couldn't bring himself to do so too deeply. 'Not a spy for the witch queen?' Pietro's eyes narrowed.

'I am here,' said Jack, forcing affront into his voice, 'on behalf of the good English Catholics. Who wish,' he added, 'to show their support and service to the true faith.' A sudden shiver of fear had passed through him. Had he been behaving suspiciously? Had his face betrayed him, as clearly as if a treacherous 'T' had been branded on his forehead? Now he was locked inside the Vatican, there was nowhere to run.

'Fine,' Pietro shrugged, 'don't tell me then.' He winked. 'Though if you need to know where to speak to the outside, you come to me, huh?' He strode away, his thumbs thrust into his belt.

Jack stared after him, his mind whirling. It was true. He was spying. Yet ... he would render only an honest account of the proceedings: who did what, what was said about England. Nothing harmful to the Church – he would close his ears to that. Even as the cardinals had arrived, he had overheard them discussing the problem of England's queen. The old pope had been a fair-weather partisan of Mary Queen of Scots – the new one might not have any interest in her plight at all. So too were they discussing the problems of France that kept so many French cardinals away from the conclave. The queen-mother there, Catherine de Medici, was said to have her own favourite for the throne of St Peter, for her own reasons. That might be valuable. There really was no telling what a man like Francis Walsingham would want to know – everything, probably, no matter how pointless or insignificant. He stored up knowledge like a miser stored rubies. Jack could almost imagine him in conversation with the creepy old William Cecil, who had apparently become a lord, casually dropping in that he knew who was the third-to-last arrival at the papal conclave and what they had said about Elizabeth. Power drove Walsingham, and knowledge was power.

Yet he would have happily given the old man nothing, had it not been for Amy. Awkward and clingy in France, moody in the Dutch Netherlands, his wife was an English girl and wanted to return. If he wanted a quiet life, the only way would be to get them back to England, and after they had abandoned Walsingham's service the previous year – run from it, in fact – the only way back in would be to visit him in France and purchase safe passage with something he could use.

If Pietro was spying too ... well, probably most of the servants were. That made him feel a little less dirty and a great deal less nervous. It was a strange thing, though, that a young man as intent on finding out information as Pietro should be so keen to avoid doing anything to come by it himself. Or perhaps it wasn't. He had long thought that spying was a lazy and corrupt man's game, little better than prostitution: it was selling your body and whispering not sweet nothings over a pillow but secrets over dead men. All too often, he thought, over dead men. A full account of the papal conclave should buy a return to England and freedom from Mr Walsingham's grubby little battalion of informers.

The serried ranks of servants had all but dispersed, men drifting through the square and through the papal apartments. Probably they would try and get some sleep. It would be best, he supposed, to do the same. Not that sleep would come easily. Since the previous year, darkness had become oppressive. In it, he imagined suffocating death.

Thankfully, there would be lights burning and other people around. At any rate, nothing of importance would be said or done on the first night. He took a last look out across the torchlit plaza. On the far side, the lights winked, fighting nobly against the full darkness that had fallen. It really did look a holy sight. He began to follow the general drift, letting out a yawn himself. Funny, he thought, how the merest thought of sleep brought on tiredness. He paused to let some other servants through the open doors ahead of him. Distantly, church bells rang out the hour.

As he crossed the hall which ran parallel and ultimately connected to the Raphael hall, something hit him on the chest.

He froze. Looked down and then up ahead. Nobody.

Crouching, he picked up a little piece of wood chip: the type kept in grates to keep gentle fires ablaze. He looked up at the carved, painted ceiling, lost in shadow. It hadn't fallen. He pouted and flicked a lock of hair out of his eyes. Someone playing a prank – Pietro probably. Two other servants had come up behind him, but they ignored him, parting to go around and out the door to Raphael and the San Damaso beyond. He made to follow.

Again, another tap.

Jack shouted out this time, irritated. 'Who's there?'

Silence.

Behind him, the hall connected to the big, chequered courtyard, but at the other it dead-ended in shadow – what lay behind its concluding wall would be the little hallway following the entrance to the Sala Ducale. He folded his arms, squinting into the darkness.

'You say something?'

He jumped. Another servant had just left the plaza and was passing through. 'Did you throw something? A … a bit of wood?'

'Away,' said the man, giving him a puzzled look before moving on. Jack held up his hands in apology before returning them over his chest in a protective gesture. As his eyes fully adjusted to the dark, he peered ahead and to the left, judging that to have been the direction his assailant was hitting him. Whilst the right of the hallway went out into Raphael's loggia, the left had doors into a tiny courtyard, the Cortile del Maresciallo; but no one went out there – it was just a headless triangle of a garden, bordered all around by walls.

A shadow moved. Jack froze. His mind worked quickly: run, chase, cry out. It could be a trap. He had no weapon, save the blunt little knife he carried for food. Before he could make a decision, another tiny chip came flying and this time he could see the outline of the thrower. Annoyance goaded him into action, making his temper flare.

'Pietro, I'll break your goddamn arm!' he shouted, leaping down the hall, statues and dark arrases blurring by. The man did not run, did not move at all, and in a couple of seconds Jack had him by the collar of a cheap tunic. 'Who the hell are you hitting …' His voice trailed off.

Soft light from the torches outside fell in stuttering waves through one of the tall windows. The dark figure had been lurking in the shadows between, half-hidden by an arras. 'Get off' The fellow shook himself, straining to get free, his cap falling to the floor to reveal cropped hair, his face a mask of irritation matching Jack's own. As his eyes grew used to the half-light, Jack slackened his grip and let the body drop. 'Oh,' he said. 'Shit.'

2

'What … how are you here?' he snapped in English, his eyes wide. Amy stooped to picked up the little cap and replaced it over her shorn hair. 'What happened to your hair? Why are you dressed like that?'

'I had to cut it to get inside,' she said. Then she looked up at him and grinned. 'It's how come I didn't get my eyebrows plucked out again too.' She waggled them up and down as if proof were needed, still smiling.

'You can't be here. It's not … you're not allowed.'

'I had to; I had–'

'Amy!' He hissed, glancing over his shoulder to see if anyone else was in the hall. It was clear. He looked at her. Instinct told him to go soft on her, whilst irritation and fear bred anger. He had always been soft on her, always let her have her way, always deferred to her rash tongue. He loved her, it was true, but sometimes the love she returned was suffocating – a fact that had only become more apparent in the year since they had come to Rome and she had demanded to know where he was going and when he would return every time he left their lodgings. It was the realisation of his own weakness as much as worry about her getting caught that drove him. He gripped her by the shoulders, hard enough to feel the bones in her back lock. 'Shut up. You're fucking mad. This is … this is madness. You've … you can't leave me alone for a day, a week. You're …' he struggled for the right word. 'You act like a woman possessed.' She stared at him, and his eyes darted down and from side to side. His knuckles had paled, and he loosened his grip, hands sliding down to her forearms. Fear had flared in her eyes and he felt an answering rush of shame burning up his neck. He had never handled her badly. His anger deflated. At the same time, hers seemed to rise, a remedy to fear.

'I can't leave you alone,' she mimicked, not troubling to lower her voice. 'Everything I've done for four years has been for you. To protect you, keep you safe. Because I'm your wife! Dragged across Europe on your … your fancy … for your religion, to see this place …'

'Why are you here?'

'Never mind. I'm going.'

'You can't go – you can't go anywhere. They'll lock you up if you try to leave. It's the conclave. How did you get in?'

A sly look came over her face. He winced. With her hair cut short and her clothes – his clothes, he realised, expertly altered in size – she looked like a weird boy. 'I copied your letter. Your letter of introduction from Hyde.' Jack stared over her shoulder into the darkness for a second. Hyde was the English lay Catholic who was the unofficial leader of the exiles in Rome. It was he who had written the letter recommending Jack for service in the Vatican during the conclave – the note on his character, trustworthiness, and piety. And Amy had copied it, the cunning little witch. All so she could stalk him. 'I remembered what was in it. I just changed the name from Jack Cole to Roberto Cole. Your brother. And brought it here and got in, all proper. I'm no fool.'

Jack stood back from her and ran a hand through his hair, flicking back his curl afterwards. 'You can't … this thing can last days or weeks. How are you going to wash?' Instead of answering she pouted, and he recoiled again.

'It'll grow back,' she said softly, lifting a hand to her head.

'I don't care about your bloody hair.' To his surprise, she burst into tears. Amy had never been one to cry. If it were an act, a means of defusing his sudden and unprecedented show of anger, it was a convincing one. He looked around again before embracing her. She punched him on the back and wriggled away. 'We can't stay here. We have to go with the other servants. Say something.'

'What?'

'Say something like … like a man. A boy.'

'Like this?' she said, lowering her voice to a throaty squawk.

'Too much.' She tried again, this time making it less obvious that she was feigning. He gave a weary nod.

'Yeah. That'll do.' Balling his fists, he put them to his temples. 'Just don't talk to anyone if you don't have to. We … we'll say you're my brother. Simple minded,' he added, with asperity. 'I mean it Amy, you'll have to keep your mouth shut.

You can't … you can't behave as you would outside this place.'

'I think I know how to keep quiet,' she snapped. 'I've been getting told to all my life.' Jack snorted in response and her eyes flashed anger again. 'And don't you forget I know how to play someone else – did I not play a lady at the French court? You're not the only one who knows how to do things.'

'Let me see you,' he said, gripping her arm and dragging her further into the light flickering through the window. She could certainly pass for a very young man, her small nose upturned and her face round. The clothes fit well enough, and she had padded the stomach of the brown tunic so that her small breasts were hardly visible: rather than a woman in disguise, she looked like a lad with puppy fat.

'I must look rotten,' she whispered, crossing her arms over her body. Then, more brightly, 'well, doesn't matter. There'll be none of … that … for a while anyway. And,' she hurried on, 'no one's said anything. Kept my head down since I came in today. I … I was watching you, but you were always with someone. In truth, I hoped to be in and out before they locked this place up.'

'You'll have to keep it down.'

'For God's sake, Jack. We were servants long enough. We know how to be invisible in a room full of people. You think any of them are looking at us?'

'They might be listening!'

'My Italian is perfect.' Her chin protruded. He sighed. It was true – and that was the problem. She had taken well to the language, but she spoke it without the learned imperfection of a native. She simply couldn't copy the laziness of others the way he could. Speaking a foreign language with too much care marked you out as a stranger as much as speaking it badly. She couldn't naturally ape new accents, tailoring speech to company.

'Do you … know where to sleep, where … to take a piss – how, even?'

'Yes. I'm not a dolt.' He could tell she was lying. One of his wife's less endearing traits, he knew, was that she would turn blue before admitting she didn't know something or hadn't thought about it. As usual, she had rushed headlong into something without a first thought about the practicalities, never mind a second.

'We have to go,' he said. 'The cardinals will be in their cells now. Or being shown to them.' He turned on his heel and began striding back down the hall, keeping to the carpet. He could hear her following and dimly wondered if she had stolen and altered a pair of his boots too.

***

The Vatican complex was not a unified building, but an unconnected series of them, some brand new, some ancient, others in various states of completion. Partly an enclosed city, partly a palace, it was wholly a building site. Pope Sixtus IV's Sistine Chapel had once housed the cardinals during conclave, twenty-five cells being maintained within its walls. It had been a good number of decades since there had been so few red-hatted electors. To house the full complement, a double suite of dormitories had been built into villas in front of the sacred building's antechamber, the Sala Regia. One dormitory, the main one, ran from north to south, roughly parallel to the great antechamber. The second, unused, ran from west to east, directly abutting the Sala Ducale to which Jack had shown Granvelle and his conclavist, Father Hernandez. They formed a rough, inverted L, despite not being attached, with a little internal courtyard formed by the old pope's private apartments on the northern side, some old audience chambers and the Raphael walkway along the eastern edge. It was along the great artist's walkway that Jack and Amy strode, she aping his loping pace: he had to hand it to her – the clothing seemed to make her move differently. To his annoyance, however, she could not resist slapping her palm against the painted walls every few steps as they made for the Ducale and the remnants of the cardinals' supper.

They entered the guarded double doors to which Jack had earlier led Cardinal Granvelle and followed a narrow passage to the wider space of the Ducale. There they found teams of men clearing up the buffets, and both drew breath. The cardinals and the conclavists who shadowed them must have been taken to their temporary homes. They had not taken their pomp with them. The Ducale, in which Jack had not yet set foot, was like being inside a giant jewel. Golds, pale blues, and marble whites stretched across the floor, up the walls, and around the curved ceiling. Geometric shapes were everywhere, and inside each more gold had been painted in cunning designs. Princely palaces with their tapestries and gilded furniture were one thing, but this was something different. Here, majesty was embedded in the floors and sang from the ceilings. The sight of it solidified a feeling he had been harbouring since dawn: that the Vatican was ancient Egypt and Greece and Rome; it was the glittering glory of the old world and the colourful rediscoveries of the new; it was jewels and paintings and everything rich from all time gathered together. It was a treasure trove of the world's eternal history.

'Christ almighty,' Amy whispered. 'Imagine living like this. My mam would piss herself if she could see me here.'

Jack shot her a warning look and then jerked his head in the direction of the activity. Several men were nibbling on leftovers, other draining wine. Tables had been set up along the walls, each laden under the leftovers. The rest of the servants were busy clattering empty metal dishes and cutlery into piles.

As they moved to join in, someone tugged at Jack's elbow. It was Pietro. 'Hey, the new pet.'

'What?'

'Jack, yes? You've been summoned, my man. No one knew the name of the lad who brought in the last cardinal, save me. His man has been asking for you. A right odd one, speaks hardly any Italian – every sentence a word ripped from his tongue.'

'Him,' said Jack, frowning. He resisted the urge to turn around and speak to Amy, though he could feel her eyes on him. 'Granvelle … I … ah, damn.' He had forgotten that the old cardinal had asked that a valet should be found for him. 'He's looking for a manservant. Pietro, would you–'

'Ha! No, no, no. He's yours. It's you that strange priest asked for – the man who brought them to the palace, he said.'

'But,' said Jack, smiling, 'if you're his man you can learn from him. What's what, I mean – the workings of the conclave.'

'Heh,' Pietro shrugged, 'I have my own ears. Don't need so much toil. No, sir – he's yours.' As if to prevent any further wheedling, the Roman moved away, pausing only to add, 'you'd better go and see what the cardinal seeks. Risking hellfire and damnation leaving him wanting, huh?'

When he had gone, Jack returned his attention to Amy. 'A-Roberto … I have to go. You … you should help here.'

'I know the job of a servant,' she answered in her husky Italian. 'It's the life I chose and the life you gave me. Go, then. Brother.'

Jack left her, hating having to do so. He was still furious, but now felt that he had to protect her – not from the others so much as from herself. All it would take would be one crossed word, someone bumping into her or giving her a dirty look, and he knew she would open her mouth. Sweat began to bubble up on his forehead as he stepped back out into the Raphael hall, now chilly from the breeze sneaking in from the San Damaso.

The large courtyard lay ahead of him and he turned left and walked farther down the hall until a gallery opened up leading to the smaller quadrangle created by the dormitories and the papal private rooms. Though it was dark, tapers had been lit throughout the little garden, mostly around statues, and he could see from the Swiss Guards outside the door which building housed the cardinals. He made for it.

Inside, he found a long, narrow hallway, doors along its length and stairs at one end. The walls were adorned with frescoed swirls of colour depicting previous pontiffs surrounded by their cardinals, and scenes from ancient Athens. Jack ignored them and began walking down the hall, unsure whether to begin knocking or to return to the Swiss Guards outside and ask for help. Just as he had decided on the latter and turned his heel, a tall man appeared at the bottom of the marble staircase. The *maestro di camera*, he saw, Casale: the old pope's chamberlain. Like Cirillo, he would be keen that the cardinals were all well housed and fed in the hopes that he might retain his position in the new reign.

'What are you doing here, boy?' he asked, suspicion on his narrow face.

'Cardinal Granvelle's man sent for me, father. He has no valet with him.' Casale's lips curled downwards, and Jack sensed that the sudden, late arrival of the cardinal had disrupted what had been a carefully orchestrated evening.

'His Grace is not down here. They all sleep upstairs. Their conclavists have offices here.' He gestured along the hall in which they stood. 'His grace is above us, second from the farthest from the chapel. You may speak only to his man.' Jack looked blank at the confusing words and knew it, as he tried to count the doorways without turning to look. 'This one,' said Casale, sweeping by him and moving towards a door. He paused at it, coughed, and then knocked. The lugubrious Father Hernandez opened it almost before the sound had died away. 'Good evening, father. My apologies for troubling you. A boy here says his Grace has asked for a valet. I trust nothing was amiss with his cell, the bed freshly made, the inkpots filled?'

'All well,' said Hernandez. And then, tersely, 'thank you.'

'If his Grace requires anything that can be granted within these walls, please do not hesitate to make use of any of our servants. And I will only be in my chambers,' he paused, giving another delicate little cough, 'my former chambers in the palace.'

'Thank you. Goodnight.' The priest's eyes had left Casale and fallen instead on Jack. He felt himself redden under them. Casale seemed not to notice, and instead bowed and began to back away, his tall form retreating from the dormitory building. As he was going, Hernandez crooked a finger and bid Jack come to him.

'Father. His Grace needs a servant for his stay?'

A delay. Jack realised that the man was translating the words, one by one. 'Yes. For one thing only. One task. Maybe more. Later.' He stepped back into his cell, which was more appropriately, thought Jack, a well-appointed bedchamber. A desk stood against one wall, a cushioned stool beside it, and the bed, big enough for two, was covered in a thick rug. Jack watched as the man stepped over to the desk and picked up a piece of thick paper, folded over. 'You speak Flemish? Spanish?' Jack shook his head and the conclavist tutted. 'You know Farnese, Cardinal?' On receiving the more positive response, he gave a thin smile – devious, Jack thought. 'You take this – give it to Farnese.'

Jack's mouth ran dry as the man held out the letter. 'Which is Farnese's room? His cell. Where he sleeps.' He mimed resting his head on his hands.

'Upstairs.'

Jack shrugged, and a small farce ensued during which Hernandez counted out with upraised fingers which room the famous Italian cardinal had been lodged in. Eventually, he understood and reached for the letter. As though distrusting him, the conclavist jerked it just out of his reach with thumb and forefinger. 'You can read?'

'No, father,' he lied.

'Good. To no one but Cardinal Farnese. None other.'

Jack nodded, took the letter, and bowed his way out of the room. He waited until he had reached the marble staircase – the priest did not stop watching until he was out of sight – and halfway up before he opened it and read.

***

Amy mechanically helped the other servants tidy up. She had not expected Jack to be displeased to see her. She had not thought through his reaction much at all, save that he would be happy when she spoke to him – not that she had been able to. It had all seemed such a good idea, as things always did before she did them. Sneak into the Vatican, speak to Jack, keep an eye on him if necessary, and leave whenever she chose. In her mind, she had even considered making light of her appearance, making some off-colour joke about her boyish figure – but she had rejected that. Even mockingly, it was always a risk poking fun at yourself – if the person didn't notice your flaws before, as she hoped Jack never had, they would certainly notice after you'd pointed them out.

She was not an idiot; she knew that the city was locked down during conclaves; yet everyone she had spoken to had told her that it was a simple matter to get in and out. She had brought along a purse of money for precisely that. And even if she was locked in, he knew as well as she did that the conclave would be short. The whole of Rome had heaved with the rumours for weeks: this was Cardinal Farnese's election – the old pope had lingered on his deathbed for so long that his successor had been all but decided before he died. This conclave was just a ceremony – a coronation – and she would not have to keep herself hidden in it for long. Jack knew this. His reaction had surprised her. She knew he had a temper – she had always known – and yet he had never unleashed it on her.

But why had she really come?

There was the obvious reason and then there was the one she shied away from. It was that the thought of him making friends and spending time with others somewhere she couldn't watch over him bothered her. It was ugly and she detested it, but it was there – the need to know what he was doing all the time, to whom he was speaking, whether he was enjoying their company more than hers. With force, she slammed down a silver goblet.

And what if she was jealous? And what if she knew that a green streak of envy made her act like a fool? It was all very good recognising your own faults; but doing so didn't tell you how to fix them. And his anger at her, that must have come not from him but from someone else who had spoken ill of her. One of those pious English exiles, she supposed. When she was out of the Vatican, she'd slice them up with the sharpest edge of her tongue.

As her mind worked, she picked up a gilt fork. Odd thing. She had seen forks before – in the French court the kitchen had had some of them – and yet still she found them strange, more ceremonial than useful. To her, the thought of eating with one was like eating with a decorative dagger. One might as well just drink out of a vase, too. She deposited it amongst the other items on the wooden tray she had gathered and made to leave.

'That Morone's a man of chance,' said a voice behind her.

'Trickster, not enough friends,' said another.

'Did you see how much he ate?'

'No manners, cardinal or not.'

'Bonnelli, he was a good one.'

'Pfft. A child, still – too young for a red hat.'

She did not turn. She had imagined that male servants, when

25

alone, would be all about the work, keeping their minds clear and their tongues caged. In truth, they were nothing more than a clutch of clucking hens, more gossipy and tiresome than fishwives.

Speaking to no one, she followed the others out of the glittering Sala Ducale, across the half-open Raphael hall, and in procession across the San Damaso courtyard to the servants' quarters – in reality a large kitchen and series of storerooms, on the floors of which they were allowed to collapse in huddles. There were no rushes, no wooden pallets, nothing that could spread fire. The safety of the building outweighed the comfort of the servants. She cracked her back before entering, spasming at the sudden pain that shot through it.

As she passed through, she noticed Cirillo's attendant standing hard by the doorway, a quill and parchment in his hands. Her heart skipped a beat, but the little man asked no questions; instead, he seemed to be counting up the numbers of servants present. Probably, she supposed, he was ensuring there were enough meals to last the number of people for however many days were expected. Clerks could always find reasons to count things. Still annoyed at Jack and yet unable to argue with him, she decided to interrupt the fellow, hopefully throwing him off his counting. 'Where do these go?' she asked in the modified growl she thought quite convincing.

'Lock them up,' hissed the clerk, not even looking up. He simply inclined his head towards an enormous wooden chest into which others were carefully depositing everything of value taken from the buffets. She followed suit, watching as the fork disappeared with a forlorn twinkle. A lonely little golden fork in a coffer full of rough metal. What Jack had said sliced into her mind: in his anger he had ranted about her following him around, about her being like a woman possessed. He did not yet know why she had come, and yet his first thought had betrayed how he really felt. The problem was that once you knew someone thought something, inevitably you suspected they had always secretly thought it; that they were thinking it all the time; that you had been a dupe and a figure of fun to them in your ignorance.

Four years of marriage and he could still shock her. Well, she would shock him when she chose.

Inexplicably, she felt tears prickle again in her eyes. What is happening to you, girl, she thought, biting down on her bottom lip. You're becoming a bag of womanly weakness – and in this place and in this guise. She thrust out her chin and turned again to face the low-ceilinged room.

Jack had been right about one thing; she would have to keep her distance from the others. As though in mockery at the thought, her bladder suddenly swelled.

The only private place she could find was a shadowy gap between two large barrels directly outside the storerooms. As the rest of the company knew, the best place to sleep was farthest from where the food and provisions were kept: the closer you were to it all, the closer you were to rats. Some men huddled near the huge, unlit grates, hoping for residual warmth: a fool's choice – sleeping next to the fireplaces ensured you would be the first kicked awake when they were lit before dawn.

When she had finished and re-laced her doublet and hose, the sound of a snick froze her in place. She crouched back down as the storeroom door opened and an old man with a thick moustache stepped out, a sly smile on his face. He turned and closed the door behind him, grimacing as he worked the handle. When he had managed to get it shut, he strode off without looking back.

Strange, she thought. And then her mind returned to Jack.

***

Jack folded the letter over again, his mind racing. Part invitation, part threat, the letter was written in Italian, not particularly skilfully, and it warned Farnese that Cardinal Granvelle had in his possession a letter from King Philip of Spain, bearing that sovereign's royal seal, and warning him that he, Farnese, was not an acceptable choice to the Spanish. If they could speak privately and come to some agreement about an appropriate candidate for St Peter's throne, Granvelle would spare the Italian the embarrassment of having the letter read out to the whole company of cardinals.

So much for the divinity of the conclave. Whatever little drama the Spanish king was directing, it was the stuff of high politics, not faith. It began to dawn on him that Walsingham and even Queen Elizabeth might as well find out all about it. If the cardinals were willing to dirty their hands obeying orders from worldly sovereigns, acting as puppets, what right had they to feign guidance from God?

Not, he reminded himself, that either Walsingham or his queen were any better, the pair of them happy to guide their own false Church for their own benefit. What an unclean world it was. The greatest trick its governors had played on normal folk was gulling them into thinking they knew what they were doing. They didn't. They were all of them living day-to-day, playing games, fighting amongst themselves to remain at the top.

Jack digested the contents of the letter as he sprang upstairs and counted his way down to Farnese's door. Bending, he slid the letter underneath and began to skip away. He did not get far. The door flew open and Farnese stepped out, his bombastic presence filling the doorway. 'Stop, boy,' he boomed.

Jack did.

Cardinal Farnese opened and read the letter silently, his face changing colour as he did so. His expression did not change, but the way he crumpled the paper betrayed his fury. 'You are Granvelle's man?' he hissed.

'No, your Grace. A hired man, a nothing, asked to deliver this letter.' He considered adding that he did not read it but realised how incriminating that would sound. 'Tell Granvelle I will speak with him.' This came out in the dry rasp of a man confounded. He glared at Jack, sucked in his cheeks, and added, a little more assuredly, 'at a time of my choosing.' After delivering this last act of defiance, Farnese retreated, slamming his door.

Jack raced downstairs, returning to Granvelle's conclavist. Hernandez answered at once. 'He caught me leaving. Said he would see his Grace.' Careful to maintain a look of slack-jawed innocence, Jack tossed his hair and then said, 'you need anything else? Wine, bread, cheese?'

Rather than answer, the priest, a grin on his face, stepped past him, closed his door, and began making for the staircase himself. Jack did not stay to watch him. Instead, he kept his hands tight by his side as he clacked across the polished marble and returned to see if Amy had managed to keep herself out of trouble.

As he passed into the kitchens-cum-servants' quarters, which cringed in the shadow of the apostolic palace like a shameful secret, he was met with a flurry of questions. They came from Cirillo's little shadow, who seemed to have been thrown out of sorts by Jack's arrival. It took a few minutes of explanation as to his name and background – and where he had been, and whether or not he had entered and left the rooms already within the past hour – before the clerk allowed him to pass.

Shaking his head, he passed through dozens of slumbering and chatting bodies, calling out, 'Roberto Cole' over and over until eventually he found Amy. He settled down beside her, not far from the storeroom. The only other nearby tenant that far from the entrance was a middle-aged man with a constant sneeze, whom they both ignored. Instinctively, Jack nearly put his arm around her, only remembering not to when he tilted his head and saw her hair. It was cut around her face and the back of her neck and looked for all the world like someone had put a bowl over her head and sliced away: which, he realised, is probably what she had done to herself.

'You won't believe what I just did. And read.'

'What?' The curtness was unlike her. He realised he had probably made a mistake in letting his surprise goad him into anger. It might take some time until she came around.

'Well, you know how everyone said Cardinal Farnese would be the next pope?'

'I don't care who's the next pope,' she whispered.

'Now, look here, Amy, I–'

'Silence, all!'

They both turned towards the sudden voice's source. His arms crossed in triumph, the clerk who had been guarding the entrance to the servants' quarters was standing next to a terrified-looking Cirillo, the old man already in a silken nightgown and cap. Behind them was a Swiss Guard, his face set.

'My man,' the old man piped, 'informs me that there is one here who should not be. A man has come into this place beyond the right and proper number of allowed and admitted servants. I command you, whoever has snuck into this holiest of places to reveal yourself now.'

Jack turned to Amy, who was staring back at him, eyes wide and a hand clutched to her throat.

3

'I give whichever man does not belong here one chance only to rise. He will be unharmed, I pledge, and conveyed only to some place of greater security until this conclave has reached its conclusion. Now, stand.'

In the shadows, still on the floor, Jack reached for Amy's hand and gripped it until he felt the bones in her palm knit. He had no intention of letting her stand, even if the idea was crossing her mind. He considered what she had told him: that she had copied out his own letter of introduction with a fresh name and passed it through to the papal household for entry into service in the city. Mentally, he followed its passage. All above board, all correct. If something had gone wrong, probably something unforeseen and quite innocent, he would stand himself and go to whichever cell they cared to take him. All of this he tried to tell her through that tight squeeze.

'I am your man.'

Dozens of voices began mumbling in unison as the speaker rose from the floor and sauntered forward. Jack gasped, just as Amy wrenched her hand free. Looking at her, he noticed she, too, was staring intently at the fellow.

'Well, should you not take me?'

Cutting a path through the sea of lolling servants was the old, moustachioed man with the crippled hands who had stood next to Jack during Cirillo's address to the staff. He was grinning, no trace of fear or shame on his face.

The Swiss Guard made to step around the *maestro di casa*, who stayed him with a hand. 'You are here without warrant? You are here to watch these proceedings and pass information through secret means?'

'What a worldly view you have, father.'

'What?' spluttered Cirillo, raising his chubby hands to the sides of his throat in a startled little gesture. He looked more like a doting grandfather than ever.

'I hear you are more interested in music. Music is an art. Art is much more pleasant that the worries and cares of the world, is it not?'

'Take him away,' snapped the priest, his nightcap bobbing. Clearly, Jack thought, the old fellow was not used to being spoken to in that way, and certainly never before a company of lowly servants. The guard complied, moving through the crowd and grasping the unprotesting old man by his upper arm. Despite his age, there was nothing grandfatherly about this one.

Though he continued to show no fear, the stranger winced. Loud enough for everyone to hear, he said, 'bear witness, friends, how these holy men treat a poor old cripple who has but wandered by chance into this place. Would God like that, I ask you?' He chuckled as he was pushed forward. 'Remember this, all of you, when you see what becomes of these creatures. When you have the power in your own hands, remember how they have treated you.' He laughed, and as the guard pushed hard on his back, he stumbled. 'Note the ceiling here, how low it is, for what they consider the lowest of people. No soaring Michelangelo here, eh?'

Once the prisoner and his captors were gone, Jack turned to Amy. 'Who the hell was that?' Then, lower, 'I thought it was you. Jesus, my heart. Who was that old creature?'

'I saw him. Earlier.'

'Me too. In the plaza, when the bishop addressed us. He was stood next to me. He–'

'Not too long ago,' cut in Amy, frowning. 'He was coming out of the storeroom.' She pointed towards it with her chin. 'Looking … not right. Like he'd been up to something.'

'What do you mean?'

'Well, it's where the food's kept, isn't it? For the cardinals. For everyone. It's all kept in those rooms, the meats, the breads, the wines, the stuff for the masses, even, I heard someone say when I was helping clear up. Everything's kept in that room.'

'Isn't it locked?'

Amy shrugged before speaking. 'He came out of it. And he had no food or drink, he wasn't fetching anything for anyone.'

'It isn't where the stuff's kept – not food, I mean. The knives and spoons and that.'

'And forks. No. They all go in a special coffer.'

'So what was he doing?'

'How should I know? Pissing?'

'I'm serious.' She seemed disinterested, quiet. Normally she would talk a blue streak and he simply listen, occasionally mumbling agreement to whichever tale she was adding arms and legs to. He sighed and took her hands. 'I'm sorry about how I was earlier, when I first saw you.' He paused; their neighbour, the wheezy man, began a sneezing and spluttering fit, wiping his streaming nose with a sleeve. Jack waited until he had pulled his cap low over his eyes, scratched himself, and returned to his fitful sleep. 'I'm sorry. I was …'

'You were a scurvy streak of donkey piss.'

'I was … surprised to see you is all. You can't blame me for that.'

'I'm surprised you didn't break my shoulders, grabbing me like that. Saying I … being so mean.'

'I've said I'm sorry and meant it.' She was not going to make things easy.

'And I confess that after the knavish way you behaved, that could only hurt and frighten me, I was hurt and frightened.' A little gleam of triumph shone in her eyes.

'Forgiven, though?'

'Maybe.'

'Well can you be hard on me later, at least?' She put out her lip. 'Good. This is serious, if that fellow was in there. And he shouldn't have been, if it's really him who shouldn't have been here at all. Why would he give himself up like that?'

'Did he seem in fear to you?' asked Amy, and Jack grinned over-enthusiastically at the grudging interest that flared in her eyes.

'No, not at all, not even a little. And just gave himself up.'

Amy appeared to consider before speaking, if only briefly. 'Then he wishes to be taken to wherever he knows they'll take him.'

'I should tell them. Say I saw him coming out of the food stores. I won't mention you.' He got to his knees and then stood, his tumble of unruly hair nearly touching the ceiling. Amy remained seated. 'Stay here.'

'Yes, husband.'

Jack looked around the room and then, in a lightning move, bent down and kissed her. 'I love you.' She only gave him a tired smile.

Satisfied she was suitably apart from the others, he returned to the San Damaso. Overhead, the moon shone down on the statuary, turning the gravel paths and marble walkways a cool grey. A light breeze had begun. Raised voices drifted from the quadrangle bordered by the dormitories, the Raphael loggia, and the private papal apartments. He made for them.

At the entrance, Casale, Cirillo, and the Swiss Guard who had led the stranger away were locked in heated conversation. Unlike the *maestro di casa*, the *maestro di camera*, Casale, was not in his nightclothes. Jack wondered if he was required to stay awake through the night, or if he chose to do so, so as to be on hand if the cardinals had any problems requiring his unctuous tongue and smooth manners. At sight of him they abruptly ceased their animated chatter. 'Father,' he said, addressing himself to Cirillo. 'I thought I should speak up about that man who was taken.'

'You know him?' The three men looked at his plain cloth tunic as though he were a wild Turk.

'No. Yet I heard him speak slanderous words against the faith this evening. When you were addressing us, father. And ... again, not so long ago, I saw him leaving the storeroom. Where the food is kept,' he added pointedly. 'I thought he had a creeping and strange look.'

The two priests looked at each other, rage and fear battling on their faces. 'Oh my. Oh my, oh my. This is all?' Cirillo asked Jack, quailing under his subordinate, Casale's, furious gaze. 'You do not know where he came from, nor his name?'

'No.'

'Nor we,' said the guard, stepping forward. A well-muscled man, he held himself with the military bearing common to all of them, but with a greater display of authority. 'He gives no name, no hometown, no state. He is no one from nowhere. Nothing about his person save some empty vials.'

'And yet I am expected to lodge this seditious mystagogue near to the most important men of our faith,' snapped Casale.

'No, Bernardino, I say it is wrong. If word of it reaches the camerlengo … A danger.' Cirillo looked as though his colleague had slapped him, and Jack had the impression that the lodging place of the prisoner had been the subject of the debate they had only just stifled. The camerlengo, the old cardinal nominally in charge of the smooth running of the conclave, was master to both men. Jack had seen him – a harmless old sack of a man called Cardinal Cornaro – and wondered at the lengths the two lower priests would go to to keep any trouble from his ears.

'Oh my. It is the best guarded place in this city,' Cirillo said, wringing his hands. There was more desperate entreaty than confidence in his voice, and Jack had the impression of a cossetted, good-natured old man utterly out of his depth in times of trouble. 'If only the commander were not fallen ill. Oh, it does look like this man took advantage of …' He seemed to remember himself as he turned hope-filled eyes to the soldier. 'Captain Moretti?' Jack noted the title. Captain, not commander.

'He shall be well guarded here, father, yes. Somewhere meaner would be fitter, but my men are in their strongest numbers nearest the cardinals. You, boy, you spoke to him?' Moretti's tone was curt rather than rude, his Italian unaccented but his voice cultivated and polite. Not a native speaker, but a polished one. Senior men were always of the better sort.

'He spoke to me.'

'With your leave, fathers, I think the boy should be taken to the creature's cell and confront him with his claims. Justice is not dead.' Jack's eyes widened – though somewhere in his mind it chimed that Roman law demanded that those accused of anything must be confronted by their accusers. 'Perhaps one of the creature's own class will have better luck. He appealed to them, did he not?'

'Sedition,' hissed Casale. 'On this night. He must have come into this place due to the poor judgement of your guards, Moretti, or those who employed the servants of your household, Bernardino.' He folded his arms. 'Very well, take the boy to him. I will not break the rules of conclave, but nor do I think he should be kept here.' He gestured towards the dormitories. 'And I suggest,' he said, speaking again to Cirillo, 'that for the sake of safety you find some means of examining the food in those chambers, lest the creature has done something.'

'I still say the vials smell of treatment for the ache and evil in the fingers.' Cirillo sounded petulant, a child whose pet idea has been scotched.

'And I say I shall not risk it. If this lad speaks true, there is a danger to their Graces – to any one of them, to all. Devise some means of testing the stuff in those rooms. And you.' He snapped his fingers at Jack. 'Come.'

As Cirillo hurried off, Casale and Moretti led Jack not into the building housing the cardinals, but towards another one of the villas. Inside, the setup was much the same albeit on a smaller scale: it was a surplus building of cells presumably designed to accommodate those cardinals who had not been able to attend the conclave. The interiors were no less opulent than the main building, with marble floors, frescoed walls, and carved niches for statuary.

'He is housed here,' drawled Casale with what Jack realised was his customary patrician distaste. He need not have explained: another Swiss Guard was standing by the first door inside the building. 'Moretti, see the boy out when you have finished. Lad, find something from him. Warn him that you know of his rude and slanderous speeches and witnessed his leaving the storehouses. That should unsettle him.'

The priest left, as Moretti nodded to his soldier, who moved to open the door.

'Is he not locked in?' Jack whispered.

'No locks,' Moretti mumbled. 'Built for cardinals and their men. Can't lock them in.'

Jack said nothing as the guard moved aside for them; silently, he supposed it made sense. If there were a fire in the night, it would not do to have the world's highest holy men and their staff locked in their chambers.

Inside, the prisoner was lying on his side, his ankles and wrists tightly bound with rope. He did not move at the intrusion.

'Prisoner, there is one come to accuse you,' said Moretti.

'This one.'

Still nothing.

'Is he … sleeping?' Jack whispered. He could feel the tiny hairs on his forearms begin to rise. There was something strange about the scene. Moretti frowned.

'Prisoner,' he shouted. When no response came, he crossed to the bed and leant over. 'Wake up.'

Suddenly, the old man began convulsing, throwing himself about on the bed as though shaken by an enormous, invisible bear. 'Jesus,' Jack cried.

'Fetch one of the physicians!' Moretti shouted. 'Now!'

***

Amy had already begun drifting into the kind of half-sleep that makes the mouth sticky when Cirillo entered, the old priest attempting to look imperious and managing instead to look fussier and more flustered than ever. Rather than addressing the room directly, he stood, his nose in the air, whilst his attendant held court. His eyes betrayed him, flicking nervously to his clerk. Murmurs and mumbles rippled through the room. Amy rolled onto her side and held herself up on one elbow for a better view. Absently, she let her finger drift in the dirt on the side of one of the barrels and smudged a makeshift shadow on her throat and jaw. For once, she supposed, it was useful that she was not a raving beauty. And still it was good that she was far from unfortunate looking. What she was and always had been was broadly pleasant and wholly unremarkable, and that held true as a woman or a man.

'It has come to our attention that the food stores have been left carelessly unguarded. It may be that someone has simply been stealing from them, for which there will be punishment. However, it might also be that the viper who swam amongst us and has now been secured is an agent from outside this place, who intends to do mischief to one of the cardinals. The enemies of our faith are legion. They are dangerous. It is thus decided that the items in the stores are to be examined.'

The low hum of conversation in the room grew louder, more unsettled.

'Obviously, there are too many of you to pour into that small space,' said the clerk, a little uncomfortably, Amy thought. 'And so, we shall require volunteers.'

No one stirred.

'Very well.' He began moving through the room, towards her and the storeroom. 'You, lad, and you.'

Of course. Though not tall, he towered over her and the middle-aged sneezer.

'As you have chosen to lie in this spot and have thus been lax in the right and proper security of this–'

'Never told to keep it close,' growled Amy. She must, she knew, speak as little as possible if she wished to avoid detection. It was infuriating. Now, for the first time in her life, the weeds of a man lent her liberty to speak and curse and she saw fit – and her treacherous voice stilled her. Colour rose on the clerk's face.

'You will not answer back.' He reached down and wrenched her up, doing the same to her fellow, who did not sneeze or splutter, but made inarticulate, groggy sounds of waking. 'Lazy. Shiftless. You'll go into that storeroom and between you you'll eat of the bread and meats and drink of the wine. You'll discover anything amiss, anything that has been tampered with. I will watch you as you do so.' He smiled. It froze on his face as another commotion broke through the room. All heads turned towards the entrance to the servants' quarters.

Amy's mouth fell open as Jack half-fell into the large, open chamber. 'Physicians,' he gasped. Automatically, she began fumbling to her feet to see if he was hurt. 'We need the least physician.' She only stopped herself from rising at his use of 'we'. Narrowing her eyes, it was clear from his face and manner that he had been sent on this mission.

Of the two physicians who were part of the conclave, neither lodged in the servants' quarters. Only Bianchi, the apothecary, was present, his seniors enjoying a cell in the dormitories. 'What is this?' squeaked Cirillo. 'What now?'

Jack crossed to him and they bowed their heads in quiet conversation. Silence had fallen throughout the kitchen, every bare servant's head twisted to the unexpected drama. After a few moments, the clerk was beckoned over; after a few whispered words, he marched through the lounging crowd to a small closet and rapped on it. Bianchi opened the door and immediately a pungent tang spread through the air. He frowned, his trailing moustaches drooping farther, but he came out, closing the door to his little chamber behind him. Another conference ensued, between Cirillo, Bianchi, Jack, and the clerk. The apothecary nodded, the dangling flaps on his round-topped hat flailing. Looking irritated, he then swept from the room in a flurry of robes. Jack looked in Amy's direction and gave a tight smile before following.

'Now,' said the clerk, moving back towards her as though there had been no interruption. 'It is time for you to begin your job of work. If there's any dark business been done in that storeroom, you two will detect it. I hope you have strong stomachs.'

***

Bianchi left the cell, his face red and his moustaches and ear flaps trembling.

'He is dead?' This was Moretti. He and Jack had remained outside whilst the examination took place. The apothecary had stepped out, to their surprise, after only a quarter of an hour. It was not yet 10 o'clock.

'Dead? Aside from the arthritis – an advanced case, I admit – there is nothing troubling him save a foul and slanderous tongue. I should say–'

Before Bianchi could finish, high, fluting laughter filled the air at his back. His face reddened again. Moretti and Jack looked at one another as the guard slammed the door. Still the laughter found its way through the cracks, wild and piping. 'Who is this creature?'

'We don't know,' shrugged Moretti.

'What did he say to you?' asked Jack.

'He … mind your own tongue, lad. There is nothing wrong with him, as I said. If there were any great tumults in his body, I suspect he laid them himself.'

'You mean he feigned them?'

'I should say so.'

'Why?'

'I do not know,' snapped Bianchi. Jack realised the apothecary was tiring of bandying words with a lower servant. Something the prisoner said had mortified him. 'He is a madman.'

'Dangerous?' Moretti asked, scratching his beard.

'Not if he is kept confined. Only…'

'Yes?'

'He had about him some vials.'

'I found those when I searched him. Empty. Were they of medicines?'

'Perhaps. There was a smell of vinegar and rue.'

'Is that a poison?' put in Jack.

'Anything is a poison if enough of it is taken, lad. Remember that even the purest water can drown a man dying of thirst. Yet it is more than that – he spoke to me. He talked to me. Of my profession. He said that in the past the Church has burnt men who delve into the more profane mysteries of the sciences, and would I not like to see one of the cardinals burnt.'

Moretti's breath caught in his throat. Jack watched his jaw clench. 'He is an assassin?'

'Why,' asked Jack, 'would an assassin get himself caught. Give himself in?'

'I can say nothing of any assassin,' sniffed Bianchi. 'He might just be a madman. Some creatures crave the care of their fellows, will say anything if it provokes them. All I can see is that he is quite well and in no danger, and that he is …'

'Yes?' Moretti asked.

The apothecary's next words came haltingly, as though he grudged them, his cheeks flaming. 'He is a man of some measure of education. With an animal sort of cunning, you understand. You intend to ask him questions?'

'Of course. We know nothing about him and yet needs must lock him up.'

'I … I should not engage him in too much conversation. As I said, he has a slanderous and viperous tongue. He is either a true madman or … or … well, I would say this if we were in any other place but this blessed and sacred city … or a possessed one.' Regaining his composure and his colouring, he announced, more grandly, 'I will see now to Commander von Brunegg. There at least is a patient respects the men who tend him. I doubt that he will eat of your table again though, captain. Too much rich food, too much.'

With that, Bianchi strode from the building. Still, Jack wondered what it was the prisoner had said that so upset the man; was it, perhaps, that he knew something about him, as he seemed to know Cirillo's love of music? Was he connected with someone in the Vatican – perhaps even one of the cardinals? Or, and at this a shiver ran through him, could he really be possessed?

'Well, if he is well enough, mad or not, he has meant only to delay us from asking him questions.' Moretti stroked his beard again, as though in thought; Jack thought that a light had kindled in his intelligent, terrier eyes. Probably he had not expected to be called upon to do anything more during the conclave than ensure the guards relieved each other at the appropriate times – and here was an enigma, potentially an assassin, dropped into one of his cells. 'He shall do so no longer. Are you ready, lad, to draw answers about your accusations from this … this?'

'Yes.'

Moretti nodded at his shoulder, and the guard threw wide the cell door.

4

The prisoner was no longer lying prone on his bed, but sitting on the stool, his ankles and wrists still bound. In the light from a single torch on the wall, his head lolled forward, a shimmering string of drool running from the corner of his lip to his chest. Something was wrong.

'Did the apothecary do something to him?' Jack whispered. Moretti cocked his head, studying the old man.

'Do you hear us?'

'Mhmmm.'

Moretti stepped forward, grimacing as he put a hand under the man's chin and began to raise it. What happened next, Jack saw first. Viciousness flickered in the prisoner's eyes, black and menacing in the low light. 'Look out!'

Moretti jerked his hand back, reaching for his sword as the old man's head whipped forward, teeth bared. Having missed his quarry, he threw it back and bellowed laughter. Jack felt the hairs on his forearms tingle again. Moretti put a stop to the laughter, cuffing the captive across the cheek with the back of his hand. He did not flinch. Instead, he cocked his head and stared at him, unblinking and emotionless again.

'Was that well done of one of Lepanto's heroes, captain? Was that the act of a gentleman? Perhaps I have been rude and ill-mannered to laugh in company. I can only blame my recent bodily weakness.'

'You seem to be recovered,' said Moretti, crossing his arms.

'Just a jest, a game, an old man's fancy to pass the time, Captain Moretti.'

'You know my name. Would you now tell us yours?'

'Us?' Sharpness came into his expression as his eyes moved away from his captor. Panic rose in Jack's breast. He swallowed, turning his attention to the wall. 'Would you be so good as to light more torches in here, captain? My eyes are not so good.'

'There is light enough.'

'Enough, yes. Just enough. I do like fire. Rome burned once, did you know that? It spread from the merchants' shops around the Circus Maximus and the people said the emperor Nero caused it to happen. Can you see it, captain, in your mind, can you imagine the cries of the poor as all the colours of an angry sun rose? Thought himself an artist, old Nero. "Qualis artifex pereo," he cried as they came for him and he turned his blade on himself. Of course, St Augustine tells us good Catholic men thought him the Antichrist. Strange, that – for God likes fire just as much. You can see why. Why he chose to put Sodom and Gomorrah to the flame. Untold death, surely, but how beautiful it must have looked.'

'Cease your prating. Will you tell us your name and from where you have come?'

'Why have you brought me this boy?' he asked, ignoring the question. 'He is not like the other. He is no failed physician feigning the wisdom of superior men.'

Moretti pushed Jack forward, but for a few seconds he could say nothing. Eventually, he stammered, 'I saw you coming out of the storeroom. Earlier this evening.'

'No. You did not. You have brought me a liar, captain.'

'Do you accuse him still?' asked Moretti, not taking his eyes from the old man.

'Yes.' Jack cleared his throat. 'Yes, captain.'

'I wonder what I was doing in there. Ach, at my age, the mind wanders. I have an itch at the back of my head. Would you unbind me?'

'Who are you?' asked Jack. The old man just looked at him, his mouth slackening. A lank streak of grey hair dropped over one eye. Unconsciously, Jack tossed his own head.

The prisoner did not answer at first; he continued staring until Jack dropped his gaze. That strange sense of panic fluttered again.

Eventually, the prisoner shrugged, his swollen hands twisting in his lap. 'Does it matter, really? We are all passing through the world and when we're gone no one will remember us. Not unless we are great. Not unless we are kings, popes, cardinals, artists. Men remember men who do things. And women. Canidia, for example, is a woman well remembered. What do you think I've done?'

'Why did you give yourself up to justice?' This was what Jack really wanted to know – it somehow seemed key to the strangeness.

'Justice? A strange word.' He tilted his head, his eyes rolling around the cell. 'Is this justice?' He smiled. 'I am treated better as a prisoner than a slave to the priests.'

'Have you attempted anything against any one of the cardinals?' Moretti asked.

'Ha! That is your worry? You claim you have seen me making mischief amongst your food and it is your betters you worry about?'

'Answer me.'

'What do you think, Jack?'

Jack drew a sharp breath. 'How do you know my name?'

'Hey! The new pet! You've been summoned.' A chill ran through him – the imitation of his friend Pietro's voice was almost exact but for the burr of age. When had he spoken those words? In the great hall of the palace. The old man must have been amongst the company clearing away the buffet. Or watching, silently, from the shadows.

It was either that or he was some kind of demon.

'What?' Moretti snapped, turning to Jack.

'He mocks me.'

'Do you know him?'

'No. He has been watching us – the servants.'

'How did you come to be in this place? All who were not to work here were expelled before the sun went down,' Moretti asked, his voice now terse.

'Do you worry, captain? About the blame of it?'

'The blame of what?'

The old man grinned, showing his good teeth again, and Moretti repeated his question. 'Oh, there will be time enough after. You, Father Casale, Bishop Cirillo – you can divide it amongst yourselves.'

'You threaten us?' Moretti stepped forward again and cuffed him across the other cheek, harder than before.

'Do you see this, violence against an old man? Why are you here, Jack?'

44

'I accuse you. Captain, he has done something. He has done something to our food. To the cardinals' food.'

Again, the prisoner laughed, but only a thick chuckle. 'Such a young boy. You are not an Italian, are you?' Jack said nothing. 'Young men … here for two reasons only, eh? To make a little money from spying on the men in red, or from a blind love of the faith. Which are you?' He paused, cocking his head. 'A fanatic, yes? A youthful madman, your head filled with the fear of damnation by priests. But you have a family? A wife?' Jack gaped. As if the stranger had willed it, sweat popped out on his back and ran underneath his shirt. His heart sped. If the old man noticed, he gave no sign. Instead, he tutted. 'I wonder what your wife thinks, having a lowly dog to husband. You know, you look like a young Carnesecchi – the image of a pretty young Carnesecchi. Before he got old. Old, and burnt. Do you remember that, captain, how the holy men took him and sliced him and burnt him?'

'You knew Carnesecchi?' asked Moretti.

A grin, sly, Jack thought. 'You recall him? Doesn't our young friend resemble him? He is taller, of course … though … yes, that might be because he still has a head.'

'If you were once a friend of that heretic, we will discover you.'

'Will you burn me too?' A look of fear crossed his face. Jack did not trust it. 'Oh, captain, please, spare me the flames.' Then his expression was again neutral. 'Of all men to behave thus to a poor cripple. Does your son know you threaten old men? That you put the fear into us of–'

At the word 'son', Moretti had launched himself forward. His fist connected with the old man's nose; he toppled from his stool. Jack stood immobile as the sound of choking laughter drifted from the floor. Again, the feeling of unreality choked the cell. Jack wanted to be free of it – of the room and its strange and, he felt sure, dangerous occupant.

'Get that stool out of here,' said Moretti. His voice was calm, but angry colour stood in blotches on his cheeks. 'Treated like a goddammned king. Not in my custody. That bed too. He shall have no comfort.' Jack snapped out of his stupor and did as he was bid, lifting the thing and moving to the door. He pushed it open, deposited the stool, and, as he returned to the room, the captain motioned him over. Together, they dragged the mattress out, and then the desk, lifting the top off its support legs. Only the bedframe remained, denuded but too heavy and awkward to shift. When the place was stripped, Moretti lifted the torch from its sconce. Throughout, the old man had remained motionless on the floor. 'You will not be so clever nor fast with your tongue in the dark.'

'I fear no darkness, captain. But what you fear … I know what you fear. And you will see it before this conclave is over.'

Moretti ignored him, pushing Jack out of the room.

As they stepped out into the hall, the captain removed his cap and ran a hand through his hair, ordering his soldier to close the door. 'If he makes any attempt to leave that cell, kill him. Come,' he said to Jack. The older man seemed to be keeping his self-control in an iron grip, but only just.

Together, they stepped out into the cool night. Overhead, scrag ends of clouds tore past the stars. 'There's something wrong with him,' said Jack. His heart had slowed to an erratic thump. Why had he mentioned his wife – what else had the old devil overheard? If he endangered Amy, he would have to find some means of silencing him himself. And he would. At the thought, his mouth dried. He cleared his throat. 'A madman, as the apothecary said. That name – what was it?'

'Carnesecchi. A heretic, beheaded and then burned … five years ago.'

'A relative, perhaps – that madman is here for revenge.'

'Or so he wishes us to think.' Moretti replaced his cap, straightened it, and then began tugging at his beard. 'Yonder creature is a liar. A common player. A magician. But I can make no enquiries into his background with the city locked up, as I have no doubt he knows. Even the captain of the guard cannot break conclave.'

Realisation dawned. 'He feigned illness. For us to go and get some man of physick, and then again when we went in. He … spoke nonsense. To delay us. Yet if he wished to delay us, to burn away time, I mean … he could have just done nothing, couldn't he? Let the bishop and Father Casale search out the … the …'

'Trespasser.' Moretti gave a curt bob of his head. 'There should be little sport in that for him. No, he means to make himself the lodestone, to guide all men's eyes, distract us. But to keep us from doing what – what does he wish us not to see as we all rush to look at him?'

'The storeroom?'

'The bishop's man will already be at work there. When you saw him leave that place, how did he appear? What was his manner?'

Jack looked at his feet. Had Amy told him? He could not recall, put on the spot. Without looking up, he said, 'He crept. Like a villain.' That seemed reasonable.

'Yet if he is as accomplished a player as he seems, it might be that he wished to be seen. To misdirect us. To have us with our noses in harmless food and our arses in the air, his designs laid elsewhere. What he said to you … that voice …'

'He spoke in the voice of my friend, the words he said in the Sala Ducale. He must have heard–'

'When?'

'When we were at work removing the buffet.' Catching the drift of the captain's questioning, Jack added, 'and he was amongst the servants earlier, standing by me when the bishop spoke to us.'

'Yes. Yes, of course.' Moretti shook his head as if to clear it. 'God, he might have lain within these walls days – before you people – you servants I mean, arrived with your papers and the general rabble were expelled. I had forgotten. It would explain how he … knows the things he knows.'

'What he said to you …'

'My son is … he is very sick.'

'Oh. I'm sorry.'

'Thank you,' said the captain, not meeting his eyes and waving a dismissive hand.

'But how did he …'

'It is no secret. Nor is my work at Lepanto, my presence amongst the company sent to fight.'

'I say … captain … what's wrong with the guards' commander? von Bruno, isn't it? I just now heard he's unwell. Didn't hear talk from the other servants, nothing about that.'

'Brunegg. He is ill.' Moretti's voice instantly took on a flatness of expression. Had he gone too far in questioning his superiors, Jack wondered, or was it that the captain disliked being thrust into a position of responsibility? Or feared it. Or …

Jack felt a grin pull at his lips, the sudden awkwardness of the conversation propelling it. Resisting, he offered, 'did you hear how much he spoke of fire?' This drew a sharp look from Moretti. He took it as encouragement. 'Nero, burning Rome … more light, he asked for.'

'You think it signifies?'

Jack shrugged, unwilling to commit himself. 'Or it might be more … uh … magician's conjuring. Trickery,' he hedged.

'If we knew who he was. He spoke of religion too. Sodom and Gomorrah. Antichrist.' Again, Moretti removed his cap with one hand and dragged his coloured sleeve across his forehead before replacing it. 'Well … it is no more your concern, lad. You can return to the others.'

Jack thought of Amy.

'Captain, if there is any danger here – if he's brought any to us – I'd like to help. In truth, I've known bad men before.' It was the truth, to be sure, but not the reason he volunteered it. Both he and Amy were spies, in the Vatican against the law, in all likelihood – certainly against canon law. What better cover could there be against being investigated and discovered than for one of them to be working hand in glove with the captain of the Swiss Guard?

'You?'

'Yes.' Jack locked eyes with him. Before Moretti could question him, a querulous voice broke in, saving him from answering and making them both start.

'You! Servant-boy! You promise his Grace much and deliver little.'

Jack and Moretti turned to find Hernandez staring at them, one hand on his hip and a slash of eyebrow puckering his dark forehead. Jack grinned, fighting back laughter – the sudden break in tension seemed to force it. Moretti said, 'Father?'

'His Grace,' said the priest, a little more smoothly, presumably having realised Jack was now in some kind of favour with the captain of the guard, 'he has need – suddenly – of a manservant. You promised him. Now he asks.' A little curl of distrust. 'For you.'

'But I …'

'Go,' said Moretti, something like a smile on his lips. 'Your duty is to the conclave. Our duty,' he put out his chest, 'is to the security of all who dwell within these walls.' He turned his smile on the conclavist, and said, barely above a whisper, 'the last cardinal … who surprised us all.'

Jack gave a last look back towards the harassed captain as he followed the scurrying priest into the main dormitory building. What did 'very sick' mean, he wondered. And what was it that Moretti feared?

***

Amy knew what poisons could do. That knowledge set up residence in her stomach even as she gazed at the shelves of food. A brazier had been brought and it cast jolly light across the glass, wood, and the richness of foods. No expense had been spared in ensuring that the cardinals would dine well during the conclave – or at least during its opening days. Some of the shelves buckled at the middle under the weight. Items were arranged with care in the small storeroom. As soon as she and her fellow taster entered, they were faced with a wooden latticework stretching from floor to ceiling, bottles of wine sticking out by their stoppered heads. Beyond the wine shelves, large barrels of unprepared foods stood, and then another series of shelves groaned under the individual delicacies: for the Polish cardinal was a selection of dried sausages; for the many Italians were regional ones; for the German were jars of pickled preserves. The servants' food – hard breads and cheeses – were on the floor next to buckets of raw materials, flour and eggs. Against the far wall stood the sacred provisions: the stuff for use in the masses.

'What are your trades in this place?'

'I'm a master baker, sir, outside these walls,' said the older man. The bishop's clerk grimaced at the sight of him, a film of snot running from his nostril to his upper lip.

'And within them?'

'Assistant to the master bakers.'

'Very good. And you?'

Amy swallowed before answering. 'Here to clean.' She had adopted Jack's role, as outlined on the papers she had memorised and copied, though since entering the Vatican she had hid for most of the day.

'I see. And I am Mr Pavesi, secretary and clerk to the bishop. I've no wish to keep either of you from your business for longer than necessary. And I'm sure you don't wish this to be a long and tedious task. Well, set to. Examine each item for marks.'

'You're telling us to drink the wine?' leered Amy's colleague.

'What is your name?' asked the clerk, narrowing his eyes.

'Giuseppe, sir.'

'Shut your mouth, Giuseppe, and open your ears.' He drew out the name as if it tasted bad. 'Examine those bottles with care. If they're unopened and untouched, they will remain so. I'll not have you having good cheer on safe wine. If they are touched, tell me. The rest,' he added, waving a hand, 'you will do the same with. Look for strange colours or odours – marks of ... marks.' He turned his back on them and stuck his head out the door, barking orders in his brusque Italian. Amy and Giuseppe exchanged glances. After a few minutes, a servant entered with a chair.

'From the apothecary's chamber, Mr Pavesi.' The clerk grinned, turning the chair so it faced into the room. He sat, still smug.

'Go to,' he said. 'I've better things to do than sit all night watching you dullards fill your bellies.'

Giuseppe shrugged before lurching over to rack of bottles. He picked one at random. 'No! Start at one end and move along. You, lad, start at the other.' Amy gave him a dark look. Since being told of her job, she had run through ways of avoiding it.

'Sir, do the cardinals not have their food and drink tested just before they eat it? Before meals?'

'Yes, of course.' The smile became a wolf-like grin. 'Their

manservants eat of every meal brought to their table.' Amy opened her mouth to speak, but Pavesi cut her off. 'And I wouldn't wish any of our guests, either the highest or the lowest, to embarrass this most holy occasion by dropping dead whilst tasting for poisons right in front of the cardinals at mealtime. Make us all look bad, wouldn't it?'

Little bastard, she thought.

'Here,' said Giuseppe, before a sneezing fit took him. ''scuse me,' he said, hunched double. Amy clapped him on the back, keeping her head down. When he had recovered, he looked Pavesi in the eyes, his own shiny-red and watering but defiant. 'Every time the seasons take a turn, by God. Throws my humours into flux. Why not let the little boy out of this, eh? Me, I'm the wrong side of forty and breathed flour and dust most of my days. I'll do what you bid.'

Amy's conscience stirred, gratitude lighting her face. But then guilt. 'He's an old man, sir. Not well, listen to his chest. We can find others, folk who'll be willing, maybe. Or … or I can do it alone.' She was sure she could spin it out or make such a poor and laborious job of it that the clerk would, in exasperation, go and find someone she didn't suddenly care about.

'Silence, both of you. Do you mean to avoid this work by running your tongues down to the roots?' They did not answer, instead staring at him defiantly. 'I can scarce believe my ears. I should wager you've never dined so finely nor eaten so much in your lives – and here you are trying to escape it. If you're careful, if you use your eyes and your noses, you'll discover any strange doings before the cursed meat or drink touches your lips.' He made a fist and banged his knee. 'And if you do, I shall see if some animal, some dog or cat, can be found to taste the soiled stuff. Don't say I'm not a fair man.'

Amy smiled a dejected thanks at Giuseppe and he returned it, sneezing again, but only in his throat.

There was no safe way out, not without drawing too much attention to herself. And, with the clerk, Pavesi, sitting there like an overgrown spider, enjoying their discomfort and fear, she would not back down. She would sip and she would nibble, and if she felt the slightest symptom of poisoning, the last thing she would do would be to smash one of the bottles and cut Pavesi's narrow throat with a shard. The thought gave her courage, and she moved over to the shelves.

Amy took up a position on the left side and reached up, her heart pounding. She extracted the first bottle in the top row and pulled it out. It was heavy, made of opaque class. But it was not full. As she withdrew it, the contents sloshed, the weight shifting to the neck. The wooden stopper was tight, but not fully inserted. She swallowed. Considered putting it back as though she had found nothing.

She hesitated for a beat too long.

'It has been opened?' Pavesi had sprung from his seat. Amy did not reply, letting the clerk peer at it. 'Yes, I see. Well, it looks a fine wine. Perhaps,' he added, scraping across the flagstones to regain his seat, 'it was one of the first opened. Served to welcome our guests.'

Amy looked down, considering, trying to recall which bottles she had seen on the buffet. Pointless. The wines had been gathered in by their own steward and presumably returned to their rightful places in this room. 'Drink.'

She scowled. Often, she had wondered whether officious little dictators reclined in their smugness after ordering servants around, thinking, 'I can make people do things'. Pavesi was the proof of it. But drink she did. God forgive me, she thought, tilting the bottle to her lips. Jack, forgive me – you wouldn't have run to them, your mouth full of tales of what I saw, had you known it would lead to this. The sour smell filled her nostrils as the flat tang of old feet and dusty sandals invaded her mouth. She pulled the bottle away, letting the foul stuff wash about before swallowing it. Vile.

'Return the bottle, please. And continue.'

She felt nothing, but that meant nothing. Poisons could act immediately, burning their way through the innards, or they could be more subtle, unbalancing the humours and discharging the guts after minutes or hours. She tried to turn back time, to imagine how her own victims had behaved after she had been forced to use poison. The years had obscured it all. Perhaps they had said they felt odd, or strange, or their stomachs were sore, or perhaps she had imagined that. She had hardly been in her right mind at the time. An impatient cough at her back brought her back to the present.

As she reached up for the next bottle, she cast another look into the room. It could take hours to examine and taste every item. Her stomach did a little somersault and she froze. No, she thought – it was only that there was something about the jar of pickles that drew her attention.

5

As bells across Rome rang out the hour, Jack placed the jewelled crucifix on its string of beads over Granvelle's head. 'Thank you very much, how kind.'

He had been brought directly to the cardinal's room, which itself sat above his conclavist's. Rather than the single-room cells of the lower floors, those upstairs were composed of sitting room and bedchamber, each fully appointed. The old man somehow looked less exhausted than he had on his arrival. Despite the puffiness around his eyes, they were alight with energy.

Jack stepped back, bowing. Hernandez had huffed out of the room, his nose in the air. On the way, he had asked Jack his exact occupation in the Vatican. On hearing he had been taken on as a sweeper and general cleaner, the priest had lost no time in denouncing him to Granvelle. 'Is that so?' the cardinal had asked in his stronger Italian. 'And do we not love the lowest as the highest?' That had shut the man up and driven him, muttering in his native Spanish, from the room.

'Ah, to be in fresh clothes,' said Granvelle, tilting his head back. Jack had helped him out of the spattered cardinal's robes – a necessary evil, the thick, rich material, for speeding progress through the countryside – and into a clean, purple cassock. It was good to have something to do, something practical and ordered. It pushed the madness contained in the villa across the way out of his mind. 'You will take those to be laundered?'

'At once, your Grace.'

'No rush, lad. I have others.' He gestured towards the bedchamber. 'Tell me, what is your name?'

'Jack.'

'You are not an Italian?'

'No, your Grace. Uh, I can speak French if you prefer it.'

'Ah, excellent.' Genuine warmth flooded his features as he switched. 'You are from France?'

'No, your Grace. I'm English.'

'English?' Bushy eyebrows rose, wrinkling the enormous forehead. Without his hat, it was apparent that the cardinal was losing a fight with baldness. 'You are amongst the exiles from that blighted land?' Jack inclined his head. 'Mm. His Holiness' bull must have driven a great number of you hither. I have heard it said, by some, that it was less than well advised, freeing your people from allegiance to Elizabeth.'

'They think us traitors,' said Jack, barely above a whisper.

'Who does?'

'Sir William Cecil. I think he's a new name now. And his man Walsingham. And … her … Queen Elizabeth.' Even saying the names felt dangerous, as though it might conjure their presence, their busy, suspicious ears.

'A pretended queen. A bastard born.'

'That is what she thinks we all think.'

'Heh. You would make a fine diplomat, young man, were you born to a higher station in life. Do you know, I recall when that pretended queen was born. I was a young man then, of course. The Spanish ambassador in England, a Mr Chapuys, he wrote to me when I served the emperor.' He put a finger to his lips. 'Her mother, the concubine Boleyn, had lost herself in the embraces of over one-hundred men. Or so her husband thought. And the false archbishop, Cranmer, declared and pronounced by way of sentence the lady's daughter to be a bastard, and begotten by the king's servant.' Jack only nodded, letting the old man revel in decades' old gossip. Yet he noticed that Granvelle's eyes didn't wander into the mists of time; they remained on him, as though waiting for a reaction. A note of resistance, perhaps – a flicker of defence of England's queen. Finding none, he went on. 'And that little bastard, declared by her own heretic church, is grown old and leads England. I understand she rules as thoroughly as though she were a man. A poor state, a mad state, that knows not what it desires, pulled first this way and then that by its sovereigns' false promises. My master was once wed to your former queen, Mary. And hoped to woo her sister. Before her manifest heresies became clear.'

'Yes, your Grace. I was born when the old queen lived.'

'The old Mary,' he said. 'A good Catholic. Let us hope her cousin and namesake breaks free her chains, eh? Then you might return to a Catholic home. Now, lad – Jack – am I ready?'

Granvelle brushed down the front of his robes and gave him an enquiring look. Jack grinned in response. At first, he had been surprised when the cardinal bid him dress him not in nightclothes but in his priestly weeds. But it was hardly his place to ask questions. Before they could speak any further, a soft knock came at the door. Granvelle's eyebrows knitted and he nodded towards it.

Opening it, Jack found himself looking down at a serious-faced man with a curving beak of a nose. He recognised him as the cardinal who had arrived not long before Granvelle's own eleventh-hour appearance: the Italian whom everyone had assumed was the last of them. They stared at one another, neither speaking, for a few seconds. 'My dear Carlo,' Granvelle said. 'I was hoping to see you before … please, come, come.'

'Do you require anything else, your Grace?'

'Jack … this is Cardinal Borromeo,' he gestured towards the little man who strode into the room, his face still intense. Jack bowed. 'Please, Carlo, sit.' Borromeo did, clasping his hands in his lap as he folded himself into a cushioned chair. There was something prim about him, his wiry body unmoving whilst the eyes burned. 'I might have need of you later.'

'I shan't go anywhere,' said Jack, a more natural smile on his face.

'Tell me, are you a betting man?'

'Yes, your Grace.' He wasn't, but he never knew what to say when someone asked an unexpected question, especially a superior.

'Then I am pleased to give you a tip.' He looked down at Borromeo and winked, but the seated cardinal said nothing. 'Forget Farnese. Put your money elsewhere.' He tapped the side of his nose before turning his back. Jack left the room as the two began speaking in low, rapid Latin.

In the hall outside, Jack paused. Granvelle had as good as told him that the favourite throughout Italy would not be elected. That information would be valuable. People crowded outside the walls of the Vatican day and night during conclaves – when they knew who the new pope would or would not be, they could sell it on to those who would sack the winner's houses, safe in the knowledge that he had found a new and even richer home.

The whole thing, he was beginning to realise, must take place during the night: the horse-trading, the arguing, the bartering and debating – the decision itself. And the cardinal had joked with him about the result. It must be expected that the servants were there to spy, to discover information ahead of the result, to make money out of it, even. There was something grubby in that, for all he liked Granvelle. When the mystery was stripped away, what remained was rather humdrum, nothing special about it, nothing magical. For a moment he was back in childhood, during Queen Mary's reign. He knew and cared nothing for religion then, but one week a series of mystery plays had been acted in the grounds of the duke of Norfolk's castle. He had watched the angels and devils caper, the reds and whites lit by the sun, the masks terrifying, and felt, as any child might, that he was seeing magic unfold. Then, later, he had sneaked around, hoping for more, and gawped at the actors, unmasked and disrobed, arguing and drinking behind the cheap wooden scenery. His father had come upon them all then, grabbing him by the hair and throwing him to the ground, cursing him for watching papistical fancies. The old man had chased the players off, helping himself to their half-drunk ale, and the illusion had gone with them.

But there was something else.

As he had departed from Moretti outside the prisoner's dormitory, the captain had said something. 'The cardinal who surprised us all.' Granvelle. Obviously the Spanish king's man had not been expected. That meant that when the stranger entered the Vatican – however he entered it – he must have shared the common run of thought: Cardinal Farnese was expected to be the next pope. That made Farnese a target – or an original target. The question was whether the last-minute arrival had disturbed a plan already in train, and if so, what could the damned lunatic do from a cell?

He padded down the staircase and ran into Moretti at the bottom, a soldier at his back.

'Captain. I've finished attending on Cardinal Granvelle. It's glad I am to see you.' Briefly, he shared with Moretti the thoughts that had been brewing. To his surprise, the captain showed no alarm. Instead, he grinned, the smile wiping away years. Jack placed him somewhere in his mid-thirties, though earlier he had thought him about forty-five.

'You are more than a simple sweep, indeed. My thoughts ran on the same path. I have been seeking a man to help me approach his Grace. In the interests of security.'

'Shall I come?'

At this, Moretti hesitated, looking between his own soldier and Jack. At length, he motioned with a hand for the soldier to stand back. 'You said to me that you had knowledge of wicked deeds. What did you mean by that?'

Jack sighed, tossed the hair out of his eyes, and swallowed. 'How long do we have?'

'Not long.'

'Hmm.' He cleared his throat and then told his story, from his service to the Scottish queen to his discovery of a plot to kill her and Queen Elizabeth. Moretti's eyes widened and he shook his head, though not in disbelief. When he had finished, Jack launched immediately into recounting what had followed – a plot against the Church by a family of murderers who had dispatched members across Europe hoping to provoke a bloody religious war. Carefully, he omitted any mention of Amy, Sir William Cecil, and Francis Walsingham. The result, he supposed, was bare bones, but it covered the main events. He bowed his head when he had finished, quite prepared for Moretti to laugh at him.

'Then you are well met in this matter,' he said instead. And then, 'tell me, is Queen Mary of the Scots really such a beauty?'

'She's bonny enough,' he said, using the Scottish word. Moretti gave a short bark of laughter. Jack got the impression that it was something he seldom did, and he recalled the mention of the sick son.

'Well, you know something of plotters and madmen if your tale is true. And if it is not true, then you are a fine teller of tales and I will buy you a bottle of good wine when this conclave is over, and that madman's identity discovered.'

'Shall I go and tell the other servants, or some of them, that there might be something strange here? Let them be our eyes and ears, like?' The sudden urge to be useful took him by surprise. The 'our' had come unbidden.

'And raise a general alarm, have men fighting one another and inventing tales over private grudges?' Jack's face fell. 'We shall not. You shall be my eyes and ears amongst the lower sort.' He turned and dismissed his own man, who shrugged and wandered off down the lower hall.

Jack and Moretti proceeded upstairs. As they marched past the frescoes, a door opened and, the occupant seeing them, immediately closed. They ignored it and went directly to Farnese's door.

The cardinal's conclavist answered and gave them a sour look. 'Who is it, Gio?' The voice drifted from the bedchamber. Jack thought that that he heard pathetic hope in it.

'Captain Moretti of the Swiss Guard, your Grace.' The older man spoke over the priest's shoulder. 'I come in the matter of the security of your person.'

This brought Farnese out of the room. The big man, so gregarious earlier, looked deflated. Unlike Granvelle, who apparently had a job of work to do during the night, he had been changed into his bedclothes. 'What? What is this? Cannot a man sleep?' Then he saw Jack. 'Why do you bring this man? He works for … Cardinal Granvelle.'

'No, your Grace,' said Jack. 'I … I'm just a general servant. Of the common run. I'm … Captain Moretti asked me to help him.' He looked at Moretti in appeal.

'That is so. We have some information from a man lately taken that there is some design on a great one, your Grace.'

'There is danger?'

'We do not know. It is possible.'

'Hmph,' said Farnese, looking towards his conclavist. 'You hear that, Gio? Not enough that they seek to ruin me, one seeks to kill me. Who is this prisoner?'

Moretti shifted uncomfortably. 'This we do not know. He appears to have no name, no state – he is a … we do not know. For the security of all within the conclave, he has been arrested and closed away.'

'Then why do you seek to enter my cell? Are you searching all the cells?'

'If necessary, yes,' hedged Moretti.

'The camerlengo, he knows of this? And Father Casale?'

'Father Casale knows that a prisoner has been taken up.' Moretti put his chest out. 'And he bids me discover what I can.'

'And this intrusion – do they know of that?'

'They each wish the safety of all in the conclave.'

'Ha. You would make a fine politician, Captain Moretti. And a finer cardinal.'

The two men stood facing each other, neither giving ground. Jack guessed that Farnese was debating whether or not to make trouble. Eventually he sighed. 'Very well. Make whichever searches you wish. One moment only.' He turned and barked something in Latin at the priest, who sidled past them all. 'You do not need my conclavist present, do you?'

'No, your Grace.'

'Good.' When only the three of them were left on the threshold, Farnese stood back. He remained standing in the doorway, watching them as they set to work.

Jack's eyes fell first on a small load of bread, well-floured on top, sitting next to a round block of cheese. A narrow end of each had been sliced away. He looked at Moretti, who nodded. As he bent to it, Farnese called out, 'it has been tasted.'

'By whom … your Grace?'

'My man – my valet.'

'And when did you last see your valet?'

Farnese did not answer. Instead he frowned, crossing his arms and turning to look outside the doorway. Moretti gave a brief smirk as Jack tore off an edge and sniffed it. He fought a sneeze at the flour but judged the thing harmless and began gnawing. His stomach rumbled in delight – he had not eaten for some time – but was otherwise fine.

'The cheese?' Moretti prompted.

Jack wrinkled his nose. 'I've gone right off cheeses, captain. Since living in France. The smell, even.'

'Oh, for the love of God,' snarled Moretti, though without any real anger. He picked up the small, blunt knife that lay next to the platter and sliced off a sizeable chunk. His eyebrows raised sarcastically, he held it beneath his nose and then popped the entire thing into his mouth. 'It is good. Italian style, not French. Good.'

After delicately dabbing as his lips, Moretti moved towards the bedchamber, from which soft candlelight fluttered. Jack followed. Inside the smaller room was another desk and a bed. It was an airless room, stiflingly warm, the only ventilation a small barred window higher than eye level. The bed was not a grand four-post affair, but a well-dressed cot swathed in scarlet. On the desk, next to a profusion of candles, was the crumpled note Jack had given the cardinal earlier. It had been smoothed out and the contents angrily inked over, spiky lines scratched across the original writing. Moretti was looking down at it, his eyes narrowed. 'A threatening note? Your Grace,' he called into the other room. 'Have you been sent any letters threatening your person?' A laugh came in response, followed by a gruff demurral.

Jack said nothing.

'Do you know how to secure a great man's bed?' the captain asked.

'No, sir. I ... my business before today was horses. Caring for them, I mean. But there were no places for grooms left this morning.'

'A noble business. A man's bed is a weak place – like when he sits on his privy, his guard is down. Come.'

Over the next twenty minutes, Moretti instructed Jack to strip the bed down to its feather mattress. When it was bare, they felt every inch of the thing, looking for concealed spaces. Likewise, they felt all along the underside of the bedframe, lest an assassin had hidden a weapon there to retrieve in the night and put to use.

Nothing.

'Help me replace it,' said Moretti, and together they hoisted the mattress back onto the frame. 'Now, throw yourself upon it.'

'What?' Moretti repeated himself. Jack shrugged and did so. 'Roll.'

Jack rolled from side to side, feeling a fool. As he did, the bitter sting of sweat nipped at him. With disgust, he realised it came from his own armpits. He had been wearing the same clothes now since before dawn and was now spreading his stink across a cardinal's bed. Only when Moretti told him to rise did he spring up. A tiny feather had come loose, and he brushed it off his chin.

'Sometimes a thin needle might be lost amongst the feathers. To pierce the body when the sleeper turns. I thought it best not to tell you before.'

Jack's eyes widened and then, without meaning to, he laughed. 'You ever seen that happen? A man wakes in the night only to find he's been pierced and … dead?'

Moretti's lip twitched. 'I do not need to see something happen to know it might. This room is clean, it is untouched. If our prisoner planned the death of Cardinal Farnese, he placed nothing here to do its work in advance. Perhaps they have had more luck in the kitchens.'

'You think that's it, though? That stranger placed something somewhere and then got himself caught?'

'Perhaps. It would explain why he had no fear of being locked away, if his design had been set in motion. And, depending what it was, who it was aimed at, he could always say that he had been carefully imprisoned when it occurred.'

'A good defence.'

'A defence, yes.' He paused, coughing into his fist. Jack followed suit. The air in the dormitories was already starting to foul, the acrid fug from candles and sconces thickening it. 'Well,' said Moretti, recovered, 'put this place in order and I shall look in on the storerooms. If all is in order, some sleep might be a welcome thing for you.'

'And you.'

'No. I do not sleep at night, not since … I have the night watch. Yet it must be near midnight. I shall speak again to that blasted lunatic in the morning, see if a night locked in the dark with no comfort has softened his sharp tongue.'

Jack made the bed, not particularly carefully, and they re-entered the sitting room. Farnese had not budged from the doorway, where his conclavist had rejoined him. 'See,' he said, not troubling to lower his voice, 'how they all pay court to the king of Spain's man?' He was looking out into the hallway.

'We are finished, your Grace,' Moretti said, bowing. 'You should sleep well tonight.'

Again, Farnese laughed. 'A thought which brings great comfort.' The cardinal and his conclavist joined by a third – the manservant who had presumably been summoned – and Jack and Moretti left the room, just as the cardinal was ordering his servant to dress him.

Farther down the hall, Granvelle's door was open; Borromeo was speeding away from it and another man, whom Jack could not recall from before, was entering. 'Do they never stop?' he whispered to Moretti. He did not have time to respond. As they marched again down the hallway, Granvelle's own conclavist appeared.

'You. Servant,' Hernandez barked. 'You are not leaving this place again?'

Jack looked at Moretti before speaking, but the older man offered him no encouragement either way. 'I thought I'd be going back to the other servants. In the kitchens.'

'Against the rules of conclave. You are become the cardinal's man, I regret. No one in or out.'

'You were out,' said Jack, immediately regretting the impertinence. But it was done. 'When I was in the other dormitory you were out looking for me.'

The priest began spluttering, apparently fighting for suitable words of outrage in Italian. Moretti intervened. 'Do you wish the boy sharing your bed downstairs?' The man reddened, folding his arms.

'I'll be back,' Jack offered, hoping a smile would defuse things. 'Oh, yes, I forgot. I have to bid the cardinal goodnight.'

Without waiting for the priest to recover, he stepped around him and knocked lightly on Granvelle's door. The hum of conversation ceased. He opened it.

'Jack?' Granvelle raised his eyebrows. 'My servant, Michele,' he said to his guest, a surprisingly young one, clad in a black-and-white habit rather than red robes. 'Would you like anything brought, any refreshment?'

The other man, Michele, shook his head. Then, almost immediately, 'perhaps a little wine. Very weak.'

'Some weak wine for Cardinal Bonelli,' echoed Granvelle, clapping his hands. 'Will you see it requested, Jack? No need to bring it yourself. Very thoughtful of you, lad, to ask.' He smiled. 'I think I shall prefer stronger wine for the task ahead.'

'Uh … Begging your Grace's pardon, but I came only to get the robes.' When blankness took over the old man's features, he nodded towards the bedchamber. 'The dirtied robes, from your Grace's travels.'

'Ah, yes.' The two cardinals remained silent whilst Jack gathered them up. 'God give you thanks,' said Granvelle, 'how kind.' He shifted his attention to the table, where a bulky little clock ticked on its springs. 'So late. I have yet one more thing to do before I can be made ready for sleep. I judge it should be some time past one of the clock. If you would return to me then.'

'Yes, your Grace.' His arms filled with a weighty bundle of red silk, he made an awkward bob of a bow and left them, using his foot to bang the door closed just as Hernandez slipped in.

Moretti now stood alone in the hall. 'Yonder cardinal's man is no friend to you,' he observed.

'He doesn't know me yet,' said Jack.

They went downstairs and left the dormitory, crossing the leafy courtyard. The dormitory which housed only the prisoner and his guard remained silent. As Jack looked up at it, he felt a chill run through him. It was a relief to leave the cardinals' closed world and return to the San Damaso.

As they made to enter the kitchens, a voice hissed from just inside. 'You are kept at work tonight, huh?'

'Pietro. My man. Not asleep?'

'Who sleeps on the first night of the …' His friend trailed off, noticing that Captain Moretti was with him.

'Good evening to you, lads,' said the older man, giving no indication of what they had been about. He marched away, through the little thickets of servants, towards the storeroom.

'What is all this?' Pietro looked at the red bundle. Jack shifted, rebalancing it in his arms.

'For cleaning. Do you know, how does stuff get cleaned here? There are no laundresses about, unless the men are doing it somewhere.'

Pietro's tongue flicked over his lips and he smoothed a strand of hair behind his ear. 'No, no laundresses. Give it to me, I'll see to it.' He reached out. Instinctively, Jack clutched the robes a little closer.

'Why? I mean … it's work, isn't it?'

'Ah,' winked Pietro, 'this stuff, for the laundry, it goes out in the morning. The cardinals' men are supposed to leave it by the doors of their building. Then it gets taken down to the entrance to the city. The guards allow it out. In the morning, some good nuns from the convent come. Gather it up, take it, return it, all fresh and clean and fit to cover a cardinal's arse. But, heh … around those gates the people of Rome gather. They throw money for any news of the conclave.'

'Have you heard any news?' At this, Pietro looked crestfallen, holding up his palms and shaking his head. 'Um … I shouldn't say it, but I did hear that Cardinal Farnese is out. He won't get it. For sure.'

'What? My favourite, huh?' He didn't, thought Jack, look all that surprised. 'It's the coming of that foreign man, that Spaniard.'

'He's from the Dutch Netherlands, I think. Speaks French.'

'Well maybe *he* is. Not Italian is not Italian. King of Spain is the king of Spain. This is my opinion.' He shrugged.

'You lost money?'

'Not if I can make enough back from this, huh?' He inclined his head towards the red robes. With a sigh, Jack held them out. 'And I have to act with haste. I saw a man earlier, creeping around in black'

'So?'

'So he might know something, be selling it out of the gates before I get there. This business, it's cutthroat. But it's exciting, no? It stirs the blood.'

'Yeah, it's exciting.' Jack, without realising it, had adopted Pietro's slouch. He straightened up. 'Stirs the blood. Well just be careful. I said I would get them laundered.' As the weight shifted to Pietro, he winked again.

'I'll guard them with my life, my friend. Thanks for the tip. When I'm a rich man I'll take you out for a drink in Rome, huh?' He moved away from the kitchens and out into the night.

***

It was near midnight by the time Giuseppe and Amy had finished sampling everything that the kitchen storeroom had to offer. Every bottle had been checked, many drunk from, and every scrap of food nibbled, sniffed, licked, or all three. Even the crate of communion bread, still only unleavened wheaten discs until the miracle of transubstantiation should transform them, was opened and the top layer of unspotted, unsullied pieces tasted. Likewise, the crate of communion wine was found to be untouched, the crate of incense crystals and powders pungent but inedible, and even the cheap, wooden cooking utensils licked in case poison had been smeared on them.

Despite giddiness from the stench of concentrated incense and wine, neither had felt any particularly ill effects, other than the surfeit of food causing flatulence in Giuseppe and an urgent need to urinate, much like the feeling she got every time she rode a horse, troubling Amy.

'Well done, both of you.' Pavesi had not moved from his chair for the better part of two hours, watching every move like a hawk.

Amy turned on him, ready to speak, but to her surprise, Giuseppe saved her the risk and the trouble. 'A rotten thing, sir, to risk us like this, the pair of us, an old man and a child.'

'Mind your tongue.'

'I'll mind it. For now,' grumbled Giuseppe, before breaking wind loudly. 'Can't mind the other end.'

'You're disgusting,' snapped the clerk, but his words were lost in Amy's laughter and Giuseppe's phlegmatic sneezes. 'Count yourself a lucky man that you have been trying me with those filth-spattered breaths this whole night, else I should have you taken to the physicians and cut open to see that no poison had got into you.'

'Is all tested and well?' All three pairs of eyes turned to Moretti, whose colourful figure filled the doorway. Amy thought him rather handsome, for a taciturn old soldier.

'This room is clean. Which,' Pavesi added with a pointed look, 'is more than I can say for the base servants who have been despoiling it. Common as muck, the pair of them.'

Moretti tilted his head back as far as his carefully angled black cap allowed, his nostrils flaring in a sigh. Pavesi began a long, tedious inventory of the items kept in the storeroom, his voice droning and monotonous. The captain opened his mouth to speak, but before he could cut off the recitation, Jack did, loping into the room.

'Captain, I …' He locked eyes with Amy.

'Jack!' she cried, drawing everyone's attention. Shit, she thought. It had been an involuntary response. 'My brother,' she offered, growling it out.

'I came to fetch wine for the cardinal, for Cardinal Granvelle, he asked for it, said I should just order it, but I thought I would come and get it, weak wine, he said, or Cardinal Bonelli did.' His words tumbled over one another and Amy realised, with a flush and rush of love, that he was trying to draw the focus of the room away from her. She had not said to anyone that Jack was her brother and supposed he had not either. It was not a lie that bore scrutiny, he over a head taller with brown hair and she short and mousy.

'This,' said Pavesi, standing and stretching, 'should please his Grace.' He brought down a bottle and handed it over. Jack nodded thanks and again chanced a look over at her. She tried to smile, noticing the wrinkle across his brow. It would not be hard for him to work out what had been going on in the storeroom.

'All's well here?'

'All is well,' said Moretti. 'Mr Pavesi assures me the room is clean. If our prisoner worked mischief, it was not in this place.' His jaw twitched. Tired, Jack thought, as he was himself. 'I must do my rounds. It will be a long night. God give you all a goodnight.' He clicked his heels and left.

Pavesi watched his departing back, and then looked at Jack. Suspicion was plain on his pinched, arrogant face – a distrust of whatever had been going on between servant and captain.

'Well, get to his Grace's service,' he snapped, pointing at the bottle.

Jack looked again at Amy. He was, she noticed, biting down on his lower lip. Again, she smiled in reassurance. As he followed Moretti from the room, it faded. Her stomach had lurched madly. A bolt of pain. Clouds drifted in front of her eyes.

***

Jack made his way across the San Damaso, the bottle of weak wine tucked under one arm. Moretti must have been faster, for there was no sign of him.

His mind had focused on Amy. It was clear she had been made to taste the foodstuff in the storeroom. It had not even registered dimly that someone would have to do it – if he had stopped to consider it at all, he would have imagined it would have fallen to the cardinals' own valets. He cursed himself. And then a hard voice of reason intruded. She had looked quite well. She had been giving little smiles – surely those were indications that she was unharmed. And Moretti and Pavesi both said the room had been clean. Besides, it was not really his fault that she had been put in such a terrible position. If she had not intruded on the conclave, if she had stayed safely at the Hydes' villa, safe in the nest of English exiles, it would never have happened. In the future, when they were out of the place, they could laugh about it – how her own rashness had got her testing food for poison.

Moretti and Pavesi had both said that the room was clean.

She was unharmed, her smile the proof of it.

The two points chimed in his head along with the bells ringing out midnight.

He had not got halfway across the dormitory courtyard when movement to his left caught his eye. He froze. The prisoner's building, visible through the thin, planted trees, remained silent. No torches or braziers gave cheer. His eyes, accustomed to the dimness, told him nothing. If someone had moved, they had done so stealthily – in which direction and from where he couldn't say.

Nothing. He was letting the night get to him. He smiled away his own foolishness. It was too easy to let fear gain a foothold in the dark. Childish terrors – who was opening and closing your door in the night, what was lurking in the shadows – never left, they just wore different disguises.

He continued on his way. The Swiss Guards were not outside the cardinals' building, as they ought to have been. Instead, they were ranged around a brazier inside. Its flames issued curling black smoke. Already it was smudging the frescoes. They ignored him and he jogged down the hall and upstairs. Granvelle's door was opened a crack at his rap, not by the cardinal himself but the scowling Hernandez. The man snatched the bottle and bid him a terse goodnight before slamming the door in his face. More slowly, he returned downstairs. Something seemed to pull at him – the thought, though he would not admit it, of returning through that neat little quadrangle with its looming villa buildings. He idled, warming his hands alongside the uncommunicative guards, before his nipping eyes warned him to return to the servants' quarters.

As he was making his return, a more definite movement intruded. It was Moretti, coming from the direction of the San Damaso. In the moonlight, he was colourless, face and uniform.

'You not bedward, captain?'

'I told you, I have work to attend to through the night. I thought … I should like to see if our prisoner has spoken to his guard. That storeroom … it might indeed be clean. It might be that there was some other design than poison laid, some other wicked weapon. I cannot rid myself of the feeling that something strange is below my nose. I will not sleep until I can be free of it. Ugh, but I would wish for this conclave to be as swift as they have all said it would be. And yet … and yet if it shall be over in a day or two, there is but little time to discover what dark deeds might be intended.'

'I'll come,' said Jack. He considered whether to say he thought he had sensed movement outside the building earlier. No, he thought – it might make him look crazy. Besides, his eyes were tired from the long day. 'I've been up and about since before the sun rose this morning,' he said instead, for no other reason than his jagged eyelids seemed to demand recognition.

The moment they entered the unused dormitory it was clear

something was wrong.

The door to the prisoner's cell was ajar, the stool smashed and the mattress shredded. Downy feathers fluttered languidly in the air. The guard was nowhere to be seen. In the light from the flaming torch on the hallway wall, a bloody handprint on the door waved at them.

6

Amy kept her face to the ground as she walked from the room. Only rarely in life had she ever drunk so much that it clouded her mind and vision. That same feeling assailed her now, making the shelves sway and the floor rise and fall towards as she tried not to stumble out of the storeroom. For a moment she was at sea, she was being tossed and swayed as she had been on the ships that had carried her from England to France, from France to Scotland, from Scotland to the Dutch Netherlands. Up and down and round and round her head sailed.

It was not poison. That much she knew.

Yet she was determined not to let Pavesi or Giuseppe suspect that it might be. She sat down in her place by the barrels. It had begun to stink of urine – her fault – from earlier. Again, the wave of nausea rose up. She lowered herself to the ground and, as soon as she had sat, the weary light-headedness passed like a cloud before the sun.

She stayed sitting, enjoying the relief, as Giuseppe left the storeroom, Pavesi at his back, pushing and muttering. The clerk closed the door and marched away, arms crossed and nose in the air. Amy mouthed the worst swear word she could think of at his departing back.

Giuseppe chortled as he sat down a few feet from her. He braced his back against a barrel and turned his head. 'It's no joke, how we're treated here.' She murmured in assent. 'You didn't see yonder clerk making for to let any food or drink touch his lips.'

'You expected him to?'

'No. I still reckon it's not right. Treating us like animals and not even trying a bite himself. Unmanly.' He wiped his nose with the back of his hand.

'Wouldn't have the stones to.'

'That's the truth, by God. It's a good thing to know where you stand in folk's eyes. At home I'm a master baker. Treat my lads right. Here I'm nothing. Not to the likes of him, leastways. No different to a bloody sweep. No offence meant to you.'

Amy rolled her eyes. It seemed she attracted people who

would not shut up, even when she had to discipline herself to guard her tongue. Desperately she longed for her books. Since taking up residence in Italy, she had begged Jack to borrow or buy the histories, on the basis that it helped her with the language. That was a lie. Luckily, Italian had come as easily as all languages came to Jack. Something about the expressiveness of it and its gestures appealed to her; it was ironic, she thought, that she spoke a much more fluent Italian tongue than she ever had an English one. No, in truth, she read because she had become fascinated with the life of the wicked Queen Cleopatra as she appeared in *Le vite de gli huomini illustri greci e romani* by Plutarch. There was something magical about walking in a city were such an exotic creature had walked, seeing the things she saw.

Considering reading was a mistake. Suddenly she ached to turn her head and drown out Giuseppe's wittering with her own new stock of facts. Before she could speak, he said, 'you going in on the night raid? I reckon you could get some revenge on Pavesi then, the little villain.'

'What?'

'The raid. I don't know what time.' He seemed to take her confused silence as encouragement. 'It's a tradition in these things. On the first night of the conclave. The servants – the lower servants – we take ourselves up to the pope's rooms.'

'Take ourselves?'

'Heh. Well the younger ones do. Aim to to strip 'em down.'

'To rob the place?'

'Ho, not to rob. It's tradition. They frown on it, to be sure, those above us. Pavesi'll try and stop it, no doubt. Hopefully get a knock about the pate if he does. But tradition's tradition. Those with the balls to do it only take anything small or lowly enough not to be willed or inventoried anyway, nothing big. The camerlengo, he'll have seen that the stuff the old boy willed is gone, so what's left, the trash – that's game for anyone willing to breach the apartments and take it.'

'When?'

'I said I dunno. Whenever the rest are up to it.' He angled his nose into the wider kitchens, where snores rippled.

'Seems a bit rotten to me,' Amy growled. 'Like, um, what you'd expect a bunch of eastern savages to do. Speaking of eastern savages, did you know Cleopatra was living in Rome when Caesar was slain?'

'Ah, Queen Cleopatra. She interests you?' Amy mumbled in assent, ready to astound him with facts until, hopefully, he fell asleep and she could find somewhere quiet to pee. His next words stilled her ready tongue. 'Doesn't surprise me. Wicked women catch the hearts of lots of young girls.'

***

Moretti held the torch aloft and pushed the door to the cell open. The eyes of the figures painted on the walls bored into him. Jack looked away from them and followed the captain inside.

They spotted the body at the same time.

The guard lay face down on the floor. Moretti stepped towards him, avoiding the cap that lay forlorn between the corpse and the doorway. He turned on the spot. 'Gone.' Jack shivered.

'Is he … he's dead, isn't he?' He said it only for something to say. Moretti passed him the torch before kneeling to examine the body. He rolled it over. The man's head lolled back, far too far. The front of his tunic was untucked and sodden, the blood looking almost black.

'The throat has been cut. Too deeply, near decapitation.' The word chilled Jack further. What was it the prisoner had said about the man, the heretic, Carnesecchi? That he had been short a head. And then burnt, Moretti had told him.

'But … where is he? How … I mean, how did an old man do this?'

Moretti did not respond immediately. In the dim light his expression was hard to read. It almost seemed to Jack as if he were looking through the body. He remembered the older man had been at Lepanto. The rumours throughout Europe were that it had been a bloody and costly victory for the Catholic faithful. Eventually, Moretti said, 'it could be this way. The miserable prisoner cries out, cries for help, feigns sickness again. And my man – this soldier – he hears the cries and enters the room. He would expect nothing, not from an old man. An old man who might be playing, giving out that he was sick. And then,' he sprung to his feet, making Jack jump and the torch veer through the air, 'he cuts.' He stood, waiting.

'Begging your pardon, captain, but … well, I mean, what with? He had been searched, hadn't he? And had no weapon about him?'

'Hmph. Anything might be sharpened. First cutting his bonds and then … and then this other.'

The rebuttal was weak. Jack pressed on. 'And … see, if he cut the guard's throat … how? Even with a weapon in his hands – and remember his hands, they're all deformed.' He considered further. 'To cut a throat. You do that from behind, do you not?' He had never seen it done, but he imagined.

'It is easiest. Yes. Yet it can be done from the side. Or the front, if the … the victim … is held fast.'

'If he didn't, though …'

'If our prisoner did not do this … this thing … then he had a confederate who freed him. And that we cannot say.'

'It would explain why he didn't care about being locked up. He knew he'd be freed. Knew that whatever he's here for, someone else would do it.' His mind flitted through all those whom the guard might have trusted enough to turn his back on, opening the door for them. A priest, perhaps, another guard hoping to peep at the strange prisoner, a servant bearing food, even.

'And yet if he had a confederate then he had no need for freedom.'

'Unless it's a job of work that takes two men.' He let the thought simmer. 'Something big, needing shifted, like. I mean, the Vatican is a big place, isn't it?' Moretti nodded, a little curtly. 'Maybe it's … maybe they're not after Farnese or any one man. Maybe not the people at all – maybe the place.'

'They … I do not know that there is any they.' Jack noticed that the captain had shifted from the collective to the singular. Moretti looked again at the body. 'Much blood usually issues from a cut throat. It pours from the neck in a foul rush.' He looked again at Jack. 'Whoever did this should be soaked in it. And yet look – barely a drop touching the floor.'

74

'The door – there's a hand of blood on the door.' Something he had heard in Scotland came back to him – there they had mentioned people being caught 'red-hand'. It made sense now. Only no one had been caught.

'Our prisoner escaping. He should not be hard to find if he is soaked in blood.' Or, Jack thought, someone else. The handprint was on the outside. It was someone coming in or someone pushing the door on the way out. 'I must assume now that there is a murderer ranging about the Vatican. That his target is a man of the faith, a cardinal. I …' He removed his cap with one hand and pinched the skin between his eyes with the other. 'My men. Christ Jesus, one slain within these walls. I must have this poor fellow removed and begin a search of this place. All of it. Jesus, but there must be a thousand places, more, that a man can conceal himself. And in the dark.'

'Should I–'

'No. No, my men might not take it well if a simple servant is charged with aiding their work, not with this deed so raw. But you might wait here awhile. Guard my man's corpse until I dispatch some others to take him to our force's chambers. I shall act in haste. Until I return, you might search about, see if there is anything that reveals what happened here. Anything broken loose, anything that might have been made sharp.'

Without waiting for a response, Moretti strode heavily for the door. He turned at it, examining the bloodstain. 'It is a mad thing. A mad thing to have the plotter taken and held fast before he kills, the killing after. Men are arrested after crimes, not before. It is unnatural.'

'All wrong,' said Jack. And then Moretti disappeared into the shadows, leaving Jack with the body. To it, he said, 'and the plot … was that laid before too? First the beheading then the burning.'

***

'Don't get yourself into a panic, Roberto,' Giuseppe hissed, emphasising the false name.

'How? How did you know?'

'And don't fall into that voice, stick with your low one.'

'How?'

'I saw you. Earlier, when the lad you called brother was by you. I was trying to sleep but you wouldn't shut up, either of you. Before the big lad ran off, he lent you a kiss. Now, I said to myself, Giuseppe, that's their business, two young lads, probably at some monks' school together. But when we were in yonder chamber, I had a look and I had me a think and I saw. And I said to myself that there's no hairless little boy but a girl.'

Amy sat back, silence and shock on her face. It gave way to anger. 'If you tell anyone, if you get Jack into trouble, I don't care where we are, I'll–'

'Oh, settle down. I'll keep your secret. I don't care. Didn't say anything to that rat-faced clerk, did I?'

'You … you would have us pay you?'

'Pay? Away, away.' He waved a hand in the air.

'Then … thank you. Thank you for keeping our secret.'

'It's yours to keep. Just out of interest, though, why are you here?'

'Jack's my husband. I'm his wife.'

'One usually follows the other, yes.'

'I needed to speak to him,' she scowled. 'In private. I hoped to be in and out of this damned place, but they locked it up before I could get him alone' She considered how much more to give. 'This morning – yesterday – I needed to speak to him but he'd already gone off, come here. So I set to work, got up and fixed up some clothes, borrowed some papers and ink and got inside in the afternoon.' She smiled. 'They didn't even search me, just took my papers and waved me in.'

'More concerned with getting folk out, eh, ahead of the conclave? So, a devoted wife not wishing to be parted from her man. You've played a dangerous game. If they find you out … I don't know what they'd do but you can bet your house you'd not like it. Reported to the big men of Rome as a spy and worse, I'd reckon.'

Amy let silence fall between them. For the first time she realised how fast her heart had begun pounding on realising that she'd been discovered. She let it slow. With it, the need to relieve herself returned. 'Here,' she said, 'I need to go.'

'Go?' She repeated herself with emphasis. 'Ah. It might not

be so good an idea to use this chamber.'

'I did before.'

'Then you were being careless.' He began spluttering and sneezing. 'Christ Jesus, I hate his time of year. No, you better go outside. Far, far outside, if you ask me. Besides, I don't like the place I lay my head being used as a pissing place. Just because we're servants it means we should piss where we sleep? No. Get you gone to some quiet spot outside, far from the San Damaso, somewhere there're no guards and no one to peep at … at you, from windows or anything.'

'Mmph,' she murmured, hauling herself up at the same time.

'Ugh, wait.'

'What?'

Giuseppe began to hoist himself up. Amy lent him an arm. She repeated her question. 'I'll come with you, lad,' he said. He chuckled at her look of horror and water began streaming from his eyes. 'To keep watch. To help you find a place. The apothecary has a physick garden with walls around it behind his chamber. Could sneak in through the back gate, though I doubt he'd thank you for despoiling it if he caught you. And the basilica is full of piles of rubble, though God wouldn't thank you for that either.' Nor, thought Amy, could she explain to Bianchi or God why she had to squat down amongst one's flowers and fruit or the other's sacred stones to relieve herself. 'Or I …' He seemed to consider something before smiling. 'A better idea. Somewhere you won't have yet seen, I reckon. Well, let's go, come on.'

'Right,' she said. Realising how abrupt it sounded, she added, 'thank you.' He waved away it away.

Together they left the space by the storeroom, and the kitchens themselves, and wandered out into the San Damaso. Giuseppe took the lead. He stopped short and drew her into the shadows with an arm as the captain of the Swiss Guard hurried past them, coming from the direction of the little courtyard formed by the dormitories and private papal block. He was moving carefully, his arm around the shoulders of someone dressed top to toe in black. Not Jack. The captain and his friend disappeared off to their left, where a path from the square ran down to the tower where the guards had their barracks.

He had been with Jack; that meant her husband might now be alone. Pressure in her abdomen insisted that she attend to herself first. 'Clear now,' said Giuseppe. She cursed to herself but let him lead her into the shadows of Raphael's covered walkway, turning right and following it. As they reached the end, they passed into a small, triangular corner chamber which joined the public rooms on the right with the rump of the private apartments on the left. The little connecting chamber comprised three shallow steps and she followed Giuseppe up them to a large, open portico on the left.

Immediately, she drew breath.

In this place, where she had not yet been, the Vatican opened up. Ahead of her, abutting the back of the papal private block, was a curving terrace, grey in the moonlight. Beyond it, stretching northward, seemingly endlessly, was an array of gardens, stone stairways, and gravel paths. The other end was so distant that it was entirely swallowed up by the night. If the whole thing was the pope's rear garden, it had to rival Eden.

'Jesus,' she whispered softly. It was beyond anything that existed in England. It was far more impressive even than the span of gardens which lay between the Louvre and Catherine de Medici's Tuileries. Dimly, she wondered what the old French dowager would make of it, and she saw only envy on her plain, matronly features. Then the face of Queen Elizabeth, briefly glimpsed, rose in her mind, her eyes two glittering currants in a stretch of white dough. Neither would quite fit here. The place was more story than reality and fit only for creatures made of poetry rather than earthly flesh.

Cleopatra, she thought. The Eastern queen she had made quite a heroine of alone seemed fit to wander the great place, teasing a gaggle of men stupid enough to place her exotic charm above their duty. Ironically, perhaps, this was a place fit for a great queen who lived only in the gilded pages of classical tales. It was crazy. Women were at the heart of over half of Europe's courts, ruling even, and here was she, locked in a town within a town full of men fighting over the next father of the faith. She shook her head. Pointless musing - it felt like it should mean something, but it was just the way of the world.

'Yes, it's some place is this. Nothing like it in the whole world, I reckon. The Cortile del Belvedere.'

'Cortile del Belvedere,' she echoed. And she was going to have to turn it into what he had called a pissing please. 'Can I … I mean … look at it, by God. It's like something out of the books. Not a place to drop breeches and soil.'

'Go for it, find you a place,' he said. She could not read his face in the dark, but his voice sounded breezy enough. 'To tell God's truth, it makes me laugh to see such a place put to real use, after the way they treat our places. Can't see it in the dark, but there's another great palace out there, built by some old pope. Each one builds his own palace and then they're left to rot. And we get the cellars and kitchens.'

'Hm.'

'Off you go then, if you need to go.'

'But you … aren't you …'

'I'll go back to the San Damaso. I'll make sure no one comes this way.' He turned his face from her and gaze a little burst of sneezes, flecks of spittle carrying on the chill wind.

'Thank you. But … no, you've done enough. I mean it, thank you – but please just go back and lie down. Christ, it's late. Go and sleep. I'll be back.'

'You're sure?'

'Yes. Thanks for bringing me to the Belvedere.'

'You like to say that, don't you?'

In response, she gave what she imagined to be a Cleopatra-esque smile.

She watched until he had gone and then returned her attention to the enormous gardens. Needs must, she thought, crunching across the gravel terrace and down a shallow flight of steps. A clump of bushes stood not far from her. She tiptoed, not only because she feared echoes in the huge space, but because it felt sacrilegious to make too much noise and, after checking the shrubs for nettles, she fought her way in between them and attended to her toilet.

Relief washed over her as discomfort poured out. A hastily grabbed fist of leaves served her turn. And then the noise came.

She stopped moving, tuning her ears. The horrible thought came that Giuseppe had lied, that he had crept back and been watching her, a sly and dirty old man in the guise of a friend. Or worse, it was possible that some other person had spotted her, pushed past him. It was possible she was taken for a thief, a trespasser, spotted from either the southern dormitory – though she knew the cardinals were housed in the western one – or even the vacant papal apartments. She would be dragged out, protesting; she would have to think quickly. Giuseppe could not save her if that were the case. She might even have got him in trouble.

Yet the noises did not sound like pursuit. She strained to see something through the tangle of bushes, but it was impossible in the darkness. Instead she let her ears do the work.

Two men, speaking in low tones. Guardsmen, perhaps, doing a search of the place. Yet they carried no lamps. The hum of voices ceased, and then what might have been a light tread on the nearby steps – someone leaving, perhaps. And then came a stranger sound: digging, perhaps, in the muck and gravel. Yes, she thought – it sounded as though someone were hastily digging up a portion of the garden and scattering the load into something else.

She sat down, a border of bushes her only protection. She could not leave until they did.

***

Jack stood against the wall whilst the soldiers lifted the corpse and placed it on a stretcher. He had searched the room as much as he could whilst Moretti had been away but found that he was less able to discover any sure signs of what had happened than to find that theory after theory flooded his mind. It might have been this, it might have been that, it might be a plot, but then it might not. His tired brain had made a chorus, mocking him.

The problem was that there was simply nothing to see. A dead guard, inside the room, his blood both inside and on the outside of the door. Jack had waved the torch all around the hall outside, reasoning that if someone had bid the guard open the door and slain him in the attempt, moving him in after, there would be some trace of it, unless it had been cleaned up. The question of when the guard had been killed was unanswerable too: he and Moretti had last seen him alive sometime before eleven, and it was now closing in on one in the morning. In the darkness outside, anyone might have come and gone. The only place that was sealed, and that imperfectly, was the western dormitory with its host of dignitaries. He thought again of the sound he had thought he'd heard before going up to Granvelle's chamber, but he had not investigated it. It might have been a gust of wind, a cat, even.

All that had been amiss was the bedframe, which was slightly chipped. With his fingers, Jack had shaved off another chunk, turning it this way and that under the light before tucking it into his waistband.

Eventually, Moretti had returned, two men at his heels. With his soldiers in tow, the older man seemed to have recovered his poise and he directed them with an air of assurance and authority. The soldiers, though their faces blanched at the sight of a fallen comrade, did their duty in sombre silence. 'Keep to the shadows,' he had warned. 'The long way. I wish to hear of no panic, no rumours.'

When the body had been carried out, bound for an outbuilding of the barracks, Moretti remained. Only then did he speak to Jack. 'What have you found?'

'Nothing, captain. I think nothing.'

'Nothing.' It sounded not like a condemnation but weary resignation. 'This man is a ghost.'

'Well …' The fear of looking like an idiot flared and he quenched it. 'Could this signify? Could this be used?' He withdrew the sliver of bedframe from his waist and held it out. Moretti took it.

'This? This to cut a man's throat?'

'Or something like it. I took it from the cot. The wood's old, it had little cracks and broken bits.' Now that he had volunteered it, he felt the need to defend it.

'Perhaps,' Moretti said. 'Though, in faith, I think it would be a hard thing for a man with his hands, decayed and bound, mind, to have worked loose a piece of wood and then wielded it as a dagger.'

'A hard thing but not impossible?'

'Not impossible.' Jack beamed, though he put little stock in the possibility himself. He had simply been desperate that it not appear to Moretti that he had sat on his arse staring into the ether whilst he had been left with the corpse. It was an odd thing: hitherto he had always disliked and distrusted men old enough to be his father. Users, all, and abusers, out for what they could get from you. Yet the captain, and the cardinal, too, had brought out an eagerness to please rather than an eagerness to depart from their company. It was not unpleasant. It was like being a child, but one who is treated well.

'Are your men out hunting?'

'I have sent them, yes. To walk the walls of the Vatican. A search of the buildings, of the place itself ... impossible in the dark. Only the walls can be walked.'

'You think he's trying to escape?' Jack sounded doubtful, and it must have shown.

'I hope that he is, and that he is slain in the attempt,' snapped Moretti. Then, more gently, 'there is little else that can be done until he is found.'

'It's just the man you're hunting for then?'

'If,' Moretti said, eyeing him sharply, 'you still think there is some confederate working with him ... have you found proof of it?'

'No, captain.'

'Then one man will suffice.'

'I was thinking, though, about what the man said when we had him. All that about fire, burning. That it might be the place he means to suffer rather than any one man.'

'You think he means to burn the Vatican?' Jack shrugged. 'It would take more than one sick old man to set this great place ablaze.' There seemed more hope in the captain's voice than assurance. 'Yet ... yet I have seen how fire can spread. Well, let us hope all the more that he is found and swiftly. I intend to join the search myself.'

Jack was quiet for a moment, thinking, and then he said, 'what time is it, do you know?'

'One, or near to it.'

'Ah, damn. I said I'd go back to Cardinal Granvelle, get him ready for bed. His meetings with the others should be over by now, he said.'

'Then get you gone, lad.'

Jack nodded and began moving towards the door. He paused, giving one last look at the handprint. 'Good luck, Captain Moretti.' A tired smile was his response.

Jack left the building, glad to be free of it, and crossed the little courtyard. He was pleased to see that the two guards who had earlier retreated inside to warm themselves were now stationed outside, as they should have been all along. Moretti had obviously had words. He made to move past them, but they stopped him, patting him down. At least, he thought, the security of the Vatican had been increased.

If the mysterious prisoner had some great plot in mind, he would find it more difficult to accomplish. Hopefully.

7

Thankfully, the cardinal was alone in his rooms. His meetings had finished, and the irritating Hernandez had pointedly retired, it being below both their dignities for him to help his master to bed. Jack saw to him, removing his cumbersome robes, fetching water up from the large basin kept on the ground floor, and putting on his nightgown and cap. That done, he went through the equally cumbersome ceremony of checking the bed, as Moretti had shown him in Farnese's room. Throughout it all, they barely spoke. Jack was as tired, if not more so, than Granvelle.

'This is awfully good of you, so very kind. You're a good boy to do it.' Jack felt warmth tingle in his cheeks. The cardinal, unlike some masters, seemed keen to show gratitude for even the smallest act. It helped write the pleasant fiction that the servant had any choice in serving the master. 'I realise Father Hernandez can be a rude fellow. In truth he is little altered in his manner to me. Alas, he has come to watch.'

Haven't we all? thought Jack. Hitherto he had thought the life of a cardinal to be one of spirituality, pleasantness, connection with something beyond the ugly world of reality. It had never occurred to him that princes of the Church were as much surrounded by spies as princes of the earth. Far from being an anomaly, Jack suddenly felt himself the lesser of the creeping watchers who stalked the Vatican.

'Will there be anything else, your Grace?' He stood to attention in the door to the bedchamber as Granvelle eased himself onto the edge of the bed.

'Just one thing.' He looked over towards the desk. 'You see that?' A sheaf of papers lay folded.

'Yes.'

'It is for Cardinal Farnese. I said I would draw it up for him after our meeting. Pray do not disturb him. Put it under his door. He might read it tonight or in the morning.'

Jack stepped over and picked up the papers, holding them against his breast. As he did so, he jerked back in surprise. For a second his father was staring back at him, drunken, red-eyed, sleepless, prowling, wolfish. Instantly his mouth ran dry. Granvelle had set a mirror on the desk against the wall, he realised, blinking away the sudden memories.

'Something wrong, my child?'

'No.' His voice felt like it was coming from someone else, even as the image before him resolved itself. It was only his reflection – he was beardless whereas his father had worn a brown thatch. A trick of the light, of sleeplessness, only. Sometimes the past and its horrors sneaked up, as if to remind you that they still had power, even if they did not wield it as often. 'I mean yes, your Grace. I'll take them to him.'

'Thank you, how kind. Tell me,' he yawned, 'what is being said downstairs, amongst the servants?'

'What about?'

'Come, you know. About this conclave.'

'Um.' Jack hesitated. He had not given too much thought to the election or to what was being said of it. Granvelle seemed to take the pause for the delicate circumspection of a good servant.

'You might speak freely.'

'They say Cardinal Farnese wished to be the new Holy Father,' he said, relying on Pietro's musings. 'That this was to be his conclave.'

'Well, you and I know better, eh? No, his Grace shall have to wait awhile yet if he hopes for the throne of St Peter. Just past fifty … it is too much for any man that young.' Jack said nothing. From his early twenties, fifty seemed bone-wearyingly old. 'Yet we have given him the choice, he shall have as great a say as any of us in choosing an … acceptable man. Have your people your own hopes?'

'My people? English?'

'I mean the common men of all realms.'

Jack studied the question a moment, his brow puckering. 'It's not for us to say. Whoever God guides your Graces to elect.'

'A studied answer, my boy.' He tilted his head and yawned. 'Elect, elect, elect. A hard thing. To balance this faction and that, to please the king of Spain, the old queen of France, the people, and our consciences. To find a tiger fit to fight the infidel on one side and the heretics on the other. To find an honest man who will stand firm in reforming abuses and please the men of tradition.' Granvelle seemed to be speaking to himself, staring into his own knotted difficulties as he did so.

'God guide you, your Grace,' Jack said, hoping the bland manners of the professional servant would be enough to conclude the conversation. Liking the cardinal as he did, he found himself wanting to hear as little as possible and thus having as little as possible with which to betray him to Walsingham. Reporting on a man's speeches seemed less duplicitous if the speeches were fewer.

'Forgive me. My mind wanders, there has been so much to consider this long day. Pray give him that note and speed him to his decision. With luck, we shall have our new pope by breakfast. And have him consecrated before nightfall.' He coughed. 'And then out of these dreadful cells.'

Jack coughed too, more out of unconscious mimicry than need. The room, though, was choking with the acrid smell of smoke, which drifted about the smudged ceiling. Each of the dormitory buildings, he assumed, had been designed to retain heat and smoke and foul airs, the better to speed up elections and lessen the time that Christendom had to spend headless. Small wonder physicians were needed in residence to take care of the old men.

Headless.

Despite the heat, the word sent a chill up his spine even as he thought it.

'Will you be requiring something in the morning, your Grace? Some food. Stuff for the mass?'

Granvelle seemed to consider. 'No, Jack. It has been a long day and a longer night. Spent, I should say, in God's good service. No, I fancy I have dispensation from celebrating mass in the morning, in the promise of being freed from all weariness of the bones later in the day. In truth,' he said, with a wink, 'I fear I shall be ill myself if I cannot sleep until dinner time. Father Hernandez will be risen, he will wake me if … if there are problems that require my attention. Tell me, what do you intend after the conclave is concluded?'

'Your Grace?'

'Your job, your trade. Will you remain living in Rome, working perhaps in some noble household?'

'I look after horses. At an inn in the town. That's my trade.'

'And you wish to carry it on?'

'Yes,' he lied. He could not tell the cardinal about his plans to return to England, still less that he had a wife. Questions might be asked, enquiries made.

'I see. I say only for your consideration that there are always places in my own household. Horses, if you like, or any other profession. It is no small thing to be placed in the household of a prince of the Church. A man can rise by it.'

'Yes, your Grace.' Jack knew all about positions in noble households, and ecclesiastical ones were probably much the same as secular ones. Resentments simmered, positions were fought for, and no man trusted the next. Even keeping your head down was likely to get you talked about, laughed at. The resentment the cardinal's conclavist had shown him all night showed just how deep suspicions and jealousies ran, and he could still hear the laughter behind his back from his time in service in England. Jack Cole, the grinning moon-man with no mind of his own.

'Think on it, my boy.' He yawned. 'But you must be in need of rest yourself. So no, do not disturb me or you. Sleep well this night and as late as you like, knowing you have played your part – been guided by the Holy Spirit in the choosing of our next pontiff. Our minds and cunning tongues and pens are but the instruments. God sets the note.' He jabbed his nose at the papers still pressed against Jack's breast. 'Goodnight, Jack. I will see you tomorrow before midday. Until then I release you. Sleep well.'

'Goodnight, your Grace.'

Jack snuffed the torchlight, left Granvelle's chambers and bumped the door closed. He looked up and down the hall, feeling the eyes of the painted figures condemning him for what he was about to do. It was always the eyes on lifelike but unliving things that frightened him. Whether statues, paintings, or frescoes, he would never understand the desire of artists to give lifeless things piercing eyes. Perhaps that was the point in the residence – to make the cardinals and their men feel that the eternal eyes of antiquity were watching them. He turned his back on them, facing Granvelle's door. And then he opened up the papers.

Granvelle's spidery scrawl covered four sides of good-quality parchment. At the head of each page was a name: Ricci, Boncompagni, Morone, Sirleto. Jack was looking at the names of the potential popes. Farnese, having been excluded himself, must have requested a shortlist and was now being invited to consider which was his pick. Beneath each name, densely packed Latin flowed over the pages. It made no sense to Jack, but he supposed it either to be the merits and demerits of the candidates, or perhaps their histories. He tried to picture the candidates but couldn't; if he had seen them enter the Vatican, as he must have, they had left no particular impression. A sudden desire to copy it all out came over him, but he stifled it as a brief flicker of madness. The names would be enough. He mouthed them to himself over and over as he began moving down the hall towards Farnese's door. Once there, he bent and pushed it under. This time he waited, expecting the door to fly open. When it didn't, he padded away.

The eyes on the walls followed him.

***

Amy hid within the bushes for what seemed an eternity. The person or people beyond it crunched away softly, she thought, but still she did not trust moving. In the darkness, she groped around at her feet and found a rock, just small enough to fit inside her closed fist. Once any sense of time had been well and truly lost, she bent back branches and picked her way out.

The Belvedere stretched off to her right, unchanged. She turned on the spot. Moonlight glinted off the marble steps she had come down. She was quite alone. The whole scene seemed unchanged. Perhaps, she thought, if she were more familiar with the place, if she had seen it in daylight before and after, she might have noticed something. As it was, whatever act the stranger had been engaged in was a mystery. Perhaps it had even been some ghosts, spirits of Ancient Rome reliving a battle or going about their strange politics. The thought, the silliness, chased away her fear.

What mattered was that they were gone.

She covered the short distance to the stairs and tiptoed up them, her shoes sliding around inside the boots that were too big for her. She turned left as the bulk of the building housing the pope's string of private chambers reared up ahead and made for the little connecting chamber running back into the Raphael hallway. Nothing bad could happen there – it was too beautiful, too close to the life of the San Damaso.

As she slipped into the deeper darkness between the private apartments and public apartments, a sudden sound stilled her.

It was someone chanting.

Worse; it was someone behind her, mumbling what sounding like Latin indistinctly.

Amy quickened her pace, torn between identifying the source of the sound and running. The language had always sounded strange to her, and, whispered and mumbled with monotony in a dark space, it was positively terrifying.

It ceased.

She stopped, more angry and curious now than frightened. Either something strange was going on, some priest saying prayers somewhere in the dark, or someone was deliberately trying to frighten her. If it were the latter, she'd give them the rough end of her tongue. In the dark no one could get a good look at her anyway. She turned around, facing the direction from which she'd come.

'Is someone there? If someone's there, come out.' When there was no response, she licked her lips before throwing out, 'damned coward!'

Suddenly a high-pitched giggling sliced through the air some distance ahead of her and she jerked back, stumbling towards the shallow steps that led down to the Raphael hall. The noise reminded her horribly of a hyena's terrible screeching laughter – a sound that still haunted her nightmares. She thrust out an arm to stop herself falling, her hand scrabbling wildly at the air where the plastered wall of the papal apartments should have been.

And someone grabbed it.

Amy reacted instantly. Her hand, loaded still with its rock, arced through the air and collided with the black shadow that had appeared before her. Whether she made contact with head, arm, body, she couldn't be sure. The sudden assault made her assailant release his grip. The figure resolved itself into the vague shape of a man, cowled, and something chimed in her mind.

Then the giggling repeated. Again, it was farther away.

Two of them, she realised, all at once – someone behind, mad, screeching and mumbling, and someone there, hiding in the chamber's shadows, close enough to be hit. And close enough to hit back.

The man in the cowl would have got her from behind if she hadn't turned to shout.

It was the realisation that send her flying, skating down the steps, the carpet folding up behind her. Pain suddenly roared through her abdomen, a wave of nausea hot on its heels. She did not pause to see if she was being followed but burst into the covered walkway and threw herself into the airier, lighter space of the San Damaso.

From the kitchens across the way, light spilled from poorly shuttered windows and the open door. She did not break her pace but continued leaping around statues and bushes. Only when she was bathed in the light of the doorway did she stop and turn around.

No one.

She cursed out into the night, shouting every Italian swear word she had learnt – and she'd made it her business to learn as many as possible. Her breath short, they all came out gutturally enough not to require any pretence at manliness. Either two men were out there, and had sought to ambush her, or one madman had a devilish skill in throwing his voice.

When there was no response, she let tears of frustration and fear fall from her eyes and cuffed them away. Before she could turn from the square, she felt vomit burning its way up her throat and she let it come, bending over to the side of the doorway. When she had done, she found that the nausea had gone with it.

And then the footsteps came, crunching their way towards her.

Just kill me now, if you're going to, she thought. I'll scream and kick and get you caught as you try it.

'Amy?' She looked up. Jack's face was a picture of concern, or surprise. 'I mean … brother. What's happened, are you hurt?' She threw herself at him, burying her head in his armpit, uncaring that her lips were still soiled. He hugged her, all the while looking over her shoulder and into the kitchens.

And then he stiffened.

'Oh God,' he said gripping her suddenly by the shoulders and holding her at arm's length. She looked up at him drunkenly, wondering what nonsense was going through his head. 'You're … you're poisoned, aren't you?'

She tried to speak, but her tongue was thick and her breath sour.

'It's my fault. Oh Christ, it was me who got you dragged into that storeroom, wasn't it? This is my fault, isn't it? He made you do it, that fucking clerk, he made you drink poison. I'll kill him, I'll make him drink it.' He let her go and punched the plaster by the doorway. Little chips of white flew. 'The apothecary, the physicians, I'll get them.'

'Jack,' she gasped. 'Water.'

'Water! Yes! Wait here!' He flew into the kitchen whilst she gulped at the night air, her head swimming. It was not supposed to be like this; this was not how she had pictured it. He reappeared moments later, a wooden mug in his hand. She let him guide her down to the ground, and they sat side by side in the doorway, their backs to the heat and light. 'Drink, drink,' he said. 'It'll make you piss, piss it out. The heat, we'll go in, sit by the fire, flush it all out.'

She swallowed the water, letting it cleanse her mouth and throat. Gradually, a sense of being in control of herself began to return. 'I'll get the apothecary now,' he said, 'Bianchi, he must have stuff that flushes poisons out.'

'No! No apothecary, nor no physicians neither.'

'But they – but you–'

'You can't. Christ, Jack, the one type of man we can't have

looking at me's the type who looks at bodies for a living.' She gave him a half-smile. 'They'd sure as fate find more than they expect if they try to examine my body.'

'There has to be something. My fault, my fault. I'm a good for nothing, an idiot.' He leant forward, his head falling into his hands and his hair drooping over his eyes. 'What have I done? Got my own wife poisoned. I wish I'd never been born. Useless. Cursed. Evil.' His hands dropped from his head and, she noticed, he balled them into fists, digging the nails into his palms.

'Don't say that. Don't ever say that. If that's what your dad said then I'm glad you … I'm glad he's dead, rotten old shit.' He had never spoken to her fully about his childhood, but she had picked up enough before agreeing to marry him to piece it together, and the knowledge had only cemented her decision. The old man had been a fanatical evangelical who had blamed his son for his mother dying in childbirth, and he had taken every opportunity to abuse him, making him pliable and desperate to please – at least until he was pushed too far. The old man had eventually pushed him too far and got what he deserved for it.

She put a hand on his back and then rested her head on his shoulder. She sighed before speaking. 'But you are a bloody daft idiot. I'm not poisoned,' she breathed, her mouth close to his ear. A pause, and then, 'I'm pregnant. You're going to be a dad and there's going to be a little spy running around.'

8

Silence followed her announcement. At first Jack did not fully register the words, and so he made no move to touch or even look at her. And then his mouth fell open in a lopsided grin, born more of shock than delight. She was looking back at him, weariness painted in the faint blue patches under her eyes.

'Is that why you're here?' He felt his voice come out in a croak.

'Yes.'

'How long have you known?'

'I … I thought I knew. Suspected. I wasn't sure, I knew something wasn't right. This morning – yesterday morning – I just knew. In the morning, I was certain. But you were up, you were away to come here. I needed to tell someone, to talk about it. Seemed like you were the right person, the first one who should know. Didn't seem right to talk to the Hydes about it.

'So I got it into my head to get in here and tell you. In and out, I thought. But it took me all morning to get your clothes all fixed up to fit me, to copy out the letter I'd seen. When I got in you were set to work already. So I hid, waited until I could get you by yourself. It got dark. They locked the place up. Are you … happy?'

He held her gaze for a few seconds and then looked out into the dark square. The stiffening breeze picked up and, as it blew over and across the San Damaso, it made a mournful, lowering sound, like someone blowing over the rims of giant bottles.

'If you're not happy I'm very sorry,' she said. He turned to her. Her face had hardened, and he realised she had misunderstood his silence. She was scared, she was hurt.

'I don't know,' he said, honestly.

'What do you mean, don't know – you're either happy or not. Don't you … it'll be our baby. Both of our baby. I always remember my mam saying it takes two to make a baby.'

'Yeah.'

They had never discussed having children. He had never let himself think about it. Children were something old people had, or young people who were blessed, who had settled lives. Or, of course, those who were cursed, and who died with their children in the gutters. 'A baby,' he said, for lack of anything else.

'Well if you weren't looking for one why did you even marry me in the first place? Babies follow marriage like night follows day, my mam always said. So … so it's taken a while longer. I just thought … maybe there was something wrong with me. Some women don't have them, and better that than having them and them born dead or sickly. No danger to the girl if she just can't and no shame neither.'

'Your mam always said?' He smiled.

'Well I can and I am. So why did you marry me if you didn't hope for them?'

'I didn't say I didn't hope for them. I …' Why had he married her? 'Because … you were a new person. And I liked you. And I hoped to be like other men. Why did you say yes?'

She looked away from him and began scuffing her feet on the gravel. His boots, he noticed, not sure why it touched him. 'Because.'

'Because why?'

'Because you needed marrying. And you made me like myself. Selfish, maybe. True though. I wished …' She blinked back tears. 'I wished to walk into a room and everyone to know that you were mine, you belonged to me. So I'd be useful. So I'd have someone to … have. To look after you and tell anyone who made light of you, slandered you, or mocked you to go to hell.'

'Christ, Amy. You've done that. Sent some of them there too.'

'Maybe. And you never told me to shut my mouth or ran from me when I didn't. So that was a good thing. So,' she sighed, 'we got married because we're both of us selfish, seeking things from each other. Still better than most of the world. We've not done so badly, have we? We love each other. I don't care what anyone else thinks anymore. About anything.'

'Are you happy?' He spoke timidly, more weakly than she had put it to him. Then, because he was unsure of her answer, he added, 'what is it would make you happy?'

'From you? Just be good. Just make me happy, just give me

that. That's all I've ever been after.'

'And this?' He gestured towards her stomach. She took his hand and placed it there.

'It makes me happy.' Tears sparkled on her lashes again. 'Oh, hell's balls.' She sniffed, shook his hand away and began kneading her own, before barking a brittle laugh. 'One thing my mam never said, my aunt neither, that getting a baby turns you soft as bloody shite. My legs going, my stomach churning – I can live with that. But this. Good thing there's no one around.' The display of hardness was her way of dealing with the show of softness. Something lit up inside him that he knew her well enough to see that. Her face changed, he noticed, and she turned wide eyes out into the square.

'If you're happy then I am too. Only ...'

'What?'

'What if it's ... like me?' He smiled, knowing how ghastly it must look. 'What if I'm like him?'

'If it's like you then I'll be glad of it. What's wrong with you? You're a good man.'

'Am I? The things I've done.'

'The things we've done.'

'What if I'm like him? As a father, what if I'm like him, my temper...' He closed his eyes but doing so did not close his mind. The old man loomed in his thoughts as he had earlier tricked him by appearing in the mirror. He could recall it all, his childhood appearing in a series of images he usually pretended had not happened: how his father used to accuse him of doing things he hadn't and then punish him; how he had been unpleasant and rude when sober, but impossible to live near when drunk; how the slightest infraction caused him to fly into a rage. Every morning forced to approach the dread figure, his bare knees sliced by the stone floor, begging forgiveness for imagined transgressions, only to be cuffed down, head spinning. He had never been sure if the old devil had believed his own fantasies or not. All Jack knew was that he enjoyed taking out his anger on anyone weaker, anyone who couldn't protect themselves. Invariably that had been Jack himself, until he put a stop to it. It had been then that he had learnt to keep secrets.

'Oh, don't be a bloody idiot. We'll be our own thing, our own family. When you get that, the old ones, they don't matter, they go away if you make them, if you desire them to. And I don't mean anything against your mam, God rest her, but I won't let the birthing get me. And I'll come back as a ghost if I have to.'

He laughed, shaking his head. 'I do love you.'

'I know it. Don't get all weeping, I've done that already. See – dry eyes now.'

'I have something to tell you too.' He sought her hand again. When he spoke, he kept his voice low. 'Why I came here – it wasn't to see the new pope made, it wasn't for faith.'

'Why then?'

'I thought … we could go back to England. Back home. If we had information to sell – to buy safe conduct back. You've not liked living about the world.' He did not add his most private hope: that finally being able to give her a home might loosen her grip on him, give her something else to possess.

'I've not minded. I never said I wanted to go back there – not once have I said that, you know I haven't.'

He bit his tongue. It was true; she hadn't. Amy had her own way of expressing her opinions on the matter of any potential homecoming, and they echoed in his mind: "Jesus, but the food here sits ill on my stomach"; "look at how the women here dress, it's a struggle to even look at them"; "this sun, it's too hot, I can't hardly take no more of it". Never "I want to go home" but always "I hate to be here." He thought it best not to mention that, though. Pregnant women were not supposed to be argued with or harassed; they were supposed to be closeted, indulged, and eventually locked away in close, hot rooms were the baby could emerge into a space not so very different from the one it came from. Just such rooms could be found in England as in Italy – if not, neither he nor Amy could have come to be.

'I know, I know, you'll do anything for my sake. But you shouldn't have to. It's been me always liking to travel, not you. You just got dragged along.' Her eyes flashed and he knew he'd said the wrong thing.

'I'm not your idiot retainer, Jack Cole, nor your henchman,

I'm your wife. I'm not doffing my damned cap. I go where you go because … because I wish to, and I have to, and it doesn't matter where we live. It doesn't.'

'I didn't mean that. But all the same would you not like to go back to England? For the baby, anyway? Don't you wish it speaking English and eating English food and … and that?'

She seemed to consider. 'Yes. I'd like it to speak the same tongue I was born with. I don't know why. But I'd like that.'

'It,' he said, without expression.

'You're in hope a boy, I'd have thought.'

'No. Not really. Saying it like that – boy or girl – it makes it sound all real.'

'It is real. I've been puking and losing my wits every few hours to prove it's real to me, I don't need words.'

'Sorry.'

'You're not after a girl?'

'A girl would be a fine thing. A good, strong girl like you. To grow up and be married and not be called Cole.' He could taste the bitterness on his tongue. He could see it – see her – a miniature Amy growing up amongst the tall grasses of England, not becoming a servant, marrying and having children of her own: grandchildren who would be so far removed from him and his that they would know him only as a kindly old man with no past of any interest. The smile which crossed his face was natural.

'One thing,' Amy said, turning his thoughts from the future. 'Don't be a cock about it, don't start … don't start playing the part of the hard man.'

'What?'

'I mean it – if you've seen other men with pregnant wives behave like strutting cocks, don't you do the same. Don't follow them in that.'

'I won't,' he sniffed. Then he smiled again. 'I'll be whatever you wish for me to be. As soon as we're out of this place we'll go, we'll go right out of Italy. Cardinal Granvelle – he's up in the dormitory – he's offered a place. It could be we join him when he goes back west, or north, or wherever he comes from, and on to Paris. See Walsingham again. I know, I don't like it either, but we'll have to give him something. Then England.'

'Pfft. If it's a lass she'll have to learn to govern her tongue in England, is the only thing. Them reformers, they're hotter on us keeping meek than even the faith men in France and Italy.'

'I–'

'Shut up!'

'What?'

'Shh!'

Amy had turned her attention out into the dark square again. Two men were striding towards them and they shifted apart a few inches. The figures bloomed into colour as they approached the light spilling from the kitchen. Swiss Guards.

'Ho, you too,' barked one, the other nodding. Jack returned the greeting. 'Have you seen a man about this place, old, hands ill-kept?'

'No. No one like that.' He could not be bothered filling the unknown pair in on his evening's engagement with their captain. Thankfully they accepted it, mumbling to one another.

'Right, nothing doing,' whispered the more talkative. 'The captain can have the care of it. He wanted the job, he can have it.'

'Yeah, sarge' agreed the other. 'We're done. Bed.'

The two men staggered off in the direction of their barracks.

'Captain Moretti's had no luck finding our prisoner, I reckon. They must just have finished their march on the walls.'

'Eh?'

'Christ, I haven't seen you. What a long night it's been. That old man, the one who stood up and went off with the bishop, he's out. Escaped.' He licked his lips before adding, 'a guard was killed. Maybe by him on his escape.'

'That's bad.'

'Bad, yeah. Worse if someone helped him. I was working with Captain Moretti.'

'Moretti. Doesn't sound very Swiss to me.'

'What? What does, then?'

'What's the commander called?'

'von Brunegg. He's sick.'

'That.' Her face was pulled in a shadowy frown. Her mouth

opened and then closed before she spoke. 'Sick, is it?'

'So I heard.'

'Well, maybe it's your captain done him a bad turn. A captain looking to a commander's shoes. Maybe that's what your new little friend is like.' Her features softened as Jack's grew hard; she might, he hoped, have realised that her jealousy was getting the better of her.

'Don't be a little fool. He's a good man. But you know what? I don't care anymore. He can go and find his man. I don't care, it doesn't matter to me. Getting out of here does, that's all.' A rising surge of excitement had begun. 'And you, and our baby. That's what matters. I'll say to the captain tomorrow I can't help him anymore. No, in fact, I'll just avoid him. The cardinal says the conclave will end tomorrow. Then we can walk away from this place. I don't care to be caught up in business with dead folks anymore, murder, spying. I just wish to take you home and see you're safe, safely delivered, and watch our girl grow. You'll need women around you.' He frowned. Amy never seemed to get on with women. Not that she got on with men much better. No matter, though; babies were women's business. He hurried on. 'We'll find good women, ones who'll take care of you, English ones.'

'Jack … I … I saw Captain Moretti a while ago. He was with someone in black. All dressed in black, his face hidden.' He looked at her, words poised on his lips, but said nothing. It was clear she had more. 'See earlier, just before you got here and found me puking – I … I think I was attacked.'

'What?' He began to rise, and she put a restraining hand on his forearm.

'I'm unhurt, I ran. But … I mean, I might have been imagining things. My head, it's been going like the clouds since …. Well, this.' She patted her stomach. 'Yet I think – I thought – that there were two men. Creeping in the dark, over that way.' He jabbed her nose across the square and to the right. 'One I thought was all in black. Like the man with that captain. Course, it might just have been two fools trying to scare me. Or one, throwing his voice away somehow. I don't know.'

'But you don't trust the captain?'

'I don't know. I'm just saying maybe you shouldn't.'

Jack frowned. Amy never seemed to like him having friends – she disliked him spending time with anyone other than herself, always had. Yet she seemed to be in earnest. 'It'll be one of his men. He's setting them to search the place for the prisoner.'

'A guardsman all in black, hood up? I don't think so.' She looked like getting ready to argue.

'I'll ask him in the morning.'

'No. He might … he was hurrying, didn't look like he wished to be seen.'

'What would you have me do then?'

'Nothing. Just have a care around him.'

'I will.'

'Things … I don't think things are what they seem to be in this place. Thank God it's not for long.'

'One night. That's it – just one night. Tomorrow, before the night comes, we'll be free of it. He took her hand and pulled her to her feet. 'And if there is someone out there, scaring you or dangerous, then you'll be safe inside. We both will. Safety in the multitude.'

He led her into the kitchens, where the scattered servants were huddled under old jerkins. It looked like he imagined a war camp might, its mass of soldiers bedding down wherever they could find a space. They picked their way through the mounds, going as far from the door as they could – all the way, in fact, to the deserted space by the storeroom where Amy had first set up lodging.

'Here,' he said. 'Let's sleep. And pray that tomorrow comes quickly.'

'Where's Giuseppe?'

'Who?'

'That old baker, the one who kept sneezing. He was fair to me – Jack, he knew I was … he knew I wasn't … like I'm dressed.'

'What?! If he's gone to tell someone – I'll knock him down.'

'No, no, he wasn't like that. He was kind to me, told me he'd keep it secret. Took me out and showed me a place to piss, private.'

'Oh right.' Something about that rankled, was unseemly.

'Well perhaps he's decided to give us privacy. Let us alone.' She murmured assent, but he could see her brow wrinkle. 'Look for him in the morning. He'll be around – probably we walked right past him just now.'

'Maybe.'

Jack squinted around the big chamber. Outside the braziers, all was darkness. No one stirred. He kissed Amy and lowered her to the ground. She tutted but accepted his help. Only she could not resist adding, once she was on the floor, 'I'm not dying. My head lightens sometimes, that's all. I can only be three or four months gone. Here, I heard there's some kind of raid on the old pope's rooms tonight. Us lot get to go and take the things too lowly to be willed. It's a tradition, I heard.'

'Not for me it isn't. Imagine the shame if we were caught doing that. Imagine the danger if you were!'

She made little grumbling sounds before replying, and then indirectly. 'So … England, eh? It'll be a strange thing seeing that place again.'

Jack crouched down beside her and stretched out his legs. He supposed she would want to whisper long into the night, probably until the sun rose, about plans, about their future. Normally it was his custom to let her talk, barely listening, waiting for her to take breath before venturing any words or opinions of his own. Tonight, though, he would let her speak as freely as she wanted, if she wanted.

Within seconds he was fast asleep.

***

Amy did not sleep. Or, if she did, it was so brief that she barely recognised it.

The truth was out now, as she had intended it to be. Yet it had not gone as she'd hoped. You spent so long, she thought, imagining how conversations might go, where they might take place, that they became almost real. And then, when they really happened, they confounded everything you had imagined.

More irritatingly, her adrenaline was still up, from being chased, from being sick, from telling Jack about the pregnancy. She was simply brainsick, and her mind would not shut down and let sleep come. All perception of time faded whilst she listened to his sonorous snores and grunts. She wondered what he was dreaming about. At some point, the room began to stir. The cooks' servants up to light the fires, she guessed.

She was wrong.

Excited chatter began to bubble through the great chamber: whispers rising and falling, giggles swiftly stifled. Then she remembered what Giuseppe had told her about the raid on the pope's apartments. She considered shaking Jack awake and thought better of it. He wouldn't be interested – in fact, he might even be condemnatory. He had as good as said no and probably expected that he spoke for her too. That was how things should be. She closed her eyes, but they popped open.

It irked her that other people were doing something, and something which might have been enjoyable, rebellious even, without her. She eased away from Jack and, using the empty barrel for support, got to her feet.

The cluster of conspirators was gathered at a brazier, by now nearly out of its life-giving woodchips. She moved to stand a few feet away from them, listening. Giuseppe's voice was not amongst them.

'Pass them out, pass them,' someone whispered, young by the sound of him.

'You joining us? All are welcome, my man.'

'Yes,' she said.

'Take a mask.'

One of the other men in the group handed her a piece of cheap cloth, oval shaped with a strand dangling from either side. She nodded thanks and tied it round her head, fingering the eye holes until she could see. 'Are we good, Pietro?' someone whispered.

'We're good,' said the apparent leader. 'Right, lads, let's take what's ours. Remember, take down that little prick Pavesi first, huh? Don't wake Cirillo – don't wander near his chambers. And don't take nothing that will be noticed or cared for.' Rapturous agreement rose from about ten mouths. 'Shut up, huh? You want to advertise what we're about? Right. Let's move. Don't tread on anyone. The old men are still asleep. Back before we have to light the fires and don't call each other by names once we're out of here, huh?'

Amy followed as the little band of men slipped out of the kitchens and into the San Damaso. There was safety in a multitude, Jack had said. She hoped he was right.

9

The late Pius V's apartments were located on the southwestern corner of the of the enormous Cortile de Belvedere, north of the angular Borgia Tower. The whole papal block of the palace was, Pietro told them as they walked, a mess of rooms, chambers, and galleries, each built over and upon as successive pontiffs sought to stamp their own tastes on the palace. They were lucky that Pius had kept the old Borgia and Raphael rooms locked up, because penetrating them would have taken master thieves.

They slipped across the San Damaso, wielding unlit tapers like poniards, in the direction Giuseppe had earlier taken earlier. She paid special attention as she passed through the chamber leading out to the Belvedere, but nothing stirred. That was almost a disappointment. Armed with a company, she should have liked to have met her attacker and done more than strike him with a rock.

Like all the other palace buildings, Pius's block looked like nothing from the outside: blocky and square-ended, it was of the same dull, muddy brown sandstone as everywhere else. The popes, it seemed, preferred as a race to spend their money on their interiors and present to the outer world a picture of bland sameness. The poets, Amy supposed, would like that – it was the job of the church after all to enrich folks' inner souls. The master builders of the world could always go to France and throw up confections which were all about the outside.

As they slipped into the building, they met their first obstacle.

On a cot, covered in thick, fringed blankets, the clerk, Pavesi, snored. To reach the upper floor they would have to pass him. Pietro, tiptoeing at the head of the group, appeared to have no intention of doing so.

'Awake! Arise!' he cried, at the same time launching himself atop the mess of blankets. Pavesi jerked awake but found that he could not sit up. Pietro, who appeared as a dark mass to Amy, was crushing down on him as the astonished clerk's arms pinwheeled. For a moment there was a struggle as the pair became an amorphous, shifting blob. It stilled. 'Done,' said the attacker, turning back to his crew.

As they moved forward, Amy saw that Pavesi had been deftly gagged and blindfolded. Pietro was even at work on his ankles. 'Is this right?' she asked, keeping her voice low, to no one in particular.

'Jests,' said the man nearest her. 'Tradition. They do the same on the outside – when the new pope's named the people strip his houses and make mockery of his folks.' He sounded unsure, she thought.

'He won't be bothering anyone tonight, huh?' Pietro laughed before gesturing for them to follow. They did, leaving the unfortunate Pavesi to writhe and mumble through his gag.

Up and along the apartments they went, their footsteps alternating between the whisper of carpets and the neat but echoing crack of boot on tile. Eventually, Pietro stopped them in a small room and lit his taper. The others carrying them followed suit and the group stuttered into half-light. They gathered in a circle, the flames bouncing off eager faces.

'In there. This here is one of his rooms. Room for meeting folks, probably. The next should be his bedchamber and chapel. I've asked the old folks, and this is it. Remember, take nothing too big for one man to carry and nothing of too great value. Come, let's be in and out before that lousy little clerk can get himself free and go crying for aid, huh?' He broke from the group, turned his back, and pushed at the tall, green door.

They stepped into the darkness. The smell of sickness lingered, stale and flat. Sickrooms never seemed to lose it, and this had been an old man's death chamber and, before that, his sleeping chamber. The smell brought back images of Amy's mother and she willed them away, hoping that the sudden intrusion of smoke and flame would beat them back. The past seemed to live in smells as much as it did in sights and sounds.

As tapers were put to the torches lining the walls, the room flickered to life. A collective, audible intake of breath shuddered through it, as the servants felt themselves suddenly accompanied by staring men and women. The pope's bedchamber was as frescoed as the other state rooms of the Vatican, despite being far smaller than most. It must have been, Amy felt, like sleeping inside the pages of a giant, painted storybook. How did the old pope do it? Was his mind not constantly stirred by the people who lived on his walls, the people who were locked in constant motion? Her head felt dizzy just looking at them. It could not, she felt sure, be good for the baby for its mother to be assaulted by such a profusion of colour and artifice.

The band of raiders scattered, each man drawn by his own instincts. The little room was dominated by the state bed: an enormous, intricately carved monstrosity made even grander than the usual monarch's bed by virtue of its lying on a raised part of the room. How small was the chamber of the king who sat above kings, she thought – the man who oversaw the Catholic world's souls, who had excommunicated the flame-haired mistress of half of a faraway island. From this little chamber, he had commanded folk all over the globe.

Some of the servants were attacking his bedposts, chipping out little gilded medallions. No one had told her that was acceptable, but she supposed it must be. Either that or greed had already overcome sense.

The bed itself was without hangings, and the walls, despite their frescoes, were likewise denuded. Similarly, much of the room was open space and the few pieces too large to be removed – the cabinets, the marble ewers, the sideboards – looked empty. Still, their doors were thrown open and hands thrust inside.

Everything belonging to a dead pope was valuable, she realised, no matter how little worth had been attached to it at birth. The men around her were much like those who went to coronations and tore up the carpets the monarchs had walked upon, eager for souvenirs. Or worse, she thought; they were like the ghouls who thronged executions and sought to dip rags in the victim's blood to show off to their neighbours or sell to travelling lovers of the macabre.

Amy wandered past a man who was stuffing a cloth into his pocket. It had come from the marble top of the ewer and must have touched Pius V's face. She passed a man chiselling away at the foot of the bed and went to its head. Beside it, on the second step by the bedhead, was a table, on which sat a huge, metal-clasped book.

'Can't touch that,' the leader of the band, Pietro, hissed. She jumped.

'Not taking it.' Her breath tasted sour as it hit her, hot under the cloth mask.

'Let it alone. Look, don't touch, huh?'

She said nothing as he scurried off, speaking to the chiseller as he did so. When he had disappeared into the shadows, Amy returned her attention to the pope's bible.

It opened easily, though she could not lift it. Staring up at her were illuminated pages and a tangle of Latin, which she could not have read even in better light. She traced a finger over the page anyway.

Many of the book's pages stuck together, whether with age or weight, and clumped closed. When the metal cover – gilded, of course – was shut, though, she noticed something. The pages no longer lined up.

Something was sticking out of the book.

Amy looked over her shoulder before using her thumb and forefinger to inch out what appeared to be little scraps of paper – book markers of some kind, perhaps. Her heart fluttered. Letters was her immediate thought: she might well be looking at some of the old pope's private correspondence, hidden and forgotten in his last days, unnoticed by secretaries or unfit for their eyes.

Walsingham, Jack had said they would go to. There was something about the old man she rather liked, though he had hitched his career to religion and seemed hot on both. What would he give for a few private letters? Jack probably would not like it, but it might make the difference between their safe conduct to England and their daughter's safety there.

Still, her conscience itched.

Amy sighed, more in frustration than anything. Her own unwillingness to simply pocket the damn things without knowing their content and walk away whistling was infuriating. Perhaps, she thought, it was some indication of weakness brought on by the baby.

To chase away the thought, she unfolded the first letter. And gasped.

At the top of the page was no polite introduction, but a somewhat crude drawing of the pope – whether Pius V or some other pope she did not know, but the clothing was proof enough of identity. His tongue was lolling and his eyes wide, and the whole head looked to be hanging at an unnatural angle as he slid from his throne. Around him, men in cardinals' robes and hats were on their knees, either collapsing in horror or bent in prayer.

At the bottom of the page, written in Italian, were the words, 'you are the last of them.'

She shuddered.

The next page lacked a drawing. Instead, it was addressed to the 'father of lies' and went on to gloat that 'there is no heaven and no earth and for the sins you commit you suffer now and not hereafter, and for the which you must know that you will be the last father of lies. After you there will be such a judgement that none shall take your throne and the men of the earth shall inherit the ruins of your city.'

The following letter was on much the same theme. 'When the conclave ends, with it shall end the tyranny of Rome.' It went on, using many words she had not learnt, to hope for the old man's suffering and to lament that so much skill had been wasted on glorifying a God who did not exist, and to tell fables in private rooms for men of politics. It finished by warning that 'the foul breath of the next father of lies shall last no longer than your own, as surely as the earth travels round the sun. Such a blow will come as the world has never seen the like.'

On the final page was drawn a grinning, horned devil and below it the words, 'when death comes to the Vatican, they shall not see its approach.' She shivered. The last letter, like the others, was undated, but they could only have come in the last months. The approach of Pius V's death had been well known, his physicians as able as anyone else to see it. He had thinned and, when Amy had seen him in the city, his skin had turned to wax paper. It was the way her mother had went in the final days, though she had been far younger.

She flipped back to the first drawing and considered it. She knew nothing about art but thought that it looked well done – better than she could ever do, anyway – yet it was indeed crude.

The lines which made up the people wobbled, as though the drawer had had an unsteady hand.

Before she could think any more about it, Pietro hissed from the other side of the room. The servants, their plunder curtailed by the lack of loot, were being recalled. She stuffed the documents into her tunic and followed. If she were caught with them, she thought, she would be killed. It did not require a theologian to understand that they had come from a man who did not believe in God.

The word in English was new: atheist.

It was sharper than the words for ungodly men and women she had been taught as a girl: heretic sounded rather fanatical – it made one think of ranting men in black, standing in market squares and claiming that fire would rain from the sky. Apostate was a word for rich men, cultured men of universities, signifying nothing to little girls or grown women. Infidel betokened foreign savages kicking up sand. Turncoat was a word for soldiers as much as religious shifters, lively sounding and providing the benefit at least of retaining a coat of one colour or other.

Atheist was new. Atheist was scary. Atheist was a word that got you killed. In her mind they denied the existence of things that existed and laughed like madmen in the doing of it. If they did not believe in God, did not believe in the afterlife, then they believed in nothing and might think themselves free to do anything. If they would torture a dying old man with threats and dark prophecies, there was probably little they wouldn't do. And what did it matter? If they got away with it in this life, there was nothing to worry about afterwards.

She would have to keep the letters close. As she followed the party out of the bedchamber, one of her fellows tugged at her sleeve, excitement overcoming caution. 'Look,' he said, matching her step, 'look what I got!' Opening a grubby palm, he showed her a string of wooden beads with a carved medallion. 'Blessed! Blessed by the Holy Father.'

'Blessed,' she repeated, without expression. That would mean nothing to an atheist. The man, disappointed in her lack of reaction, moved on. As they passed into the next room, she considered whether the author of the letter that, with every step, crinkled against her heart, was connected with the men who had attacked her, with the old man arrested at the start of the night, now escaped and wandering.

There was a connection, she decided. This was no coincidence – the old pope had not simply had a poisonous writer tormenting him in his last days. A plot was afoot. She wondered if the late Pius had told anyone, if it meant there was security around, or the entire thing was already discovered and guarded against. Probably not, if the strange, voluntary prisoner had managed to get in and then turned himself in before escaping. Probably Pius V had read the letters and discounted them, tucking them into his bible after reading to rob them of any power the words and images had. It was well enough known that private letters could carry the spirit and mind of their writers, and if that mind was corrupted and had penetrated the Vatican...

She burned to read them again but couldn't – not until she was back in the kitchens.

'When the conclave ends, with it shall end the tyranny of Rome.'

The conclave would end the next day. How would the rule of the popes end with it?

'Judgement.'

What did that signify – a trial, a reckoning?

The dead pope in the drawing.

Was it Pius or was it his successor, slain in plain sight before his cringing cardinals?

'The breath of the next father of lies shall last no longer than your own,'

That was threatening enough. The death of the next pope was intended and, putting that threat together with the earlier, it was intended to happen at the close of the conclave. Only then, after all, would the new pope be known and proclaimed beyond doubt.

That really gave them very few hours left to stop it.

As they passed out of the palace's private apartments, Pietro drew up short, causing each man to bump into the one ahead. 'Shit.'

Pavesi had already broken free of his bindings. He was gone.

A shiver of worry passed through the group, voiced in muttering and the occasional puppy yelp of anxiety. As they passed back out into the night, fear had begun clawing at the edges of the party.

As the fresh air hit them, a piercing cry joined it.

'There! That's them!'

Amy swallowed, hard. Pavesi, his face a shade darker even in the moonlight, was standing with two guardsmen, whom he had evidently dragged from their sentry duty outside the cardinals' dormitory and brought around the old block.

Pietro darted into the night, leaving the looters helpless.

'What is this?' asked one of the guards, stepping towards them. Everyone began talking at once, Pavesi's voice rising above them all.

'Take those masks off. You are all under arrest.' He stood in the light of the guards' torches, his arms folded and a smile splitting his face.

'I'll take 'em back to the kitchens?' offered one of the guards. The group quietened.

'What do you mean?' Pavesi spat. 'Arrest them. Lock them up over there.' He pointed a thumb vaguely at the bulk of the private apartments. 'I'll now be up the rest of the night guarding against further intrusion from more of their rotten lot.'

'Captain won't like us to be away from the cardinals' cells for too long,' said the other guard. He then began speaking rapidly to Pavesi, who joined him eagerly in argument.

As Amy's eyes travelled over the pathway leading back towards the San Damaso, a sudden shape caught her breath. The man in the black hooded robe who had assailed her earlier leered into her memory. But it was not him. It was just a priest with dark hair taking the air, probably woken by the commotion and alarmed by the disappearance of the guards. She looked back at the argument between clerk and guard. With luck, the whole rabble would be locked up, if they were to be locked up, as one. No one would pay any attention to the individuals. When she looked back towards the connecting chamber, the figure had retreated.

Jack, she thought. What might she have gotten him into now?

As the dispute rumbled on, the soldier who had offered an escort back to the kitchens, mumbled out the side of his mouth, 'fuck off, all of you. Back to where you came from.'

Amy and the others needed no further invitation. As one, they took heel and sped away down the path by the Belvedere, into and through the connecting chamber to the Raphael loggia. In twos, they leapt over the low wall separating the hallway from the San Damaso. Pavesi's indignant shrieks followed them, shattering the early birdsong. So too did the reluctant and, Amy thought, rather amused commands from the two guards that they stop, come back, go nowhere.

When they reached the kitchens, they each removed their masks, tossing them into burning embers, and the party broke up, some going off in pairs, others alone. If Pietro had returned, he was already in his own bolt hole. Tradition, it seemed, had been enough to keep the guardsmen at bay. Already the kitchens were starting to come to life, the bakers and lighting-up boys beginning to stir the ovens. The sky outside had been as star-studded as when she had left, but she supposed some instinct taught those who knew their trade when it was time to rise. If she could, she might manage a few hours of sleep before the whole company of servants was roused and put to work.

Where was Giuseppe? The old man had said he assisted the bakers. He might be up and about now, the one man who knew her secret and bound himself to keep it. But she could not face asking around and pushing sleep still further back. She would just have to trust the old man, as she had decided to do earlier.

If her luck held, Pavesi too would say nothing – he did not seem the type to wish to advertise his embarrassment to his superiors. She dragged her feet back to her hidden little crawlspace by the barrels. As she sat, the crackle of paper again stirred her mind and she cursed it.

She lay down next to Jack and this time her eyelids felt weighted. She considered waking him but as her arm jostled him, he mumbled, 'I'm pregnant' in his sleep. Right you are, she thought. Tomorrow she would have to reveal what she had been up to. If he were angry or tried to rebuke her, she could always plead her belly. That was something she fully intended to enjoy in the coming months.

In the morning, she would show him the papers, the drawings, all of it. If there was a plot to murder the new pope, he could take it to his old friend the captain and they could do whatever it was that men did to prevent murders. She yawned and immediately felt little needles pressing under her eyelids. Everything felt heavy.

What kind of weapon brought death without anyone seeing it coming?

She was dead to the world herself within seconds.

10

Sleep wrought by exhaustion is often dreamless. If dreams were born of the mind, it lacked the strength to conjure them. If sent by God, He was merciful enough to spare the sleeper.

Jack had not dreamt or, if he had, he could not remember it. He only knew he had slept thanks to the trickle of drool that ran from lip to chin. Were it not for that, he might have simply had a long and uneventful blink. One of the good things about service was that it bred instant alertness: from the moment his eyes popped open he was ready to stand without sluggishness. His first thoughts, however, were not of the day's work, but of Amy, and before he rose, he made sure she was there, solid, breathing, and still fast asleep.

He decided to let her sleep on.

Already, the kitchens were buzzing. Smoke wafted around the plaster ceiling and the smell of baking bread was thick. Men trooped in and out of the storeroom, giving him a moment's pause. But the storeroom, at least, had been cleared of suspicion. Moretti's suggestion of distraction came into his mind. The prisoner had wanted them to waste time nosing about in there. That could only mean that the true danger lurked elsewhere.

Yet Amy claimed to have seen Moretti passing through the San Damaso with a stranger, a man in black with his face hooded, before she was then attacked by just such a figure. He would have to think of some means of finding out what that was about. Thankfully, he had time. Though, he thought, pursing his lips, he was not sure how much. The activity told him it must be mid-morning.

Jack washed his face and armpits at the long trough of icy water adjacent to the entrance. It was already thick with scum and floaters – a further indication that he was a late riser. Once he was presentable, he gathered up a board of bread, weak wine, and cheeses, and stepped out into the San Damaso.

Thick mist shrouded the square. It was hardly an unusual sight in Rome, as the noxious airs rose up from the Tiber, but it made the going slower. It also seemed to still the chatter of those other servants whose work took them outside, many of them clinging to the sides of buildings as they moved. He pressed on towards the dormitory, his hand over his nose and mouth to keep out the thick, oily sewage smell.

After a cursory check by the guards, he paused outside Hernandez's door on the lower floor. He began to walk away, thought better of it, and returned to knock. Some shifting and scuffling inside told him to wait, and eventually the priest answered, his dark hair a thicket. 'You.'

'I brought the cardinal something to eat.'

'Late.' Hernandez looked like he'd had a sleepless night, and as he stood, he massaged his right elbow with his left hand and cracked his neck to one side.

'You slept well?' asked Jack, trying to force a warmth he didn't feel.

'Ha. In a cell? No air? No sleep. You are late.'

Jack sighed. 'His Grace said to let him lie this morning.'

'Hmph.' Hernandez tilted his head back, eyes narrowed. Then he plucked an edge of bread off the board. 'This is tasted?'

'Yes,' lied Jack. The priest gnawed on it, his Adam's apple bobbing like a cork, before tearing off another piece.

'Good. Thank you. Rouse his Grace. This is the last day. I dress myself.' He slammed the door.

The last day, thought Jack.

He took the stairs. Cardinal Granvelle opened the door at once. As Jack stepped into his cell, it immediately became clear that the old man had been up for some time. Papers littered the desk and the vinegary smell of ink stung at his nostrils. He did not speak first. It was good practice, whether stable lad or groom, to say nothing in the morning until the master had indicated whether his mood was for conversation or silence.

'God give you good morrow, Jack.'

Conversation it was. Granvelle spoke in French.

'I hope you slept well, your Grace.'

'Very well. And you have brought me something to eat. How kind.' Jack set the board down. 'Although, between us, I confess I have never found a cheese I favoured.'

'Me neither, your Grace,' said Jack, grinning. He looked down at his feet. Too familiar.

'Alas, it is bread for us both. Have you eaten?'

'No.'

'Please, join me.' Jack's mouth fell open. 'Yes, that is a good start. Eat.'

The cardinal sitting and Jack standing, they shared the bread between them, leaving the cubes of cheese.

When they had finished, Granvelle poured out more thanks and Jack helped him to dress. This time, he had selected a fresh set of red robes. 'Did you get the other fouled red off to be laundered?'

Shit, Jack thought. 'Yes, your Grace. I saw that it was sent out to them.' That was not quite a lie, although he wondered if bending the truth to a cardinal was sinful. Had it been a secular master, he would not have been bothered, but something about the red robes, the crucifix, and, above all, Granvelle's pleasantness made it seem grubby.

'Very good. Thank you. There is no great rush. I will be wearing this same scarlet this evening. I shall have only a little labour today to soil it.' Mischief played on the cardinal's face as he looked at Jack, his balding head making him look like a great toddler caught doing something naughty. 'If the French can be shepherded, we shall name our new Holy Father at vespers.'

'There … there are French cardinals here?'

'Heh. You are observant. No, the troubles in France have permitted none to travel. And yet the French king's mother…' He made a little tsk sound, more amused than irritated. 'Her Majesty has minins enough even without Frenchmen. She will have this, she will not have that.' He shook his head, clucking again. And again that little stab of distaste flared in Jack, that feeling of seeing a mysterious and magical thing unmasked and found to be nakedly human.

A knock at the door. Granvelle nodded and Jack went to answer.

Hernandez stepped in and immediately began speaking in fluid Latin. The cardinal put his chin in his hands and stared for a space. Then he said in French, 'Cardinal D'Este. Speaking of minions of the French dowager … Well, he knows his conclaves. If I must, I must.' His eyes sharpened. 'Jack. You are relieved. I suppose I shall see you at dinner. Nothing heavy. I do not wish to lead the French on too full a stomach.'

Jack bowed his head, gathered up the board, and left the room and the dormitory. As he passed the disused block, Captain Moretti fell into step with him and they exchanged greetings as they parted the mist. The older man looked exhausted, his eyes pink. Bodily odour wafted from him with each step.

'When this lifts,' said Moretti, plucking a fist-sized piece of cheese from the board and munching into it, 'I can organise a fuller search. Of buildings, inside.'

'So he wasn't abroad on the walls, then?' Moretti mumbled in the negative through a mouthful. 'I don't guess he could have found some disguise?'

'A disguise?'

'Robes, a cowl. Something with a hood that hid his face.' Not subtle, but it got the job done. Moretti stopped walking.

'You saw someone in a hooded robe?'

'No.' Jack felt control of the discussion slipping away. The urge to ramble was too strong to resist. 'It's just I thought that if I were to try and get away from somewhere, as if I had to hide as it were, you know, until I could make a good escape … I'd get in something that covered up my face.' He began walking again. 'It was just an idea came to me in the night. In the dark.'

'And do you still cleave to the thought that our man worked with another?'

'I don't know, captain. Not my work to think on that, is it?'

'No.'

Jack kept his head down as he picked his way along the little path from the papal courtyard to the San Damaso. He knew the words had come out tartly, but the question of why Moretti was making such a friend of him remained. 'Do you want to finish this cheese?' Moretti gave him a hard look before taking it.

'It has been hungry work, I own. I have not eaten since yesterday.'

'You've not slept?'

'No. The day brings my sleep.' They came into the San Damaso. 'Thank you, son, for the food. It has bought me the will to see to the guards before I retire.'

'Where do you think he is?' There was no need to clarify whom he meant.

'I cannot say. I … there is some devilry in him, I think. It can give a man devilish strength and wiles. If you hear anything amongst the servants, pray come to me before I retire. If I am abed, one of my men will listen. I have set them to lend their ears to strange rumours.' He clicked his heels and disappeared into the mist.

Jack returned his board to the kitchen and then found Amy. This time he woke her and waited as she rubbed sleep from her eyes. 'My mouth tastes like feet.' Her hand flew to her breeches. 'Ugh, thank God you woke me. I was dreaming. Dreaming I was pissing into a good, clean pot. Just a dream.'

'How are you? How is … how are you?'

'I …' Fogginess seemed to lift from her face, though it wrinkled her brow as it went. 'Jack. I need to tell you something.'

'About the captain? I've spoke to him. He was odd, he–'

'No, not him. It's … I found something.' Her face, he thought, turned foxy. Even wearing his dirty clothes and a hideous bowl-cut, something of her prettiness shone through. A tingle ran though him, and he squeezed her arm, not bothering to look around.

'What is it?'

'I went to the old pope's rooms last night. Raiding, with the others.'

His squeeze became a vice and, when she yelped, he let go, mumbling an apology. 'What? I told you – I said …' This time he did check behind him before leaning into her face. 'You have my baby and you do mad things. You could have … anything could have happened. Why would you do that?'

'I did it,' she said, 'because I …' Tears filled her eyes, whether born of her condition or of her guile he didn't know. But he relented, and she blinked them away. 'Never mind why I went. I did and that's flat. It's what I found, though. In his rooms.' She patted her bosom, before extracting some papers.

Jack leafed through. As he did, he felt his throat constrict and

118

his mouth run dry. 'Devil drawings.' Something about them raised the hair on his arms, as it had been raised when listening to the mad prisoner's rants. Drawing such things was an invitation to them to cross from the black world they inhabited, the world of painful, crushing, nothingness, and enter into the world of man. Even now, demons might be passing from the pages into the air around them.

'The words, Jack, read them.'

He did.

'Jesus.'

She nodded. 'So, see, it's really a good thing I went. They were hidden in a bible. Must have been sent in the last weeks. Threats. And I've been thinking. You know the Scottish queen?'

'What?' Jack had only been half-listening. The image of the grinning devil, its horns inked to points, its hooves cloven, had sent little claws of dread up his spine.

'The Scottish queen. The one you couldn't take your eyes off back in England.'

'What about her?' He disliked speaking of Mary of Scotland with Amy. He knew that his wife disliked her as much, or more, than he had found the willowy lady attractive. A tacit understanding had grown between them that they would simply never speak of her – she was part of a sorry episode in their life together.

'The husband she killed, the Scots' king.'

'She didn't kill him.'

Amy rolled her eyes before speaking. 'King Henry. He was blown up, wasn't he?'

'His house was. He was strangled, or smothered, or something. By the rapist, the earl of somewhere.' He paused, and Amy smiled at him, a look of smugness spoiling her face as she seemed to wait on him catching up. 'Shit.'

'See, if death comes but isn't seen coming – well, I thought, that king must not've seen it coming. Else he would never have bedded down in a house that had been mined.'

'This whole place might be mined.'

'Gunpowder.'

'In vaults, in cellars, packed anywhere. We were set to think on poison but that old bastard, that old man, he'd saw powder placed somewhere. Then he could get himself settled in a cell. Didn't matter – the plot was laid already. But ... then why escape?'

Amy shrugged. 'Maybe something went wrong. Maybe ... maybe he was put in a cell too close for comfort.'

'So his friend would have to free him.'

'What friend?'

'I don't know. Doesn't matter now how many are in it. We have to stop it.'

She nodded. 'What do we do?'

'We don't do anything. You have to stay safe.' He looked around the room. 'Should be safe here. No one cares about blowing us to heaven. We're nothing.'

'Speak for yourself, Jack Cole.'

'I have to tell Moretti. Warn him, set a search. We have time, right? I mean, these letters say stuff about the last pope, the end of the popes. So we have time, don't we? The madman won't light anything until ... until vespers. That's when they're set to name him.'

'Yes.' He thought there was little certainty in her voice, but he appreciated her desire to assure him. He gave her arm another light squeeze. 'Only ... remember what I said about that Moretti. I swear I saw him, Jack. I wasn't lying.'

'I know you weren't. But if he doesn't do anything ... if he's ... if there's something strange about him ... I'll go to the cardinal. He'll tell the camerlengo and make a great stink and it'll all be stopped anyway. But Captain Moretti first.'

She said nothing, and he stood up and skipped from the kitchens, folding the papers inside his tunic as he moved.

Moretti had not got far; Jack found him standing in the Raphael walkway. He told him what had happened, claiming he had been part of the raiding party, and repeating his and Amy's suspicions about gunpowder. 'And that's it. It makes sense, doesn't it? It could be why he was happy to give himself up but then had to be freed, if we were too close to where there would be a great tumult, to wherever's set to explode.'

It was only at the word 'explode' that Jack paused for breath. As he did, he realised that all colour had drained from the captain's face. 'You believe me, don't you?'

'Powder.'

'Yes. Lots of it. Somewhere.'

'That prisoner, that stranger. He spoke of my fears. He said I should see them.'

'You fear powder, captain?'

'As we all should. I have …' He swallowed, before removing his cap. He threw it to the ground, making Jack step back. 'I have seen what it can do. At Lepanto. It does not cut a path to the enemy. It kills all, neither caring for friend nor foe. The fire it issues, there is no stopping it.'

'It's like I said,' Jack ventured, unsure of the sudden change in mood, 'about them wishing to reduce the place. Not just the people, the new pope, but to destroy this place. The whole Vatican might be threatened. When they killed the Scottish king, it was said his whole house was made rubble, not one stone standing above the other. A blast here would do that. And the fire, like you said, would ruin the rest.'

'Yes.' Moretti seemed to collect himself. Points of red began to prickle out again on his white cheeks.

'But we have time. Cardinal Granvelle said to me they hope to elect a new Holy Father at vespers tonight. We have time.'

'Mmph.' Moretti cleared his throat, put a hand against the wall to steady himself, and reclaimed his cap. With both hands, he fixed it on his head. 'Time. Yes. To hell with that devil. If this is true, then he has found some hole in the farthest reaches of this place. Near a gate, I should imagine, an exit. He can be found later. First, we must discover the places where an attack might be made.'

'Captain!' a new voice cut in and a guardsman emerged from the mist, his face ashen. 'Sir, you must come.'

Jack and Moretti stared at the man. His eyes were wide with shock. 'What is it?' the captain snapped.

'Our men, they have discovered something terrible. An unholy terror.'

'It's not the commander, is it?' Moretti asked. Jack let his eyes slide towards him, but neither the captain's face or tone betrayed anything.

'No … I … he lies abed, I think, captain. His stomach still poor. We dare not trouble him with this … this violence.'

'Then what?'

'You must come. Bodies. Slain foully. It is the devil's work.' Again, those little fingers of dread tickled their way up Jack's back.

11

Jack had not yet been in the Piazza San Pietro, which he found dominated by the broad facade of the new basilica, large but plain and not particularly impressive with scaffolding surrounding it and an empty drum that should, if work ever continued, support a great dome. At the centre of the square stood a strange-looking covered fountain, its roof supported by pillars and decorated with exotic birds. Beneath the ornamented roof, water running down its sides, was a huge stone pinecone.

It was against the base of the fountain structure that the bodies lay.

Swirls of mist still laced their way around them, but the weak spring sun was beginning to burn it away. 'Christ Jesus,' said Moretti, crossing himself. Jack and the guard who had led them through the entrance courtyard and down to the San Pietro did the same.

One of the bodies belonged to an older man. His back was to one of the fountain's low walls, his legs jutting away from it, bent at the knees. His left arm was crossed over his stomach and his slumped head appeared to be gazing down at it. His right arm had been tucked up over his head, palm spread. It took a few moments – death and the strangeness of the position altered him – but Jack recognised the corpse as the old man who had been tasting food in the storeroom with Amy. The thought of a slow acting poison stopped his heart, but only long enough for him to accept the soaked front of the man's brown tunic. His throat had been cut.

The other body, Jack saw, belonged to Bishop Cirillo's clerk, the weedy Pavesi. He lay just to the old man's left, and was likewise leant against the fountain's wall, though angled slightly on his right side. His hands were clutched over his chest, gripping at his neck, an outstretched finger tapping his left cheek, and his head faced down to his right, eyes open. There was no mistaking how he had died. Dressed in a cream-coloured nightgown, the reddish-brown splashes down the front spoke of another slit throat.

In the big, open courtyard, unseen birds chattered, uncaring of the gruesome scene to which their songs provided accompaniment. The festive chirping turned to mockery in his head, the birds into demons. Eventually, left to themselves, they would turn on the dead, pecking and plucking at eyeballs and soft flesh. Everything that seemed good, that seemed beautiful, turned out to be rotten in the end.

'Does the bishop know of this? Bishop Cirillo? Father Casale?' As Moretti spoke, Jack pictured the masters of household and chamber, and wondered if they would care about the man they had worked with, or only about how a dreadful murder might hurt their chances of finding favour with the new pope.

'No, captain. Only just found. The mist, and our boys all scattered around the walls of the place.'

'Good. They must be told but … I should like to understand more of it first. Fetch me the physicians. No. No, that will alert the cardinals, alarm them. The apothecary. And have men brought who can take them from this place.'

The guard saluted and hurried off.

Moretti removed his cap and wiped his brow with it. 'An obscenity.' The sight, Jack noticed, did not drain his colour in the same way the mention of gunpowder had. 'Christ Jesus.'

'That old man, he was in the storeroom. Tasting. Do you think he found something?'

'I cannot say. And we can hardly ask him now. It is the death of this fellow that troubles me.'

'You think he saw something?'

'I have no idea. It troubles me because this cannot be kept close as easily. The bishop will be alarmed. A very godly man, Bishop Cirillo. He will take this to be the devil's work.'

'Is it?' Jack locked eyes with the captain, but the older man said nothing.

***

Amy ate ravenously, needing food more than she needed to be washed or relieved. She then wandered around the kitchens, keeping her head low but her eyes active.

Giuseppe was not around. Pietro, however, was.

She knew it was a danger to engage too openly in

conversation with anyone, but she didn't care. For one thing, there was danger at large, and for another, the whole thing should be over by the time night fell, one way or another.

'Wake up,' she said, nudging the sleeping man with a foot.

'Huh?'

She repeated herself. 'You left us last night.'

Pietro murmured and cursed groggily for a few seconds. Then he grinned. 'Every man got to make his own way. You get much?'

'No.'

'Well, I'm sorry for that. But you had your chance. Let me sleep.'

'It's morning.' Even in his prone position, he managed to shrug. 'You were hard on that Pavesi man last night.'

'He's a prick. I'm tired. Wake me in an hour, huh?'

Amy considered haranguing him further. There was something about him she did not trust. He had been altogether too rough with the clerk during the raid. Not that Pavesi didn't deserve to be roughed up, but with matters so strange, any odd behaviour was suspect. But Pietro rolled away from her.

As she made to move, a Swiss Guard marched into the kitchens and the servants who were scattered about stood a little straighter. The new man ignored them, heading straight for the door to the apothecary's chamber. He beat on it three times with his forearm.

After a few seconds, Bianchi answered, straightening his hat. 'What?' Seeing it was a guardsman, he shifted tone. 'Good morrow to you. What news? There is some trouble?' Amy could not hear the guardsman's whispered response, but she could tell from Bianchi's widening eyes that something was wrong. The apothecary stepped from his chamber, banged closed his door, and followed him out of the kitchens.

Over the next few minutes, a buzz began to thrum through the servants. It reached Amy without her asking, in the way that gossip will.

They're saying someone's been killed.

There's been an accident.

Murder.

Death.

Amy did not stand around and join in the exchange of news. Instead, she took off running. In the San Damaso, she could see some others heading for the Raphael walkway, and she followed. The little drift of excited servants became a throng, all headed in the same direction. They crossed the chequered entrance courtyard. On the far side, more guards were forming a barrier stopping people entering into the parallel San Pietro. Nevertheless, servants were standing on tiptoes, craning necks and arching bodies to get a look at whatever was going on beyond. Amy joined them.

'What is that?' she heard. 'Is that people? What's the apothecary looking at? Can you see?'

***

'Throats cut,' was all Bianchi could tell them, stroking at his moustache.

'I can see that,' said Moretti.

'Then why did you call for me? I am to see to Commander von Brunegg. I do not like the colour of his movements. As for these … they are beyond my help. Beyond all earthly help.'

'Did they die together? Can that be said?'

'I am no surgeon. You ought to have sent for a surgeon.' Distaste coloured the apothecary's words. But he bent down all the same. 'I should say the old fellow died first. A neat job of work.'

'How do you know this?'

'See here,' he tapped on the corpse's upraised arm, 'it is held aloft. Stiffening. The other, poor Mr Pavesi, he is yet soft and moveable.'

'Where they killed here?'

'I cannot say. Killed here or moved here, what does it matter?'

'Pavesi lodged far across two great courtyards. If he were killed in his bed and dragged here, should not there be blood, a great trail of it?'

'No,' said Jack. Both older men looked at him.

'Who is this?' asked Bianchi. 'He's hardly your boy. I saw you last night, did I not?'

'A friend,' said Moretti. 'Go on, lad.'

'The killer I think is the same who killed your man.'

'That devil prisoner.'

'Maybe.' Jack frowned. 'Or someone helping him.' Before Moretti could argue, he pressed on. 'He cuts their throats and uses the clothes to soak the blood.'

'Is that possible?' Moretti directed his question to Bianchi.

'Perhaps. As I said, a surgeon might tell you about these gory matters. Yet even if the blood could be well soaked up, how might a man move a body – two bodies – about this place unseen?'

'In the dark? If he had the strength, with ease. Pavesi is small. The other is older, weakened by age. No hard task.'

'Are there no guards? No men to stop him?'

Moretti crossed his arms. 'My men had other business in the night. Seeing to the security of all.'

'I daresay your men think they have a holiday with the commander lying abed. They are not seeing to our security at all, captain, if we can be slain in our beds, even honest clerks under the protection and employ of the bishop.'

Jack leapt in to defuse the unfolding argument. 'Does it matter? I mean, it doesn't really matter where they died, does it? It's where they were found.'

The three pairs of eyes turned up to the fountain and then, as one, to the unfinished front of the basilica. In the grey morning light, it looked like a crumbling old temple straining not to fall down, rather than a new building eager to be finished and beautified. 'A threat. This is a threat against this conclave, against this sacred place. A foul blasphemy.'

'I should say there is practice of sorcery in it,' agreed Bianchi. 'Yonder fellow you had me examine last night. I said nothing of it but after thinking and praying … there might have been devils in him.'

'And he wanders free.'

'What?'

'He killed his guard and escaped. We have sought after him all night and been up, like the owls, without sleep. Nothing.'

'Or someone killed his guard and freed him,' said Jack. Moretti's refusal to accept an accomplice was becoming irritating. Or, he supposed, Amy had made him so suspicious of his new friend that he was ready to see strange behaviour in everything. Besides, he had no proof of another man helping.

'That creature could have done it alone,' said Bianchi. 'The devil might have taken possession of his hands, made them work for evil purposes.'

They paused their conversation at the sound of the men approaching with boards to take away the bodies, each one already loaded with sheets. The guards seemed to move forward on a chorus of sound. 'Captain, there's one back there, a servant, making trouble.'

Jack's heart sank.

Pushing through the guards and marching towards them was Amy.

'Captain Moretti,' she announced.

'Your brother?' he said, raising a quizzical eyebrow to Jack.

'Yes, sir.'

'Dr Bianchi, thank you.' The apothecary, apparently delighted at his promotion, bowed and walked away. 'Gentlemen, please cover these poor fellows and remove them.'

'What are you doing here, Roberto?' asked Jack, trying to keep the anger out of his voice. 'You've not been well. You know that.'

Amy had fallen surprisingly silent. She had got a proper look at the bodies. 'Oh, Giuseppe.'

'You knew him?'

'Yes, captain. He was my friend. Someone's killed him.'

'I'm afraid so.'

Her face hardened. 'I saw you last night with a man in black. That man attacked me.'

Silence.

The small group of men who were attending to the corpses froze, turning from their bent positions to look round. Jack balled his fists. For the first time, he felt like striking her, striking his pregnant wife, and the urge, quickly extinguished, frightened him.

'You hold your tongue, boy,' said Moretti. His voice was low, starved of all emotion.

'But I did, I did see you. And now my friend's been murdered.'

'You say your brother has been unwell?'

'Yes,' said Jack.

'And yet here he stands, looking passing well.'

'I'm well enough,' said Amy. Jack silenced her with a look.

'Well enough not to question your betters, you young whelp. You say this man was your friend. And the other, Pavesi, he set you and this friend to an unpleasant task yesterday. You might have reason to see both dead.'

'What?' Amy suddenly looked unsure of herself. She really did, thought Jack, look like a lost boy. He hoped so, anyway.

'Item: Mr Pavesi had you eat and drink what might have been poisoned.'

'But it wasn't. I didn't do anything.'

'Item: this other old fellow–'

'Giuseppe. He was my friend. Why would I hurt a friend?'

'Friend. Sometimes friends discover our secrets and we look upon them with less than friendship, is that not so?'

Jack jumped in. 'My brother was with me. All the time. During the night.'

'And yet you have been with me and working for your new master, the cardinal. This … lad … has been alone enough to spy upon his betters. What else has he been doing, one might ask.'

'Please, captain. I can speak for my brother in this, in all matters.' Panic had begun to tear at his chest. It was Amy's fault, but he could not risk her paying for her mistakes. Not now. He added, meaningfully, with the barest glance at Amy, 'our mother would not forgive me else.' He lingered on the word 'mother' for just a beat.

Moretti took a deep breath and let it out slowly. He turned and barked at the men behind him to get back to work before returning his attention to Jack and Amy. 'I speak only to show that false accusations might be cast upon anyone.'

Jack exhaled relief. Then he said, 'but why these two men? What did they do?'

'The wrong place, perhaps.'

'Both were out in the night,' said Amy, her voice low and, Jack chose to believe, remorseful. 'I saw them too.'

'You have been busy.' It was difficult to tell if Moretti was amused or exasperated. He had a remarkable way of speaking – he could be utterly dry when he wished to be. 'When?'

'During the night. We … we went all together on a raid on the old Holy Father's rooms.'

'That.' The captain rolled his eyes.

'The man who took us, he's called Pietro, he was hard on Mr Pavesi.'

'I heard that masked men abused him. Broke in upon him, tied him down. And when he escaped and sought aid, they ran into the night. Most annoyed, he was. Yes, he was up in the night. My men returned to the dormitories and Pavesi would have walked alone to his lodgings. Perhaps he meant to keep watch himself, hoping to catch more thieving dogs.'

'And Giuseppe took me to see the Belvedere. I didn't see him again after that.'

Moretti tugged at his beard. 'Two men, alone, in the darkness. It would take but seconds to cut a throat. Longer to move them here.'

'Easier with two,' persisted Jack.

'This Pietro you spoke of. Jack, do you know him?'

'Er … yes. He's … he's somewhat of a friend of mine.'

'Do you trust him?'

Jack looked at Amy and then at the captain. 'Yes. I don't know. Yes.'

'Bring him to me. You, Jack's brother. You accuse him – you bring him.'

***

Amy had to drag the protesting Pietro from his slumber. The young Roman seemed to have a knack for understanding, and it seemed he understood that no good could come of his being called before the captain of the guard. Still, he went, grumbling all the way.

As Amy retraced her steps, Pietro in tow, she crossed paths with the guards carrying their covered stretchers. The spectacle drew the attention of those servants who had crowded the edge of the piazza, freeing up their passage.

'Shut up,' she hissed back at her charge. Throughout the jog to the kitchen and back, she had been cursing herself. As soon as she had caught sight of the corpses across the square, Jack's back moving around before them next to Moretti's, something had kindled inside her. It had overcome reason, forcing her through the guards and demanding that she confront the captain. She knew he was hiding something, and she knew that Jack would not drag it from him. In doing so, she seemed to have triggered something in the older man, bringing out the hard, unpleasant side to him that she supposed all captains must have. Yet she had also seen her husband's expression when she had appeared, the sudden fury, and she remembered too his rage when she had first revealed herself to be in the Vatican. That had only been the previous evening, and yet it seemed so very long ago.

Was it the baby that made her act out? She didn't know, but neither did she think so. It was a desire to provoke, to have her say, to make things happen when others wouldn't. It was the same desire that now dragged Pietro along behind her.

'This is him?' asked Moretti.

Pietro stood before the captain, one hand on his hip. 'What is this, huh? Jack? What's happened, my man?'

'Speak when you are spoken to.' Amy noticed that Jack looked overwhelmed. She had not stopped to consider what she might be doing to him. He had developed some kind of friendship with Moretti and with Pietro, and she had forced him into deciding where his loyalties lay. The battle played out on his face as he bit at his lower lip. She had engineered the confrontation, and it was plain that he could not avoid it.

'Did you make threats against the late Mr Pavesi?'

'Pavesi is dead?' Pietro paled. Moretti repeated his question. 'Jack, what is this? Am I accused?'

'No,' said Jack. 'It's just some folk are saying you were a bit rough with him. He's been killed in the night.'

'I didn't do it!'

'No one's saying that, are they captain?'

Moretti said nothing. Instead, Amy noticed, he was staring,

unblinking, at the flustered young Roman. Silence drew out a while. 'It was a tradition, a jest, we didn't hurt him, none of us, we saw him after, with your men, sir, he was fine, unhurt. I didn't do it!'

'What is your knowledge of this man?' Moretti asked, addressing himself to Jack.

'We met yesterday. He is … a friend.'

'See? See, he speaks for me.'

'Have you spoken to him since?'

Everyone's eyes fell on Jack. Amy felt her heart breaking at the confusion on his face. If only Moretti had had him speak in private. If only he hadn't been forced to discuss a friend in front of that friend. If only she could have kept her mouth shut. 'Yes. Yes, I gave him the cardinal's robes to take to the laundry. After supper last night.' He put his palm to his forehead and rubbed.

'Yes,' gasped Pietro, his head nodding in a frenzy. 'He did. I took them, I took them right away.'

'Red robes,' said Moretti. 'Very good for soaking blood and that blood remaining unseen.'

'What? No!'

'Where are these robes now?'

'I don't know! I left them out by the gate.'

'The gate. My men saw you?'

He turned evasive. 'I left them there. Maybe they saw me. Jack, huh? Do you know?'

Jack gave one sharp shake of his head. Amy tried to catch his eye, to communicate reassurance, but he would not look at anyone.

'Until we discover the truth of the matter, you will be confined. You laid hands upon a man now dead. And my young friend here has said for hours now that there are two pairs of hands at mischief in this place.' She saw him stiffen. His unruly fringe fell over his face but he did not bother to flick it away.

'Confined? But … Jack, speak for me. I'm a free Roman, I've done nothing. Nothing wrong. Speak for me.'

'Captain…' But Moretti was already shouting across the San Pietro. One of his men strode over and, taking Pietro roughly by an arm, marched him off.

When they had gone, the captain passed his gaze between the men Amy hoped he still thought were brothers. 'Now. Since you are both here and you, lad, are not so unwell as Jack thought, I hope you will help put an end to this madness.'

Amy bowed her head in acquiescence. When she looked back up, Jack was staring at her with cold, implacable anger. She opened her mouth to speak. Before she could, Moretti spoke again. 'And before we set to work, I will have something else from you. I would know why you have been lying to me.'

12

'Lies, lies, lies. And from you, lad, in whom I have reposed trust.' Jack felt Amy move around beside him. Almost instinctively, they began backing away from Moretti until both were facing him across a cane's thrust, two schoolboys before a disapproving master. He felt her fumbling for his forearm, and he shook her loose.

'Sir … I …'

'You spoke to me of this merry jetting about his Holiness' apartments,' said Moretti. 'Yet you withheld that your young brother here was with you. You withheld that yonder wandering vagabond Pietro was your leader and mishandled one of the dead men. You break trust.'

Jack looked up, a grin spreading. Moretti reddened in apparent anger at it and he forced his mouth into more natural lines. 'Sir, I sought only to protect my brother. He is … poor of wits.' He saw the captain's doubtful eyes shift towards Amy's bowed head and sped on. 'He can't hold his peace or his tongue. He says everything he sees.'

'A fine thing when the case is as strange and dangerous as this. Rather I think it is you, Jack, have been too close-mouthed.'

'To protect him only, sir, I promise. He … I didn't want him getting into trouble for the raid. Or anything.'

'Is that so? I wonder.' He paused, as though to let them stew a little. 'Or perhaps the pair of you are in league with that old devil, have been hiding him.' Before they could react, he continued, 'a powder plot would be weeks, months, in the making. It would take men to transport the stuff into this place in servants' weeds, little by little, never enough to arouse the suspicions of the commander, of any of us.'

'But we wouldn't tell you, would we, if we'd done that?' Amy was indignant and thumped at her side. It seemed to do the trick.

'Wouldn't you? Some heretical plot, then, and you two seek to turn my eyes from it with false talk of powder. Else you are sent here by some enemy of one of the college of cardinals, interferers. A conspiracy, perhaps, laid by heretics and enemies, involving I know not how many.' Moretti seemed to run himself dry and, when he finished, he turned his face up to the sky. It had turned the colour of marble, thickly veined with white, grey, and violet. A single spot of rain landed on Jack's cheek before the sun bellowed forth through a break in the clouds.

'You don't believe that, do you, captain?' he said, trying to maintain the dignity Amy's outburst had lacked.

Moretti made a little exasperated noise before speaking. 'No. Yet I still say the matter is strange, a marvellous thing, and neither of you deserve true and faithful trust.'

'I've only acted for the safety of the cardinals. And to protect my brother. If I had to lie or hide anything, I'm sorry.'

'Well that, I suppose, is fair.' The captain seemed to relax, the rant having released some of the pressure which must have been building in him overnight. 'Have I not offered you friendship and trust enough that you might speak to me openly?' Jack said nothing. He had seen Moretti's face when Amy had burst amongst them and spoken of his consorting with a stranger. He could not speak back to the captain, but nor would he feel guilty about withholding things from him. The thing was to keep the attention focused on himself. Amy had acted like an idiot, a broad-mouthed fool who did not think before speaking, but that was a problem he would deal with in his own way, in his own time. Before a stranger he would protect her.

'I'm sorry, sir.'

'As am I. Sorry and,' he screwed his eyes shut and held them that way, 'ugh.'

'Are you well? Shall I go and get the apothecary back?'

'No. Tiredness.' Moretti opened his eyes and Jack noticed that the redness had been compounded by the heavy bags under them. 'This is my time to sleep. And I can have none. You,' he said, turning to Amy. 'Go forth and send my men to me. A group, tell them, with sharp eyes and lanterns fit to be lit. And then visit the gates.'

'Which gates?'

'All of them. Every gate in and out of this place. Seek out who visited them in the night. You did not trust young Pietro and so you shall find the truth of him. Discover if he truly took those robes to be laundered. If they are still there, bring them. If not, ask the guards about his manner, the time at which he came to them. Use your head.'

Amy nodded. 'Jack, will he come?'

'No. He will stay by me. Close by me. I do not intend that either of you should conspire together nor that he shall be alone. He has been close to this matter from the start.'

'You don't trust me? Sir, you don't think I'm part of any of this?'

'Trust is earned, boy. You, go.'

Amy began to move away, reluctantly. Jack saw her making faces at him, wide-eyed, worried looking. For the sake of the baby he gave her a tight smile in return but did not let it touch his eyes. Before she could depart, Moretti spoke again. 'Do only as I say. And remember, Roberto, that I am not the fool you might take me for.' She said nothing, gave no sign of understanding, but walked away from the square.

'What now, captain?'

'I intend to discover if there is powder hidden.'

'Where?'

'Everywhere. If there are only a few hours left until this place meets a terrible fate ... then we must use them wisely. All trusted men must take part.' Jack noticed he laid emphasis on the word 'trusted' and he lowered his gaze to his boots. 'Orderly, that is what we must be. And I cannot forget or lost sight of the fact that these dead fellows were placed here. But why?'

'A threat, you said. I mean, it could be like striking at the heart of the place, couldn't it?' He stepped around the fountain and looked up. Not only was the front of the new St Peter's Basilica under construction, rising high at unequal levels, but the round shape of the old building clung to its left. Further left again a huge, sword-like shape stabbed at the sky: the Egyptian obelisk brought by some emperor of antiquity.

'If powder there is, our villain cannot know that we know of it. Yet he likes display. He likes to taunt.'

'We saw that last night. He was a madman. He mocked the bishop, he mocked Mr Bianchi, he ... mocked.'

'And there lies his failing. And his falling. It might indeed be that in displaying his devilish power before the basilica, he reveals something he has intended for it. We search it and if there is nothing we continue to search, onwards and northwards,' he pointed his finger, 'in that direction.'

'What if we don't find anything?'

'Then these places are clear. And I shall turn my men to covering the Sistine. The chapel shall be the most guarded place in history during the ballot. Not a single man shall come and go excepting cardinals and their creatures.'

Jack stood back whilst Moretti splashed his face in the fountain and drank. Again, he screwed his eyes shut and wobbled slightly on his heels. 'Maybe you should sleep, captain. Leave this all to someone. To all of us, we can search.'

'I am well.'

Jack said nothing. If Moretti wished to kill himself working without rest, there was nothing he could say to stop him. He supposed the older man could not or would not risk disaster occurring due to his having been asleep. Better that, even if something bad fell upon them all, he was at the helm when it did; he could say that he'd done all he could.

They waited in silence until the crew of Swiss Guards arrived, lanterns swinging. Their leader claimed that a strange boy had been snooping around the barracks and claimed he had been sent to fetch them.

Amy, Jack thought, relieved that she was doing what she'd been told. Yet he noticed that the captain turned sharp at the mention of snooping, asking where exactly, and what the boy had found. He only relaxed when the guardsman assured him that he had found only the crew.

Whatever secrets the captain held, he would not share them.

Moretti introduced Jack to them, and he grinned. They seemed a little resentful at the interloper, until their captain informed them what they were searching for and the breadth of the undertaking. At the mention of gunpowder, most of them stood more erect, and glances of horror passed between them.

Jack wondered how many of them had been at the Battle of Lepanto, and what they might have seen there to make powder blasts such a terror.

'We begin,' said Moretti. He took up a position before them, his legs slightly apart, hands on his hips. 'First, through the new basilica and then the old. Discover anything that might explode, might reduce the place. I need not tell you that if the buildings behind us were well mined, the great tumult would fall upon us all, upon the whole Vatican. Fire would rain down, with burning stone and metals. This holy place would resemble the deepest pits of hell.'

One soldier coughed, and Moretti nodded. 'If there is nothing in the basilica, captain?'

He glared at the man who had spoken. 'You go back, I have no need of you here.'

'But captain–'

'I mean no offence, lad. Return to the barracks. Secure weapons. Firing weapons. And then command a small force, the better sort, to search the dormitories, both of them. Tell them what to look for, barrels, bags, anything that might be stuffed with powder. Look in waste places, ditches, on the outside too. Especially on the outside, and in any cellarage. He might have sought to undermine.' He rubbed at his eyes. 'I want the cardinals' living spaces assured. And the papal apartments, too, anywhere that might appear forgotten.' It was a lot of ground, thought Jack, but it could just about be done with enough men. Something in Moretti's manner made it all seem professional, clean, organised. 'But no fear, no panic. The weapons first. See to it.'

'Guns, sir?'

'I think … no, I think not. Longbows. We might have need of them later. If we find nothing here.'

'Should … ought we to have someone tell the commander about this? See if he has any knowledge?'

A silence followed this, the majority of the group turning their gazes groundward. 'No,' said Moretti. Then, more powerfully, 'do we wish to intrude on a great man in his sickbed, or do we wish to tell him, when he stands tall once more' – a little ripple of nervous laughter burst forth, the men having presumably heard that the commander's bowels had turned sour – 'do we wish to tell him that we have been lost without him? Or that we have done him proud? That we men of the guard have discovered and defeated a lowly old man who sought to trouble us?'

A small, half-hearted chorus of cheers. The soldier who had spoken looked doubtful, but he saluted and set off the way he had come.

Another man, perhaps keen to be relieved of the mission, persisted in the line of questioning that had got his comrade sent back. 'What if there's nothing in there?'

Moretti's answer sent a shudder through Jack and, he thought, the rest of the company. 'Then we go under.'

***

After leaving Jack and Moretti, Amy kept her pace up, despite the stich developing in her side and the tearing pain in the small of her back. She had made a mess of things, but she would not run away from them. Instead, she would work as hard as anyone to set them right. If Pietro was innocent, he would be freed if the real calamity could be averted. If he was guilty, he was rightly locked away. And if the disaster could not be found, whether gunpowder or otherwise, they might all be dead in a few hours, and none of it would matter save she and Jack and their baby would have bought their way into Heaven by trying.

But she would not let that happen. If anyone was trying to kill Jack, to kill her baby, she would put them in a grave herself and shovel the dirt over them as they cried out for mercy. Just thinking it boiled strength up inside her.

The guards who had formed a cordon along the edge of the square had melted away, as had the throng of servants eager for a peek at what had been going on in front of the basilica. With the removal of the covered bodies, the show had gone on the road, like a mummers' fair taking its business to a new innyard. Returning all the way to the San Damaso, Amy took the path eastward, to where she knew the barrack houses of the Swiss Guards were. An old-fashioned round tower dominated the area beyond the kitchens and palace block, and scattered around its base were the neat, one- and two-storey sandstone buildings that, by their flags and pennants, were what she sought.

She turned in a circle, searching amongst the cluster for signs of activity. Momentarily, her eyes landed on a section of the wall which jutted out from the main curtain and had a small door built into it. Potted cypress trees lined it, obscuring even the old door. It certainly wasn't anything of use to the guards.

She made for the grandest building, and passed through an unlocked, metal-studded wooden door. Ahead stretched a single, low-ceilinged hall, with an unlit fireplace and several bits of good furniture. It was evidently a private chamber, probably the fallen commander's, for it contained a single desk against one wall with inkpots, a cushioned chair, and a side oratory. Chests stood around the room, one of them open, revealing suits of guards' clothes in their profusion of colour. She ran a hand over them, enjoying the silken feel. Then she jerked it away.

Hidden amongst them were a selection of black cloaks.

Amy lifted one out, feeling around it. It had a hood. She darted a look back towards the door and then replaced it, tossing the colourful items back over. A sound overhead made her start, and she wheeled around, a child caught snooping. The doorway through which she had entered was still empty. A flight of wooden steps stood in the corner of the room and she inched up it. At the top was a landing with a door to the floor above. She raised her hand to knock. Stopped. Put her ear to it instead.

From within the upper chamber, a low keening sound rumbled. Laughter followed. Ice ran in her veins. But it was not quite the maniacal laughter of the man or men who had stalked her the night before. She put her hand to the metal handle and tried to work it without making a sound, but it was no good. The door was locked.

'Who goes there?'

Amy nearly tumbled down the stairs.

In the hall below, a guardsman had come in. She went down, shaking and mopping a brow that had suddenly developed a sheen. 'Good morrow.' She coughed, dragging raggedy phlegm into her throat to give gruffness before repeating herself.

'This is the commander's chamber. Are you here to clean it?'

'Yes. No, I mean.' That did her no favours, she thought.

'Captain Moretti sent me. I've to find men with good sight and able bodies. A group. To go over to the San Pietro. He wishes a search to be made. Safety for the cardinals. And to bring lanterns too, he said.'

'And you sought us up in his bedchamber?'

'I don't know this place. Don't know the rooms.' Something slid into place in her mind, bringing relief with it.

'I see.' The guardsman stared at her for a few seconds, as though willing her to be a thief and admit it. She held his gaze until he exhaled through his nostrils and nodded assent. 'I will muster a company. You've no need to be about this place. Captain cleans it himself. Come.'

'Yes, sir. And I suppose the commander is upstairs. We all heard he's unwell, taken to his bed.'

'Commander von Brunegg? No. He lies in a smaller outbuilding, closer to … closer to the privies. Captain Moretti has this place for the conclave.'

'Oh.' The little puzzle piece tore itself away, mocking her.

Amy followed him out, dragging her feet as much as she dared, her head tilted to one side lest any further noise from above make itself heard. There was nothing. The queer sensation passed through her that whatever was up there was listening as well. 'You frightened of dogs?' asked the young guardsman, pausing and turning in the doorway.

She continued walking towards him. 'What?'

'Dogs. You frightened of them?'

'No.' Confusion must have wrinkled her face because he laughed, a little too brightly.

'The cap keeps a mastiff. Big brute. Always trying to get its use allowed in searches, security.'

'Is that so?' She put a finger to her lip. 'Well, if that's so, hadn't you better go up and get it? Might be a help in his search.'

'He didn't ask, did he?' The trace of humour had departed the man's face. 'Come.' Cursing at having to admit defeat and leave her curiosity unsatisfied, she followed him.

The soldier led her to a shabbier building, and she followed him inside. It was a bunkhouse, the hammock-cots lining the walls. He shook a few of them, tumbling the men cursing to the floor. As they began to undress, she averted her eyes and wandered through a door to a larger, open chamber.

She drew breath.

Death skipped through the air, tickling her nostrils. No corruption fouled the odour; instead, it carried a low, slightly sour note, like overripe fruit smelt from another room.

Here were bed-like bunks, but their tenants would never rise again. A guardsman lay in one, eyes closed, his arms crossed over his chest. On the next lay Pavesi, similarly positioned. Atop one on the other side was Giuseppe. His eyes were open and staring and his position unnatural, the limbs and legs bent.

'Couldn't straighten him. They go stiff after a while, bodies.' The guard who had led her to the building had followed her into the room. 'My boys are ready. We're off. San Pietro, you said?'

'Yes.' Her eyes were still on the old man, and her voice sounded distant in her ears.

'Stay away from the captain's lodging. He won't be happy if you creep about.'

'Yes.'

The sound of curses, oaths, and laughter from the men in the bunkroom dissolved, capped off by the door banging shut. Still, Amy stared down at her dead friend. She closed his eyes with a hand; the eyelids, at least, were amenable. 'I'm sorry,' she said. Had it not been for her, Giuseppe would have been asleep in the kitchens all night. He would never have been prey to some madmen stalking the shadows.

Then anger flared.

It was not her fault. Both he and she should have had full liberty to wander wherever they felt like wandering, whenever they felt like doing it. Had she not been quick enough to turn and fight back, she might have been lying in one of the cots too. It was never a victim's fault for becoming the target of a madman; it was always the madman's fault. She had not set the old man wandering in a wolves' den, where the animals lacked reason, but walking through the holiest place on earth. His killer had reason enough and had chosen to kill. That was his fault, whoever he was, and only his. 'I'll find him,' she said aloud. 'Find him and cut his throat.' She meant it. Giuseppe had not mentioned a wife or children, but she swore silently that she would discover that when she was free of the Vatican and its unfolding madness, and she would visit them in person to tell them that she had avenged him.

She left the room and the building and set off towards the nearest gate. She would do as Moretti had bid her, but she did not trust him. Even his show of anger, accusing her and Jack of being part of whatever was going on: was that genuine, or was it a sham, a clever design intended to fool them both?

If he was part of a plot, a powder plot or some other wicked design, it would suit him well to play along with their suspicions, join eagerly in the searches they thought necessary, all the while knowing that he and his men would find nothing he did not wish them to find.

13

The ground floor of the basilica was neatly laid enough, although the entire interior still had the sad air of a building unfinished. Statues inhabited some niches; others lay empty. Some porticoed spaces had elaborate stone tombs filling them; others lay empty. Irregular columns of light sloped in through gaps in the ceiling and high, unglazed windows, making illuminated stages for dancing specks of dust.

Jack and the guardsmen had each been sent in different directions by Moretti, instructed to look for boxes, for bags, for loose floor tiles, and even for tombs which looked to have been disturbed. Although it had not been instructed, Jack ran his hands down behind statues, wiggling his fingers for the tell-tale feel of something that didn't belong.

Nothing.

There came a natural point – he had no idea of how long they had been at work or even what time it was – when the crew came together in the nave. 'Hard to believe there could ever be anything bad happening here,' said Jack, his voice bounding around the open space.

'Bad things happen everywhere,' said Moretti. 'Here, most certainly.'

'That's the truth!' cried out one of the soldiers. 'When was it, captain?'

'1527, men. Remember, always, your fallen brethren.' Jack looked around him as the guards, as one, saluted and then crossed themselves. 'A great massacre,' said Moretti, 'took place on the steps outside. In 1527, when the imperial forces of Charles V sacked Rome. Our brave boys made their last stand, fought like tigers.' A chorus of muted cheers passed through the men, magnified by the open space. 'And were slain like men, true men. Of nearly two hundred, but forty-two survived. We are their true heirs and shall defend this place to our dying breaths.'

It was clear that the captain had made the speech before, that his men had heard it before, and that they enjoyed hearing it again.

Moretti's voice echoed around the room, 'there has been no powder here since Bramante the Ruinante began reducing the old place to the ground.' A little murmur of laughter rippled through them. Jack did not join in, and Moretti silenced it with a glare. 'Yet I have not forgotten the remains of the old basilica.' He pointed to the group's left as they faced the nave. 'The rotunda still stands. And with it the tomb of the late Holy Father.'

He led them to the little altar of San Angelo, south of the nave. Jack had noticed it earlier, from the outside of the building: a circular chamber which clung to the side of the emerging new building like a sorrowful reproach. Tombs still filled it, some of them ancient, clearly untouched for years, their painted colours faded, and lids having lost all chance of being opened without great tools.

The late Pope Pius's, however, was freshly carved, the gilding complete. They searched all around the box-like structure. The question of opening it up remained unasked. Yet the thought had occurred to Jack and must have occurred to Moretti. The old moustachioed man, the prisoner, the fellow that the captain insisted was some kind of devil, had a twisted enough mind, as must whichever man Jack knew was helping him. Minds such as those, which had tortured the old pope at the end of his life, might well have sought to use his tomb as a means of execution in death. It would be cruel indeed if Pius's remains proved to aid the end of his successor. Eventually, Moretti crossed himself and Jack locked eyes with him. The captain put his hands on the edge of the lid. Jack followed. In turn, each man moved to help, and together they opened the tomb.

The embalmed face of Pius V stared up at them, waxy but wholly uncorrupted, his white hands held together in prayer. There, thought Jack, is the old man who had been the custodian of his soul. It felt like an intrusion, a monstrous intrusion, yet somehow also strangely peaceful. It felt almost as if the old pope was giving them a posthumous blessing, accepting what they were doing as necessary rather than lurid. 'Is that right that he should be so untouched?' one of the soldiers said, wonder in his voice. 'I've seen men turn to rot under the sun in days.'

'It is a mark of true saintliness,' said Moretti. 'There is nothing hidden here. God bless you, your Holiness.' Together, they heaved the lid back over the tomb.

'What else is there?' Jack asked. The thought of going underground sat ill with him, but there seemed no other choice.

'The grottoes, one floor below us. They say, too, there are mausoleums below that. Old Roman tombs hidden below the earth. Yet no man has seen them. If they are truly there, they have not been got at by any man alive.' An audible, collective sigh sounded up to the roof of the rotunda.

Moretti led them to the lower floor, more a large basement that a subterranean grotto. Yet it was dark under the curving ceilings. They paused to light the lanterns. 'Have a care,' hissed the captain. 'Let no lick of flame touch the ground. If there is a even a scattering of powder...' He did not need to finish.

Darkness pressed down on them, the lanterns doing little to relieve it. It caused the men to focus their eyes on the nearest floors and walls, and without discussing it they formed themselves into a tight-packed square, like the old Roman legionaries were said to have done. As a unit, their little troupe of light-bearers moved ahead, hugging the left wall as they passed through a small trio of chambers. They shone on nothing but old columns, empty recessed spaces, and the occasional box that turned out to be filled with bricks. There were no elaborate paintings, no frescoes.

'Jesus!' one of the men cried.

Jack felt his heart scud against his ribs.

In the beam of the lantern, a body lay sprawled.

'For the love of God, Antonio,' Moretti said, not unkindly. 'It is a statue.' As the group looked on, the captain stepped forward with the lantern he had commandeered and shone it upon a plain, white woman, her sightless eyes half closed as she cradled nothing. Laughter again rumbled through the group, Jack joining in this time. It relieved the tension of stalking through the confined space.

They continued on their way. Throughout, Jack could not escape the feeling that it was a fruitless search. There accompanied him the firm but unshakeable resolve that one never found what one was searching for. Things, good or bad, only turned up when you knew for sure they were there, or else when you didn't expect them to be at all. Still, they were now underneath the basilica and might as well make a thorough job of it.

The light began to pick up the sweat on the other men's faces, despite the relative chill of the grottoes. At such close quarters and with every second man carrying a lantern, the heat began to feel oppressive. Moretti, however, led them around every corner and into every recess.

Nothing.

St Peter's Basilica was clean, up above and down below. If gunpowder was intended, no vast stores of it had been built up to destroy the grave of Jesus' apostle. Doubt crept into Jack's mind. Gunpowder had seemed so likely a weapon – it could be struck to life by anyone, unseen by the intended victim. He refused to let it go. Just because the basilica might be crossed off as a place of disaster, it did not mean that powder was absent from the Vatican. Far likelier, in fact, was that the dormitories were mined.

Something Moretti said suddenly struck him. Distraction. Always distraction. The two dead men were not intended to threaten the basilica but rather to keep the Swiss Guard busy at it, away from the real site of catastrophe. And they had fallen for it, wasting what felt like hours blundering around in the dark. He debated whether to say anything to Moretti immediately, considering how it might stand with his men to point out such an error. Better, he decided, to wait until he could get him alone. He continued, keeping his own counsel.

'Let us be off, then,' said the captain as they made slow progress through a tight, sharply cornered passage. 'Yonder lies the way out of here. We can move on knowing that this place is not to be sent skyward to fall down upon our heads. Who – who has broken off from us?'

Jack looked up from where he had been tracing the progress of his feet along the undressed stone floor. He followed Moretti's profile and squinted. 'You, which of you is making a run for the way out? Have you taken fright at the thought of another damned statue pretending to be a corpse?'

Farther into the darkness, a little light bobbed. No one answered. As Jack peered, he thought he saw a hooded figure holding it.

And then the little flame became a bigger one, as it fell to the floor and blossomed. Fire cut off their path out of the grottoes.

***

Amy found nothing at the main entrance to the Vatican, the one through which the cardinals had arrived, save an almost threatening chorus of voices from outside: a drunken mob, by the sound of things, doing what drunken mobs did best. It seemed that huge crowds had gathered and were involved in some sort of carnival beyond the gates. The rumble of hundreds of voices occasionally burst into wild cheers. Apparently, word had gotten out that today was the day. It was odd – she had only been one night closed up in the Vatican and yet the enclosed city had managed to instil a fear of those outside. The rabble over the wall, unseen and rowdy, seemed almost like dangerous besiegers.

She continued on until she reached the next port: a tall, painted door with smaller doors and windows cut into it. It was unguarded. Next to it stood a large wooden coffer. She lifted the lid and found it empty. If it was the laundry chest, it had been emptied and the fouled stuff passed out of the Vatican.

A loud tapping.

Again.

Amy looked up and down the wall, stretching off to her left and right, and then she stood on her tiptoes and grabbed a metal pull affixed to one of the small windows. As she jerked it open, the door itself did not budge.

She jumped back as something came flying in, landing just behind her. Her first instinct was to duck, her second to stretch back up and close the window. Closer to the ground, however, she saw that it was a small purse. 'Who goes there?' cried a voice on the other side of the door.

'Who goes there?' she hit back.

'Pietro?'

'Yes.'

'What news?'

Amy swallowed, trying to remember the lazy sound of the boy's voice. 'You get the cardinal's robes, huh?'

A paused. 'I know not this code, boy. It is me, Reynard the Fox. What news?'

'The black robed man walks at night.'

'What? Pietro, is that you?'

Amy could not resist smiling at the confusion. 'Bugger off.' She reached up and closed the window on the enquiring voice.

Two things, she thought, trying to organise them. Pietro was selling information to a stranger on the outside, and no guards seemed to pay much attention to this door. Probably they got a cut of the money.

Three things, in fact. If Pietro had indeed dumped the missing cardinal's robe by the port, it was gone.

She reached down and picked up the purse of money, jiggling it before tying it to her belt and pulling her tunic down to cover it. She considered what to do next, whether to return to Jack and Moretti or complete her tour of the Vatican gates. She had not time to decide. 'Who are you?'

Amy wheeled around. A familiar-looking guard, paunchy and picking at his teeth with a sliver of metal, was regarding her. 'I was … Captain Moretti sent me.' It hit her; he had been out the previous night with a fellow – the pair had interrupted her and Jack as they had sat on the threshold of the kitchen, talking babies. He stood a little straighter and, she thought, looked uncomfortable, his eyes shifting to the gate. He did not appear to recognise her.

'For why?'

'A lad's been arrested. He … uh, he stole a cardinal's robe. Left it here in the night. So he says. Have you seen it?'

'Robe?'

'Have you seen it?'

'I wasn't here in the night.'

'Nor in the day,' she said, tilting her chin. It was a mistake.

'I don't report to no hairless messenger lad. I'm Hasler, Sergeant Hasler, of Lucerne. Kin to folk whose arses you're not fit to wipe.' Amy crossed her arms but gave no ground. 'The captain had the men at work walking the walls all through the night. Not guarding doors already well locked. Get out of it.'

'I'll report you for not being here. Now I mean.'

'You do that. And you'll leave the Vatican with your breeches pulled up so high that voice of yours won't never break.'

Amy felt her cheeks inflate as she struggled for something witty to toss back at him. 'To hell with you!' She began marching away, his laughter following her. She turned around and stuck a finger up; but mainly she wanted to see if he remained at his post. He did, picking his teeth again. Before she could get too far, he seemed to have second thoughts and shouted over to her.

'Wait! The captain, he sent you? I thought he wanted weapons and arms.'

She gave a chin-heavy smile in return. 'Yes. You've all to be getting ready weapons. But he especially wants to know about that robe.'

'Mm. Lad dumped a robe on this here coffer last night.'

'What time?'

'Don't know. Sometime before he was out there wagging his chin with the priest. He didn't touch it. Come to think, it were gone by the time he came.' He scratched the side of a wide nose. 'I didn't see the robe again after the lad dumped it.'

'Did it go out to the laundry?'

'Nah. Laundresses' servants come in the morning. Nothing for them this morning, no point. Everyone knows the conclave ends today.'

'Which priest?' She had begun stalking back towards him. 'When did you see a priest?'

'Can't say.' He held up his hands. 'Don't ask questions of priests. Late though. Or early if you look at it that way. I didn't see that cardinal's robe then, though. Now you mention it, I'd forgot all about the thing. Lad threw it on the lid, I had business away from here, and I never did see it again.' He shrugged. 'Only saw the lad again later on, before I turned in. Him and his pal the priest. Odd that.'

'Did he have dark hair, curly, the priest you saw here?'

'Not here. Didn't see no priest here.'

'Where, then?'

Hasler sucked in air. 'Out by the San Damaso. Head bent with your little friend of the robe. It was dark. Look here, the captain knows what goes on. As long as the doors are locked, there's no harm in nothing. Can't a man meet his friend and share news in the night? No crime in that. They were neither of them the old creature with the crippled hands we were set to find.'

Amy said nothing but turned and left him again.

So, she thought: the side gates, though firmly and securely locked, were left unguarded for much of the time. On the other side, she supposed, were agents of the French ambassadors, Spanish, probably dozens of others.

On the inside, men like Pietro, and, again, likely dozens of others, would use the windows to send out information and take in payment. At night, especially, areas like those where the guard now stood were probably the busiest places in the Vatican. She thought of the priest she had seen after the raid. At the time she had thought him to be roused by the loud fuss caused by Pavesi, but it was more likely he was out to speak to the folk beyond the gates. Depending on his nationality, he could have been talking to anyone.

It seemed, though, that Pietro had been telling the truth in one thing at least. He had taken the red robe and left it at the gate. From there it had disappeared.

But things didn't disappear. Someone had taken it, and the stupid, lazy sergeant hadn't bothered or even noticed the theft. The only question was whether it was important or a red, silken distraction.

14

The men did not panic but edged away from the column of flame that stood between them and the exit from the grottoes. 'Back,' Jack shouted, 'we go back.' He could hear the ragged edges of his voice.

'We cannot let the place burn.' Moretti's steadying voice brought calm to the whole group. 'It is a small fire. It will not catch stone.'

The captain, handing his lamp to a soldier, placed a steadying hand on the arched ceiling overhead and crept towards the light. Jack craned his neck to see what was happening and watched as he began stamping on the flame, his boots alternately putting out and sending up smaller flames. In less than a minute, the fire was extinguished. Jack and the soldiers moved towards Moretti, who was patting down his smoking boots with the back of his hands.

'What was it?' asked Jack.

Moretti leant down and, with his fingertips, lifted the rags of material that had been set alight. The lamplight showed them to be a blackened red. The sting of burning material filled a dozen pairs of nostrils. 'Someone is jesting,' said the captain. And then he threw the scorched cardinal's robe to the ground in a sudden show of fury.

'A threat, captain, against a cardinal?' offered one of the soldiers.

'But which?' asked another.

'None. All.' Moretti threw the robe down and kicked at it. 'Why?'

'To prove Pietro innocent,' said Jack. 'I mean, maybe there is some group of conspirators in on this, each looking after the others.' It sounded hollow to him. 'Did anyone see who set the thing to flame?'

'I saw a creature in black,' said one of the soldiers. 'Captain, I...'

'Silence. It might have been anyone. Black robes are not hard to come by.'

'Should we go after him? I can run. If it was that old cripple you spoke of, he can't have got too far.'

'No. By now he could be halfway along the Passetto.' It was no old man, thought Jack, to be running about setting fires. Moretti sighed, as if reading his thoughts. 'If it were the old man. We must accept the possibility that there is more here than a single madman working alone. The better question is who knew we were down here. Someone watching from outside, else a member of the guard is informing someone. Or,' he said, looking at Jack directly, 'someone outside the guard. A friend or relative of one here.' Jack said nothing but forced himself to meet the captain's gaze.

'This is Cardinal Granvelle's robe,' he said, surprised at how level his voice sounded. 'His Grace is become my master. I gave it to my friend to leave at the gates. My friend who is now arrested.' He moved towards the captain and stooped to pick up the charred cloth.

'It might have been that whoever killed the men above used this to soak the blood, to keep himself clean.'

'I can see no blood on it, can you?' Jack held it out to Moretti, who angled his face away from the still-smoky material but kept his eyes on it.

He grunted before speaking. 'It might be burnt away. The bloodstained parts might have been set alight to destroy evidence.'

'But not by Pietro. He's under arrest. So … so someone else took the thing. Then whether it was bloody or not, they kept it until now.'

'An attack,' announced one of the soldiers, drawing everyone's attention. 'This is an attack on this stranger, this Cardinal Granvelle. Some enemy of his, captain. By your leave, might we not attend upon his Grace, some few of us escort him wherever he goes. There might be no powder here, no great plot – a simple threat against a cardinal by his enemies. He is, what, a Frenchman, a Spaniard? It is he who is in danger, not this place.' He looked around, his chin held high.

'It might be so,' said Moretti. He put down his lantern for a moment and scratched at his beard, swaying as he retrieved it. 'Or it might be that that deformed plotter taken last night wishes us to focus our minds on the politics. And in doing so, we ignore a greater threat. Yet,' he added, with a watery smile, 'you may be right. And your point is a good one. Worthy of consideration.'

Jack did not think that the soldier looked mollified. He said, 'if it's so, if my master is in danger … I'll look out for him, taste his food. But the man who threw this, he saw us coming down here and tried to kill us.'

'Kill?' asked one of the other soldiers, seemingly goaded by the murmuring that broke out amongst the rest. 'A little fire can't kill the Swiss Guard. Look how easily it were put out.' The men, Jack thought, were becoming cocky, restless. Their captain was doing well to manage them.

'A thing of opportunity,' said Moretti. 'To delay us. Frighten us, perhaps. Are we frightened, men?'

'No!'

'Never!'

'Not us!'

Back slapping and hurrahs passed through the soldiers, Jack excluded. He cleared his throat. 'Could it be, maybe, that the man we had held prisoner, or a friend of his, did this to … to keep us thinking that the basilica is threatened.' He picked up his pace, warming to the idea as it came out of his mouth. 'You know, like as if to say, "oh no, you are on the right path in this place and I will try and stop you". So that then we make further search of the place. But, in fact, we aren't at all. There's nothing here.'

'It might be,' said Moretti, his tone noncommittal. 'Myself, I think our man is a false sorcerer, conjuring plans and mummeries as they occur to him. That, I think, means whatever he intends, if it truly exists, if it is set in motion, is less secure than he would wish. It shall not take us from our path. Do you hear me, men? Are we not Swiss Guards? You see, now, that we have an open enemy. He has shown himself, revealed that he still walks amongst us. Fears us. It is our sacred duty to protect this conclave and all within it. It is plain that his goal is to destroy it. Will we let him?'

Another chorus of nos. 'But what next, captain?' This was one of the soldiers.

'Onwards.' On saying the word, he snatched the robe from Jack and began walking towards the exit. Everyone followed. 'The basilica is clean, whether the villain who stole this robe and set it to harass us wishes us to think it or not. We continue our search.'

Jack coughed again. 'Um, what time is it?'

'I cannot say. Have any of you heard the bells toll?' Murmurs of demurral. 'Around noon I should think.'

'But … the robe, it reminded me – I have to get my master his dinner.' Jack felt his cheeks heat up at the chortles that ran through the group. Moretti did not answer at once.

'We must all serve someone,' he said. 'Go to, then, lad. We will see you out.'

'What will you do? I mean, if it's noon there might not be much time left.'

'The Cappella Paolina, she is next. We search our way northwards. An orderly search.'

'Shall … shall I come and help you after dinner?'

'Yes. The more men the better.' He drew up short as they stepped outside. The square in front of the basilica was empty. Above, the sun continued its struggle to be seen and felt. It offered no clue as to the time and it was not kind to Moretti, who staggered blinking into it. If he had looked tired before, he looked positively ragged after the search. He turned his red-veined eyes on Jack. 'But have a care, lad. If you or your little brother are in any way playing false, it will come to light and it will go hard for you.' He spoke low, so the other men could not hear. The effect was somewhat muted by the burbling rumble from his stomach.

Rather than quailing under the warning, Jack sucked in his cheeks. The same, he thought, to you, captain.

As the soldiers made for the next church, Jack began his jog back towards the busier parts of the Vatican, wondering whether it would better to lie to the cardinal about the fate of his robes or tell him a mangled version of the truth.

***

Amy completed her tour of the Vatican's gates. About all she could ascertain was that all of them were left locked but largely unguarded, and had been especially abandoned during the night, when the Swiss Guards' boots had pounded the perimeter. If anyone had escaped, they had not done so over walls or through locked doors, unless they could shrink in size and clamber through one of the little windows.

She considered returning to the basilica and speaking with Moretti, but her back was beginning to ache. Instead, she asked around and found that Pietro had been taken to the disused dormitory block, to be lodged where the mysterious last prisoner had been taken. A little stab of guilt had taken up residence in her lower back, and no amount of stretching would rid her of it. It was her fault the stupid boy was under lock and key.

She went there.

Inside, she found a guard outside the cell, and she grudgingly passed him a few coins from the purse she'd found to gain passage inside. The new prisoner did not have the carefree attitude with which the old had given himself up. Instead, Pietro was curled up in a ball on the floor, his eyes raw from crying. He was a changed man from the cocky creature who had led the raid on the papal apartments.

'Pietro,' she said, cursing that she hadn't thought to bring him anything.

'You. Am I freed? Did you find anything? The robe, it is gone to the laundry, huh? They know I speak true, don't they?'

'It wasn't there.' She was conscious of how dry she sounded, and licked her lips, trying to force a lighter tone. 'But it'll be found if you spoke true.'

'Oh God,' he began sobbing, 'they're going to kill me. I hurt no one, no man. They're going to hang me.'

'Not if we prove you innocent. If you are innocent.'

He seemed to clutch at the word like a safe haven in a turbulent sea. 'Innocent, yes, I'm innocent, you know it.'

'Knowing and proving are different.'

'How can I prove it?'

'Tell me everything you've been doing. I'll tell Captain Moretti. My brother is thick with him, friendly. Tell me what you were doing and what you've been saying and who you talked to.'

Pietro, rubbing his eyes, began spilling his secrets.

***

Jack knocked on the door, enjoying the smell of cooked meats. When it opened, he stepped away from them and into the bitterer world of herbs and potions. Bianchi was not inside; a door from the small chamber led out into a walled garden and he could hear whistling. He coughed, letting his eyes wander over the chests, bottles, powders, and bunches of tied-together stalks.

'Who is there?' The apothecary stepped into his inner doorway. 'You. Come outside, lad. What ails you?' Jack followed him out into a small enclosed space. Though it was not sunny, the air was fresh, and insects buzzed lazily in the air.

'Dr Bianchi,' said Jack, knowing it would endear him, 'When you left the San Pietro this morning, did you see anyone? Anyone hiding about it?'

'Hiding? No, no. I was not looking. Why, what's happened?'

'Someone attacked us. As we were below the basilica.'

'Attacked? Is anyone hurt?' He began to move towards the door. 'Not another murder.'

'No, no, we got away. They started a fire. More to frighten us, maybe. Captain Moretti put it out but the fellow had run off. I just wondered if he'd been watching, and maybe you'd seen anything.' It was a lie, but it seemed to work. Having wrapped his visit in plausibility, he pushed on. 'I wished to ask you about the captain. I think he's unwell.'

'Unwell how? His guts, his head?'

'He is overworked, I think.'

'As are we all.'

'Yet he won't stop. He hasn't slept, I don't think.' Jack paused. In truth, he had hoped to learn more about Moretti, and he suspected that asking the guardsmen would be fruitless. They seemed a clannish, loyal lot. Cardinal Granvelle, of course, would have no idea. 'Do you know him well?'

'Not well.'

Damn, he thought. 'I think he's a good man.'

'I'm sure he is.'

'Yet he is devilish secretive.'

'Why are you here, lad. What's your name?' Jack told him. 'What is it you wish to know?'

'Doctor, I … is it possible that Captain Moretti is keeping someone secret? I thought I saw him last night. With a man in black.'

'I see.'

'Who was it, do you know?'

'No. Did I smell dinner cooking out there?' This time he did make for the door back to his chamber, grasping Jack by the arm as he did so. 'You and the rest must have work to do. I know I do. All of you, should you not be clearing out and getting the cardinals fed?'

'I was on the point of it, doctor.'

'I'm no doctor,' Bianchi said tightly. He pushed Jack out of the door before he could speak further. Standing on the threshold, he said, 'if the captain has friends he seeks to protect … that is his business. I suggest you ask him. And if he is unwell, I suggest he retires to his bed immediately and lets younger, fitter men see to our safety.' Confidence poured into his voice. 'Yes, you tell him that from me. Tired men make errors. He will serve this place better by taking to his bed and letting the young folks get on with finding their murderer.'

The apothecary slammed the door in Jack's face. He stood there for some time, going over what the man had said, but there seemed to be nothing useful.

Then he tried imagining what a trained man like Walsingham would do. He would tease out the secrets of the heart. Bianchi, he felt sure, did know what Moretti had been up to, but he, like the guards, would protect the captain. Either Moretti was a good man who inspired loyalty, or he was a frightening man whom no one wished to divulge the truth about. Walsingham would tell him to watch. And to wait.

Unfortunately, the reality of being a servant meant having, as Bianchi had said, to give dinner to his master.

***

Amy emerged from the dormitories and stood in the papal

courtyard. She gulped down lungfuls of air. She had a name, another piece of a puzzle that seemed to show more than one solution. And names did not reveal the nature of plots. Whether gunpowder or something else, Pietro had known nothing of any secret weapon.

She stood, her back to the wall, watching servants scurry backwards and forwards, their arms laden with trenchers, boards, jugs, bottles. Her stomach danced and she felt another one of her lightheaded spells come on. She bent until it passed. As one servitor slouched by, she begged some scraps from his load and, on seeing her face, he handed them over. She must, she felt, look sufficiently dreadful to warrant charity.

Eventually, she saw Jack entering the courtyard from the gallery leading to the San Damaso. His face was red and sweat had tracked paths down the high, stiff collar of his tunic. She launched herself away from the wall and stumbled towards him.

'Amy,' he said. Then he seemed to remember he had been mad at her. Before any words of condemnation, he asked, 'are you well? Is … is everything well?'

'Just a little sick. All the running around.'

'Yeah. Well, maybe you wouldn't have needed to do it if you could keep your mouth shut.'

She ignored that. 'I went in there to see Pietro. I've been to the gates. The robe is missing.'

'The robe,' he said. She kneaded at her temple as he told her what had become of it.

'Someone tried to kill you.'

'I don't think so. To frighten us.'

'I'll kill him.'

'If we can find him. It's not that old man from last night. He's hiding somewhere. It's his … his conspirator.'

'Then I'll find him and bash his head to jam.'

'You'll do nothing. You have to stop this, Amy, stop being part of the world like this. The dangerous world.'

'How can I not be part of it? What, should I do nothing to help, hide, maybe be blown up or burnt to death or whatever the hell is laid as a plot?'

'Just let the men deal with it.'

'To hell with you,' she said. 'To hell with you, Jack. Men. I'll tell you what men have been up to this past night; Pietro told me. See your Cardinal Granvelle? His man, his conclavist or whatever it is they call themselves, he's been paying Pietro to carry tales out to the gates. Hernandez.' This was the name she'd drawn out of the imprisoned boy – the man whom he had made an arrangement with, meeting in the night. 'Black, curly hair. Oily. Creeps about in the night like a … a … creeping Spaniard. Well, the Spanish ambassador's men have a camp right by them and pay your little friend again to receive the news. And the guards, they don't care. Their true master is sick, and they have only your little friend to lead them. They can get away with murder. They either look through their fingers from laziness or they're paid to do it. And that captain–'

'What about him?'

'Pietro said he saw him, same as I did, with his stranger. Guiding him about like he was leading a disguised mistress in some love game, some dance. And that's not all about your friend Moretti. He poisoned the commander at dinner, for sure. And now he has that stranger hidden upstairs in the big guardhouse.'

'Did he know who it was? Who was hidden?'

'No. Only his men and the richer sorts will know that. Look after each other, those men will.'

'I … I have to go, Amy. Have to get this up to the cardinal. Then I'm going back to the captain. Got to help him search this place for powder.'

'Fine, you do that.' She sighed. After a good rant, she always felt deflated. Now she could add exhausted to it. 'Are you going to tell the cardinal what his man's doing? Trading in secrets?'

'You say that,' Jack said, looking down at his board of food, 'as if it's not what we do.'

'We do it for us, not for money. Are you going to see if grand Granvelle knows?'

'I don't know. No.'

'Fine. I'm going to see Moretti.' She thought, but didn't say, that he lacked the guts to ask his superior anything; that he was afraid of learning that his new cardinal-friend was as crooked as his minion. How like him it was to find a reason to go. It was ever his way; when he couldn't defuse a conflict he would seek to escape from it before his own temper burst forth. 'You dawdle up there and enjoy the reek of crusty old men in their crusty old palace.'

'You're not going to say anything, are you? You're not going to cause trouble?'

'Oh, trouble. Three men dead, my friend dead, and I wouldn't want there to be trouble, would I?' Jack said nothing, but gave her a puppy look of reproach, making her feel small and shrewish. 'No. I'll tell him I did what he sent me to do. Where is he?' Jack told her, pointing in the direction of the chapel. She began to stride away, stopping only to say, 'you realise, though, that whatever's going on here, they could all be part of it? Maybe there's a whole pack of them sick of their faith and corrupted, like a witches' coven of devil worshippers. Maybe we're being led one hell of a merry dance. And given the blame of it, like Pietro, when it's all done. Watch, just watch, and then take it all to France. Well look what you've got yourself into, Jack Cole.' She did not even enjoy the wrinkle in his brow her words drew.

There was the truth of the faith he had embraced spread before him, and he a lonely child imagining a dream, laid bare and ugly and real.

15

Amy did not go directly to Moretti after her tour of the Vatican gates. Instead, she decided to take a risk, firmly putting reason aside.

In the servants' kitchen quarters, she knocked on the apothecary's door. There was no answer. She bit at her nails, looking around. Perhaps she had been making a dreadful mistake, trying to put herself in front of a man who might immediately notice that she was not what she pretended. Fate might have been telling her to leave, to abandon her idea; the other servants said the apothecary had returned from tending the sickly commander, but some quirk of chance might have deafened him to her sharp knock. Turning from the door, biting at her nails, she almost cried out when it flew open.

'What the devil is it now – I said the captain is without gui – who are you? What do you wish? Can't a man rest his eyes after the sights he's seen?'

'I … I was told to enquire about the health of the commander. Captain Moretti sent me.'

'Captain Moretti is searching the basilica,' said Bianchi, his narrow face narrowing still further in suspicion. Amy bowed her head.

'He's done.'

'There is no change in the commander, tell him.' Amy gave the lowest nod she could manage. Her mind worked quickly.

'The captain said he's worried. Feels sorry for … well, you know.'

'Ah, it is nothing. Some touch of rich food. I hear he served the commander herring when they dined the other night, pickled. It has turned his stool to water. It is but a simple flux.'

'Yes, he said that,' she lied. 'I think he just doesn't want the commander put to worry…' She trailed off, knowing that the more she spoke the more precarious her situation.

'He will be well enough in a few days. A week at the most. I have ordered he should be given nothing but strongly boiled and baked foods. Nothing raw.'

'Thank you. I'll tell him.' Amy turned on her heel.

'Wait!'

She swallowed, wondering whether a half turn, or a full turn would be better. Did she appear more the counterfeit in profile or from the front? She opted for the latter and stared at the apothecary's feet. A good servant should not be too bold anyway. 'Yes, sir?'

'Where is my chair?'

'Sir?'

'It was taken from this place.'

'Oh, that. It's in the storeroom. I can fetch it for you.'

'No. I'll get it myself.' A pause drew out. She chanced a glance up to find him frowning first at the cluster of servants milling and chatting behind her, and then on her. Her eyes fluttered downwards. 'You have sharp little ears.' Her heart leapt into her mouth. He was obviously inspecting her. 'What news of the new pope?' She relaxed.

'No news.'

'Nor when the mass and the announcement will be?'

'No, sir.'

'Blast. It must needs be this evening. I have lost money enough already to our sick commander by it not being announced after matins. He had evening.' As though remembering he was talking to a minion, he added, 'a gentleman's wager, you see, can prove a powerful restorative in turning a sick man's mind from his troubles.'

'Yes. I must get back to the captain. Thank you again, sir.'

'Wait!' She said nothing this time. 'You might carry this to your fellow slaves. I'll thank you people not to come stealing things. There are dangerous decoctions in my chamber. A sneaking servant will swallow anything he thinks might give him vigour. And might instead find himself with something worse than the bloody flux.' She shrugged, wondering dimly if her silent thoughts, which were 'tell them yourself then, you mouldy old fart', showed in her downward-gazing boy's face. With a haughty little sniff, Bianchi slammed the door in it regardless.

She stood for a few seconds until her heart resumed a regular beat.

So, she thought, Moretti had dined with the commander of the Swiss Guard, and the commander had then gone down in a puddle of his own shit. Jack's stern-faced older friend might well be a poisoner, who had sought to remove his superior to take his place. Just as she had first thought. Perhaps he hoped to kill him; perhaps it was simple ambition. Or perhaps he just wanted him out of the way during the conclave, so that he could launch whatever strange, murderous enterprise was currently unfolding.

The thought became a certainty as it formed in her mind. The only question was how to prove it. That done, she could only try not to be too obviously happy about telling Jack the ugly truth about his newfound friend. Then he might finally see what she had always known and what experience should by now have taught him: that everyone in the world, especially friends, were rotten to the core and could never be trusted. Far better to stick with one person and thumb your nose at the rest of the world. With a spring in her step, she bounced out of the kitchen.

She found Moretti slumped by the wall outside the Paolina, the nondescript little chapel facing the chequered entrance square to the Vatican, the one Jack had spent most of the previous day sweeping and re-sweeping. The morning mist had lifted entirely, and wavering sunlight had started to bring a pleasant spring heat. It looked a fine day to elect a new pope. Daylight brought the illusion that all would be well, she thought - light chased things into the open; it denied secrets their shadows.

Yet the light was not kind to the captain, whose face was colourless, almost waxy. Dark bags hung under his eyes, and he was mopping his brow with his rolled-up cap. He quickly unfurled and replaced it as he saw her coming. 'What news?'

'I ... I followed your orders. And spoke to the boy, Pietro. The one in ward.' He gave her a hard look, both suspicious and questioning. Before he could point out that he hadn't ordered that, she rushed on. 'He says that he had some arrangement with one of the cardinal's men. Cardinal Granvelle. For money. This man, Hernandez, this conclavist, he was paying Pietro to carry news of the conclave out to the gates and over. To the Spanish ambassador,' she added with a flourish.

Moretti did not, as she had hoped, look either surprised or angry. He gave only a shrug. 'News about the deaths of three men is what I seek. News of the stranger who has breached these stout walls.' Amy did not reply. For some reason, the urge to cry came upon her, to shake him. The word 'conspiracy' flared in mind. There had to be some great conspiracy involving the whole pack of them – Moretti, Granvelle, Hernandez, the guardsmen, Bianchi, everyone who sought to take Jack into their confidences. A conspiracy of secrecy and silence, of protection. They were all up to something. Or was that simply madness groping at her mind? Vainly, she struggled to remember if she'd ever heard about pregnant women falling victim to fond and wild fantasies.

'I followed your orders,' she said at length. Her mouth was running dry. 'Spoke to Sergeant Hasler.'

'Good.'

'He wasn't good. He wouldn't help me, even though I said your name. Said I was under your orders. He was rude in his manner.' She let the words linger, hoping both to embarrass the surly guardsman and his master. There, she thought, and that for your assumed authority.

Before Moretti could reply, his men emerged from the chapel. Their faces were coated in dust and grime, with little tracks of sweat cutting pathways through it. 'Clean,' was the assessment, delivered by the tallest man of the crew.

'Unlike yourselves, boys,' said Moretti, giving one of what Amy took to be his leading grins. It looked like it cost him. He gestured behind him, where a large portico opened onto a covered, shallow staircase. 'We move on.' Then, as they started trooping upwards, he turned sharp eyes on Amy. 'You. See to the weapons I have ordered, chase my men to the Sistine with them. I want them brought to us as quickly as can be. We must find fit places for men to be stationed.' He looked upwards and she followed his gaze around sun-dappled stone rooftops, shimmering red. 'Hm. No good to us.' She had to agree. Most of the key places in the Vatican were hidden under the same sprawling roof. The shallow staircase led to a complex of holy chambers which were all enclosed by a linked network of roofs. He looked down at her again. 'No one has gone in or out of the city?'

'Not that I was told.' Then, impulsively, 'though I heard that there's trouble with dogs.'

'Dogs?'

'Loud dogs. Up in the grand lodging. Lots of strange things going on in this place if you ask me. Men in hoods in the night and loud dogs.'

For the first time, she detected a note of threat in the captain's stiff and formal demeanour. He leaned close, too close, she thought. 'No need for you to worry on that matter, is there? Only little girls need be afraid of loud dogs.'

***

Granvelle nodded his thanks, smiling as Jack nibbled bits of bread and cold meat before he himself partook. 'Thank you, my boy. You need not wait. I believe I shall pick, like the cows in the field.'

'Don't leave it unattended, your Grace.' Jack turned as he spoke towards Hernandez, who stood with his back to the wall, arms folded. The word 'poison' began to spread out in his mind. Amy had again said Moretti had poisoned the sick commander. There hadn't been time to question her on it, to find out if she had discovered something or was shooting her mouth off wildly, as she often did in a temper. Hernandez's hostile gaze proved an antidote to that train of thought.

As soon as he had left Amy, Jack had tried over and over to think of clever things to say to let the conclavist know that he was aware of his dark dealings. He had come up short. It would not have done to bluntly threaten or make too-loaded hints, as Amy might have done; but neither was he capable of the kind of sophisticated wordplay that was the stock in trade of educated politicians. The moment passed. 'I shall have a care,' said Granvelle. 'It is good of you to worry. I appreciate such loyalties. And reward them.' He winked. 'The matter is decided, is it not, Father Hernandez?' The conclavist only glowered. 'Cardinal Boncompagni, do you know him? Ugo Boncompagni. Formerly a lawyer of Bologna.'

Jack thought, but he could not envision that particular cardinal. Only the name rung a bell – one of those on the shortlist he'd delivered to Farnese. 'He is the new pope?'

'He will be. The matter is quite settled. It remains only for agreement of the … ah, the lesser of our most sacred company – I should say our good companions – to signal Boncompagni. There is fine play with words.'

'Is it well known?' Jack's words drew the cardinal's eyebrows together.

'What is that?'

'I … I've become a good friend to the captain of the Swiss Guard, your Grace. I think he'd like to know who might need … special protection.'

'Oh. I see. I imagine it is well suspected but known only to those of us within these walls.'

Jack leapt upon the opportunity, swivelling his head towards Hernandez. 'Then, your Grace, we should hope that it's kept close. If it becomes known and Cardinal Boncompagni is endangered, I think the captain should wonder who has a loose tongue.' There, he thought, not the most subtle intimation, but it certainly thinned the sour conclavist's lips. Granvelle seemed to ignore the exchange, inspecting instead a crust of bread.

'Close, close,' he said. 'Yes, although the world shall know in a very few hours. I believe we shall have a mass of thanksgiving this evening and let the world know, shall we not, father?' Hernandez mumbled assent, still glaring at Jack. 'Ah, but it shall be a fine thing to get out of this wretched place. The airs, they have turned so foul already.'

'I hadn't noticed, your Grace,' said Jack. In truth, it was impossible not to. In addition to the heat, the entire building had taken on the smell of a hospital. Amy had been right about that. Gathering the highest clerics in Christendom together did not produce an air of wisdom but an air one might expect in a house of invalids.

'You are a sweet boy to pretend. The fumes of the place choke. It is small wonder we disdain the meagre food. Ah, what a different world is a conclave from the lives we lead outside. At the very least you need not play the acrobat upon my sheets before my head touches them tonight. You have my leave to go. Make use of your knowledge only upon your honour.'

'Yes, your Grace. And I'm sorry again about the robe. An unfortunate accident.' He had decided to claim that the robes had been taken for trash rather than for laundry, blaming the guards who, he claimed, had promised to see to the cost of them out of their own pay. Granvelle had waved this away and, to Jack's surprise – or suspicion – Hernandez had made no issue of it.

He bowed, picked up the mercifully lidded chamber pot, gave one last look at the conclavist, packing in as much meaning as he could, and then walked backwards from the chamber, easing the door shut.

He gulped down the air in the hallway, which was no fresher. He had done something, at least, to warn the conclavist that he knew what he was up to. Still, it irked him that Amy had mocked him as a weakling. Pregnancy could only excuse so much. In fact, he might have been swept up in her suspicion.

He tried to sort through what he knew. A strange, railing prisoner had given himself up and then his guard had been killed. He had hidden out, or been protected, through the night. In the morning, two more men were dead. That was all clear enough and hinted at a lone madman attempting something against the new pope. On investigating such a plot, someone had tried to frighten the searchers. Again, all was clear. It was the rest that added complication. That madman might well be being helped along by someone, or some people, unknown. Amy suspected Captain Moretti, whom she claimed to have seen with someone hooded and strange in the night. Moretti's guards and apparently even the apothecary, Bianchi, knew something about that and were keeping it quiet. His own friend, whom he felt sure was innocent, was now taken up, having been abroad himself in the night and having threatened one of the victims. Now it seemed that that young fellow was in league with Father Hernandez in a quite different bit of business – corrupt but not murderous. And Amy was accusing Moretti of poisoning the sickly commander.

Nothing was clear. Having disordered bits of knowledge was

almost worse than having none at all. And what good had it done to suggest he was wise to Hernandez if the conclavist was up to no good? He should never have let his wife goad him. If there was even a small chance that Hernandez and Pietro were killers – or in league with a killer – then he had as good as painted a target on his own back. It was one thing blundering towards answers; it was another just blundering. He tossed his head, setting his unruly curl bouncing, as though to clear it.

Leaving the dormitory, he emptied the chamber pot, rinsed it, and left it in the sun to dry. He then wandered around the complex of buildings, asking other servants where Moretti had last been sighted, until he found himself in the indoor hallway called the Sala Regia, the cavernous antechamber to the Sistine Chapel. The space was stuccoed, but only partially decorated. Like everywhere else in the Vatican, it smelt strongly of fresh paint and plaster with a sweet undercurrent of incense. It was deserted, but the great door to the chapel lay open. Voices and the sound of boots reverberated out and up to the vaulted ceiling.

Jack crossed the hall, feeling small and insignificant, and stepped into the chapel.

And his breath stopped in his throat.

16

If the Sala Ducale, in which the cardinals had had their welcome party, was like being inside a giant jewel, then stepping into the Sistine Chapel was like entering a giant jewel case with embroidered interiors and gold fittings. Though it was not a huge chamber, its craftsmen seemed to have worked miracles in tricking the eyes. It was empty but did not seem so. A dizzying whirl of reds, blues, flesh colours, golds, and purples swirled up the walls and across the ceiling, picked out in the forms of men, women, angels, clouds, instruments, columns. They seemed in constant motion, pressing down on the real humans who crept about. Here, the living were interlopers – breathing people were less real, less alive, than the unreal. The floor was painted in black and white geometric shapes, with concentric circles seeming to invite those who dared enter to stand in the middle and be judged.

Outside there might be corruption, politics, murder. Inside was the heart of the Catholic faith, pure and glittering. It was as though God has distilled all the beauty of which man was capable into one chamber.

'Step out, men. Under those chairs and up above, too.' Moretti's voice echoed up to the ceiling, cutting in on Jack's awe. The soldiers began moving forward, through the space between a golden screen and into the chapel proper. Along the walls on either side of the nave were arranged, at intervals, solid gold chairs with red velvet cushions. On these, Jack presumed, the cardinals would sit for whatever official ceremonies were required on the election of the new pontiff. Irreverently, Moretti's men began lifting and prodding at the cushions. 'Have a care,' the captain shouted. 'Ensure that no powder lies hidden in anything.' He himself was scanning the upper mezzanine. 'I want men up there. And during the mass, one on either side.'

Jack tiptoed across the nave himself, moving towards the altar. In the middle of the room he threw his head back and almost fell backwards at the dizzying sight of the ceiling frescoes. How anyone could have scuttled about, spiderlike, painting those images mystified him. He shook his head clear and moved towards the altar, genuflecting self-consciously before climbing the few stairs up to it.

Apart from its cloth, the marble altar was bare. He had always wondered what lay behind them and he moved around it, crouching to peep into the box-like space behind and within. Some golden candlesticks, an empty golden receptacle, nothing more. It seemed a fruitless search. It had seemed fruitless, too, in the Paolina. They were simply not going to find anything. He had never heard, in fact, of a plot being discovered by searchers prior to its unfolding, and he should know; he had once considered firing a gun on the English queen. The conspiracy had failed because he had backed out of it, not because guardsmen had assiduously sought out and found the gun. No, plots collapsed only when something went wrong in the doing of them, when a plotter opened his mouth – not because soldiers chanced upon caches of weapons or powder.

He shook his head, running his hands over the cold marble for the sake of it, conscious of the blaze of colour at his back. Turning, he looked upon the main fresco. His eyes trailed across it, up and down, side to side. At eye level, a verdant landscape and river, complete with boat, were beset by human misery. Dwarfing it above was an enormous expanse of blue sky, densely populated with semi-dressed divines.

'The Last Judgement.'

Jack started. Moretti had reached him and was standing by the altar. He moved to stand beside him. 'What's that?'

'The great artist Michelangelo's gift to the world. The Last Judgement. Seven years it took him, and he an old and bent man already.'

'It's big,' said Jack, realising the shallowness of his words. 'Beautiful,' he added.

'For the glory of God, so we think. See how it seems to lean inward?'

'Oh. So it does.' The whole wall, in fact, seemed to lean towards the two men. 'Made it easier to paint, I suppose. And to clean now.'

'Perhaps.'

'He … um … he liked well-proportioned men.'

Moretti gave a pained looking smile. 'Yes, it looks like a scene from some old Roman bathhouse. Look there,' he gestured to the left side, under the cross, 'even the women painted there look like men. Well, I should imagine the great artist liked his jests. It is said he has hidden Jewish images within this thing, but I have never chanced upon any. I see only Christ Jesus and the blessed Virgin.'

Jack's eyes rolled towards the centrepiece of the painting, where Jesus and Mary were poised.

And his heart skipped a beat.

***

Amy ate whilst watching soldiers march across the courtyard outside the servants' quarters, their arms laden with guns. She burped, pulled down her cap, and stepped out. The afternoon was speeding along now. If something was going to happen, it would happen soon. The word amongst the servants was that a new pope had been chosen and the cardinals were only waiting now for the evening service, to which they would progress in state from their dormitory, to give out the official announcement. Everywhere money was changing hands. Someone called Boncompagni had apparently been elected, though no one quite knew the source of the rumour.

She could not shake the feeling that the next few hours just needed to be gotten through, for good or ill. What would happen would happen. Tenseness and excitement seemed to hang in the air. It was not unlike the days before the northern rebellion in England, when whispers and worries seemed to form a cloud. Back then she had come close to killing the queen of Scots, the fragrant Mary Stuart. If she had done so, the whole world would have changed in a moment, and no one would have seen it coming. So it would be today. The soldiers might be searching for powder, but if plotters were at work, their enterprise would be done in an instant no matter what the Swiss Guard did – like the swallowing of poison and the sudden sweep of death. If she could detach Jack from Moretti, she fully intended to drag him to some obscure part of the city and hide with him until the whole business was over, pleading womanly frailty if need be.

But first she would have to get to him.

She joined the nearest group of soldiers, careful to ensure that the man she had encountered at the gate, Sergeant Hasler, was not amongst them. 'Captain Moretti sent me with a message,' she announced. 'To see that guns and munitions were taken to him.'

'We've run ahead of your message, lad,' said an older soldier, good-naturedly. 'Looks like you shouldn't have taken time to fill your belly. Sergeant Hasler says these have to be given out to the men guarding the dormitory first. You've heard who the new pope is?' Amy nodded, getting a wink in return. 'Won't hurt to make sure he's protected ahead of their progress out of that old place, will it?'

'Then you'll go to the captain? He was going into the Sistine Chapel.'

'I daresay. You can run along now.'

'But I … Captain Moretti said I was to have a bow.' She swallowed her pride and put on a manly growl. 'I've been training ever so hard at the hunt and the captain's taken a shine to me.'

The old soldier barked laughter. One of his fellows had overheard her and joined him. 'Give the lad a bow,' said the younger. 'If he shoots the new pope by chance, I'll owe you five ducats before we hang him.'

Amy took the weapon, weighing it in her arms, before trailing the men as they crunched across the courtyard. It was not dissimilar to one she had fired the previous year. Quite why she wanted it she did not know, other than that it made her appear manlier and would, if it came to it, be useful in protecting Jack and the baby in whichever hiding place she found them.

***

'I see it,' said Moretti in a croak. 'By God's body, I see it.'

Jack had taken some time to understand it himself. He still didn't. The figures of Jesus and the Virgin, painted high on the wall of the chapel, had struck a chord with him, but at first he couldn't say why. It was something in the postures rather than the dress or the expressions. And then it had hit him like a thunderclap.

The two dead men who had been bizarrely posed against the

fountain had been arranged in exactly the same natural and yet unnatural manner. The dead secretary and the old man had had their arms and heads twisted to precisely resemble Michelangelo's mother and saviour in The Last Judgement. 'Sacrilege,' said Moretti, his fist balled at his side. 'I was so eager that they be moved, that they not be seen. I did not see this.'

'I didn't know either, not till I saw it. It just looked … looked like I'd seen it before. A cruel joke.'

'Or more than that. It is sacrilege, truly – a devilish mockery. A dagger thrust at the heart of this holy city.' Jack said nothing for a while, still staring up at the image, which had transformed from ethereal beauty to horror. Perhaps that was the point. The whole painting was as gruesome as it was awe-inspiring – one fellow even appeared to be carrying a full human skin. Whoever killed the two men might well have been drawing attention to the supposed cruelty of the Church.

'Someone who hates the Church,' he whispered. 'Our prisoner seemed to. This was his doing. He spoke of art.'

'Hm.' Moretti stroked his beard. 'But why this? Why this painting? Were we supposed to spot the posture all the sooner and speed our way here?'

Jack digested this in seconds. 'What … do you mean … are you saying we were being lured here?'

Moretti looked down at him, his eyes widening.

At that moment, one of the soldiers who had been searching the chapel cried out. 'Oh shit!' All eyes turned to him, some in surprise, some in disgust at his language. He was standing near the door of the chapel, but slowly backing away from it. 'Captain,' the man yelled. 'Captain Moretti. We're in danger. Treason! Treason!'

***

Amy and her company reached the Sistine Chapel through the circuitous route of the entrance yard, up the Scala Regia, and into the Sala Regia. To her annoyance, the unlikeable Sergeant Hasler had taken charge of those heading towards the chapel, leaving others to guard the dormitory. Thankfully, he said nothing to or about her, simply giving her a half-amused, half-contemptuous look. The others seemed to have adopted her as a mascot, shucking her chin and slapping her back to send her flying. Soldiers, she had always heard, were superstitious, and loved having along a lucky whipping boy.

As they reached the high ceiling of the chapel's antechamber, a shout of alarm went up from Hasler. He held up a beefy hand to halt the men. There was no awkward barrelling into one another; instead, they achieved a neat stop. 'What is this?' the sergeant bellowed. 'You, you lousy old bastard. What are you about? Quite this at once.'

Amy had to stand on tiptoes to see over the shoulders of those in front. When she did, her blood ran icy.

Standing in front of the doorway to the Sistine Chapel was the old man, the moustachioed prisoner who had given so much trouble the previous night: the man who had almost certainly killed his guard, the secretary, and poor old Giuseppe. He grinned up at them.

On the floor around him were piled mounds of gritty, brown-grey powder – bucketfuls of the stuff. He was holding a torch above it, casting wavering light across the partially-painted walls. 'Boom,' he said, throwing his head back and laughing.

17

'Touch him not, men, touch him not!' Hasler boomed. Half turning, he gave a trace of a nod to the soldiers, who instinctively spread out across the chamber, taking up positions with their backs to the far walls. Weapons were raised, but no one fired. Amy followed them, her own bow aiming at the old man's heart.

Jack was in there. That thought alone compelled her to remain. If the devil was going to kill her husband, she was going with him. At the thought, she imagined the baby stirring. Again came the urge to run, to escape, to leave this madness and him to his fate. Images of twisted bodies – Jack's and her own – flashed in her mind. Did gunpowder flare in one almighty bang, wiping out life as one might blow out a candle, or did it send out flames to slowly lick and scorch its victims? She didn't know.

'What kept you gentleman?' purred the old man. 'I have been concealed for some time awaiting this interlude. It is always a fine thing to have an audience, is it not? You have fair luck – you will get to participate in the last act of this great tragedy.'

'Shut up,' snapped Hasler. 'Keep that light away from the powder, you son-of-a-whore.'

'That would make a damp end to the whole, would it not? Antigone without a rope, Haemon without a dagger.'

Someone called something indistinct from inside the chapel. Hasler appeared to hear it and when he spoke, his voice had the strangulated tone of someone choking back anger. 'Look here, man, we only want a word. Put that torch out. We can talk, man to man. Get you transported out of this place, eh? Can't say fairer than that.'

'Leave? Why should I want to leave, if by leaving I leave this house of papist art standing? So much talent, don't you think, wasted in the painting of these trifles. Did you see my own artwork?'

'You can leave in safety. I'll promise you, my friend, I'll escort you myself. We needn't even break the conclave. There's a passage by our bunkhouse, ain't there, men?' Hasler turned briefly away from the madman. Sweat gleamed on his pink skin.

'You fail to listen, sir. Did you like my artwork?'

'What the fuck are you talking about?' snapped Hasler. Amy bit her lip. It was important, she realised, to keep the creature talking. He might at any point move far enough from the powder that if he fell, even with the torch, he would not ignite it. It would be a risk, but it was risk enough to have him standing over the stuff. A stray spark might send them all out of the world. She gripped her bow tighter, ignoring the stiffening in her arms and the whitening of her fingers.

'The two dead men. I can no longer grip a brush, you see, so I must do as needs must with larger tools.' To demonstrate, he let the torch wobble in his bent fist. A murmur of alarm rippled across the chamber, drawing more derisive laughter from him.

'You … you killed the bishop's clerk?' Hasler swallowed, before rubbing at his neck. If it was a sign, no one took any notice of it.

'And a poor old man, most unfortunate, he had seen too much. Yet you care nothing for him, do you? Yes, it was all me. I fancy I achieved a good likeness to the great Michelangelo's work. One of the greatest sculptors the world has ever known, yet never did he work in flesh. And you see what work your Church set him upon? Painting scenes of fancy for a few half-blind prelates. It is small wonder he mocked you all in his great fresco – hating you as the Romish Church strangled true artistry. Now imagine, if you will, a world in which the arts were not constrained by doting priests and popish prejudices. Where our universities encouraged men to question rather than burning them for doing so on the orders of proud tyrants in red. Is that not a goodly imagining?'

'How?'

'How?'

'How can it be that an old cripple like you killed two men?' At the word 'cripple' more voices drifted from inside the chapel. Amy strained her ears but could not make out who was speaking or what they were saying.

'Perhaps the devil is in me.' Silence followed this. 'The say the devil can infect any mind he chooses. I am his vassal, do you not think? He gives me strength that surpasses that of the poor, weak cage of this body, and I do, and I do, and I do. And now I shall pass Satan's judgement on you all and fly singing his name to hell.'

He's enjoying this, thought Amy.

'You'll do yourself to death too, you crazy old bastard,' Hasler muttered, edging closer.

'Stay back.' The sergeant stopped. The old man raised the torch a few inches. 'It will be a glorious inferno. It will be seen for miles around. We shall all die a merry death.'

***

'What's he saying?' Jack asked. Sweat had begun to trickle down his back.

'He speaks of the devil,' whispered one of Moretti's men. 'Devil gave him strength to kill the clerk and that old servant. His guardsman too, must be.'

The whole group of searchers had clustered not far from the door. It was dangerous, to be sure, but there was no safe place within the chapel if the flame touched the gunpowder. Probably it would be better to be killed outright in the blast than to die more slowly by burning.

Jack's fingers dug into the damp palms of his hands. He had been wrong. There had been a plot, the old man had been behind it. And there was gunpowder. Where it had been hidden he had no idea, and it hardly mattered now.

'We could rush him, captain,' said one of the other men, his cap pulled off to reveal a young, beardless face. 'Push him forward, away from it. He's looking at them out there, not us.'

'It is too great a danger,' said Moretti. 'It is not our lives alone that stand in peril. It is the cardinals, this ancient place, the whole of Christendom.'

'The windows, then,' pressed the guard. They all looked up doubtfully at the upper mezzanine, above which stained glass stood out in ordered rows.

'Yes. Yes, you men get up there. Get out, break the glass if you must. On to the rooftops and away. I shall stay.'

'No.' The general refusal was echoed. 'If you stay, we stay. We'll stop him without fleeing. We are Swiss Guards. We're sworn to protect this place, not to leave it to ruin.'

'Good man. Good men, all of you. If we live through this, I shall see to it that the commander knows about the sacrifice you have made. You will all be sergeants in your turn, and captains too.'

Some smiles passed across frightened faces, but the conditional kept them from breaking out into cheers.

'He's raving about art again,' said Jack, edging his way closer to the door, his head tilted. 'Is he a mad Lutheran, an evangelical? They hate our faith.'

'He's possessed,' said the young soldier. 'Possessed by the devil.'

'That damned Hasler must keep him talking until either a man out there or a man in here can disarm him,' snapped Moretti.

'Why hasn't he done it?' asked Jack. 'If he means to kill us all, why is he still talking?'

'The devil –' began the soldier.

'He is mad. Madmen run loose of tongue. By God, we cannot just stand here waiting to be blown heavenward.' The captain took off his own cap and stared at it dazedly. He put it back on, straightened it, and then said, 'I mean to close that door. It might not save us when the blast comes, but … it might save some of you. And it might discomfit that wretch. Perhaps then … perhaps Hasler will be able to do something. They must have weapons by now – longbows with no powder about them, no spark of fire. Perhaps they can do something.'

No one questioned the captain, though Jack could tell from the falling faces that most wanted to. They turned their attention as one to the double doors: huge, thick wooden panels. As he suspected the rest were doing, Jack calculated how likely it was that they could withstand a direct blast from gunpowder. Not very, he supposed. Even thick oak would have turned to matchwood. He had once escaped an explosion by jumping through a window. The house itself had been ruined, consumed by fire. He knew what gunpowder could do, and how quickly and viciously it could destroy men and matter.

'I'm afraid of powder,' he said. He wasn't, no more than of any other deadly substance, but he recalled that Moretti had seemed terrified of the stuff. If he was to die, he could satisfy his curiosity about that at least.

'It is a cruel thing, crueller to those who survive it than those who die from it,' said the captain, his voice low. The other soldiers looked at their shoes. 'If it is to be powder that does for me, I do not intend to breathe ever after. I shall go down in it instantly.' If it were meant to be a rousing speech, it failed. Yet Jack suspected otherwise. The captain's determination fuelled rather than satisfied his interest. 'I shall count. When I speak three, I will run at the doors and push them home.'

'I'll get the other one, captain,' Jack said. No one protested.

'Very good, boy. You have a stout heart. You would have made a good soldier.' Jack grinned. 'Would have' – not that he had ever wanted to – had an air of finality about it. It would be fair to go out on a smile, he thought, and all would be sudden enough that he need not brood on the life he stood to lose. Before he could let his treacherous thoughts turn to Amy and the child, he focused on Moretti's grim face. 'One … two … three.'

***

Hasler had failed to make headway with the torch-wielding prisoner. In fact, the madman had simply warmed to his theme, reciting the names of devils, sending shivers through the assembled soldiers. Weapons wobbled in unsteady arms.

Just one lucky shot, thought Amy.

'Reckon there's gold enough to buy you passage anywhere,' said the sergeant. He had not given up on coaxing and had now gilded his promises with bribery. 'You might walk out of here a rich man, richer than any of us, eh lads?' No one provided encouragement.

At that moment, the doors of the Sistine Chapel began to move, diverting everyone's attention. Even the man who held them in thrall gave a half-turn. For the briefest second, Amy swore she saw Jack's face on the other side, and then it was gone, replaced by polished wood.

'It seems,' said the old man, 'that I am not welcome in the holy of holies.' He shrugged. 'No matter.'

'Your game is up,' said Hasler. 'You see, they've shut the

doors upon you.'

'But not upon you. If the men in there burn, it is to their misfortune. We brave few out here, we shall have the more merciful deaths.'

'Look, Mr ... what's your name? Let's talk as friends, can't we?'

He shrugged. 'Call me Legion, is that not what the possessed man said in the foolish old tale?'

'Mr Legion, then. Can we not talk as friends?' The sergeant had grown wheedling. It was not very convincing. In other circumstances, it might even have been amusing to see a haughty, red-faced, truculent man reduced to sweet-talking an urbane, elderly lunatic. 'It's obvious to me, to all of us, right lads, that you don't want to do this. Else you'd have done it by now.'

'You are an astute man, sergeant. I have been tiresome. It has always been my curse. I like to talk, to discuss art if I can no longer make it. But I can see I have bored you. And I confess that this torch is giving my poor old hands no end of trouble.'

'Then throw it away, throw it to me. And I'll escort you from this place. To a place of greater safety.'

'Do you know, I think I shall. Gentlemen of the Swiss Guard, I bid you adieu.'

'No!'

The chorus of cries went up around the room, men falling to one knee. Amy's mouth fell open. As though time had slowed, she watched as the old man opened his swollen hands and let the flaming torch fall to a mound of powder on the tiled floor below. She screwed her eyes shut, no time to think of herself, of Jack, of their child.

And silence followed. Nothing happened. After what seemed an eternity, only the lilting giggling she had heard the previous night pierced her consciousness. She opened her eyes.

On the floor, the torch lay fizzling on its bed of unlit powder. 'It doesn't burn!' shouted Hasler, relief and triumph giving his voice a high pitch. 'You fool, your powder is ruined. We live! We live, men, we live!'

'Powder?' laughed the old man, his laughter subsiding. 'You

181

thought this harmless gravel taken from the sacred Belvedere was powder? Ye Gods, but you soldiers have ugly, suspicious minds.'

'To hell with you,' snapped Amy, tension draining, anger flooding, and a rush of angry energy animating her fingers. This was the world now: a world of terror, of hostages, of the threat of sudden, violent death. She could either be a victim or take up arms against it.

Without thinking further, she narrowed her eyes, kept her bow aimed high, and loosed an arrow straight at the man who had made her fear for her life.

18

The old man fell to the ground, puffs of powdery, harmless dirt drifting up around him. For several seconds, the Sala Regia seemed populated by statues. Then, at last, one of the soldiers began laughing. Fear clutched at Amy's heart; she thought for a second she had missed her mark before she realised who it was.

Hasler reached the fallen man first. 'He lives,' he shouted. 'But by God, boy, you did a fine thing. I'd reward you myself for this.' He spat in their captor's face. 'Fucking dirt, dust! You'll go to the dust, you old son-of-a-bitch.'

Amy stumbled towards them, her legs quivering. 'He lives,' she echoed.

The old man was curled on the floor, his face chalky and his lips pulled half in grimace, half in grin. The arrow had gone in through the fleshy part of his shoulder. Still it skewered him. In one violent jerk, Hasler pulled it out, the backwards-facing points of the arrowhead tearing a scream from his lips. 'A good thing you didn't kill him. We'll be having sport with this old fucker tonight.'

Amy looked up at the great wooden doors. Hasler followed and banged on them with his forearm. 'Captain Moretti? It's Sergeant Hasler, sir. The danger has passed. Your little servant lad is made a hero.'

At length, the double doors began to open. The captain and his men spilled out, Jack at the back of them, looking wonderfully like a lanky boy playing soldier. It was a good thing, too, that he had lingered behind; the press of the others stopped her from throwing herself at him. Instead, she offered up a silent prayer, full of confused and irreligious thanks. 'He lives, captain. What'll we do with him?'

'What happened?'

Hasler explained, with Amy keeping her head down when her part was rehearsed. She gave only a brief smile when the men cheered her. 'Good lad, Roberto,' said Moretti. She noticed he put little heart into it. 'Jack, you have a brother finer than yourself, which few men like to hear.'

'Then the threat is over?' asked Jack. Amy looked at him, and the smile died on her lips. Doubtfulness was written across his face.

'So it would seem. We must lock the creature up. In his old cell. Let that brain-sick boy, what was he called?'

'Pietro,' Jack offered.

'Yes, throw him out of the cell. He is no threat, a common broad mouth. He can walk free. He cannot escape the city.' He nudged the stricken man with his foot. 'Take him there and put him in chains.'

For the first time the old man spoke, his voice a hoarse rasp. 'You cannot constrain the devil, and I have him in me.'

'You'll have my boot up your arse,' snapped Hasler. 'Playing us for fools with mountains of dust.'

'With Satan's art and more time, I should have made it powder enough to bring forth the fires of hell.'

'I … shut up.'

The old man said nothing, but his words had had an effect on the guardsmen, who backed away. Even prone and bloody, he managed to scare them. There was something disconcerting about him. There had been, Amy realised, from the beginning. Sick and crippled people often had that effect on the superstitious, but this one seemed to revel in his illness, and, further, used a vile tongue to conjure images of demons. 'If there be devils in him,' said Moretti, 'then it is not meet that we should have anything to do with him. That is the priests' work.'

'Curse your priests,' laughed the prisoner. 'I'll spit fire at them. You see, my wound scarce bleeds. I have stopped it by the dark arts.'

Hasler made the fatal mistake of leaning down to look. He was repaid for his earlier behaviour with a gob of spittle in the face. 'Ha! You see how marked you are now with devil's blood. The unholiest of all.' Anger blossomed on the sergeant's face, but only for a second. It was replaced by fear, his hand flying up to wipe his dirtied cheek. 'Captain, let's get him away now. Bind him fast and leave him.'

'See to it,' said Moretti. 'Conduct him there now. I will find fast chains to keep him. The rest of you return to your duties.

The search for powder is over. It is now our mission only to see this conclave to its conclusion without trickery. Find secure spaces from which to watch over the procession of the cardinals.'

Moretti's men dispersed, two of them reluctantly prodding the prisoner to his feet and out of the Sala Regia with the ends of their bows. None seemed willing to touch him with their bare hands.

Seeing Jack remain, Amy did so too. 'Am I relieved now too, captain?'

'Yes,' said Moretti. Irritation flared in his voice. She had the impression that he wanted some time alone. Strain upon strain had weakened him, seemingly almost to breaking point. 'The danger has passed. He was a low, wicked murderer and meant only to frighten us.'

Amy looked over towards the staircase through which the man had been taken. She swallowed. It was a few seconds before she realised that Moretti was trying to take the bow from her. Unconsciously, stubbornly, she maintained her grip until he coughed. Her attention returned and she released it.

'But,' said Jack, 'I … to kill those men, it's a big thing. Wicked, like you say. To then just play a trick with false powder…' He too was staring out after the departing soldiers and their strange burden.

'Come to your point, man,' said Moretti. 'I am … I am tired.' He blinked emphasis into his words. It did little to improve the redness in his eyes.

'I just mean … couldn't it be a feint?' Moretti closed his eyes in response. 'Couldn't it be that he wants us to think that the danger's past, so we stop looking. Let our guard down, like.'

'What would you have me do?'

Amy sensed the captain's simmering resentment – probably because Jack's assessment made sense, even if he didn't want to admit it – and she crossed to stand by him. It took a great deal of self-restraint not to reach out and grasp his hand. 'I don't know.'

'Why not ask him?' Amy offered. Both men looked at her. 'You have him prisoner. He gave himself up, really.'

'You shot him,' said Moretti, his voice level.

'Couldn't have done that if he'd not led you to the chapel here and then just … announced himself. That's twice now he's given himself up. Ask him what his game is.'

'The man speaks in devilry and riddles.'

'So knock forty different shades of shit out of him until he speaks sense.'

'He spoke of devils,' said Jack.

'You believed all that?' she asked, turning and looking up at him. 'You don't think he meant to frighten?'

Jack looked between her and Moretti, before shrugging. 'I don't know what to believe. But if there's devilry … I mean, can there even be devilry in such a holy place?'

'I am no priest,' said Moretti. 'Yet even I know that the devil will seek to strike where he might work the most evil.'

'We're in the Vatican City,' growled Amy. 'There stand about fifty cardinals within pissing distance. A bishop. Monsignors. The whole lot.' The blank stares of two exhausted men met her. 'Ask them. It's beyond our understanding, this devilry and religion. It's them are the learned men, the divines. Ask them.'

'Quite right,' said the captain, gathering himself together again. 'As it was your idea, you might shoot a message rather than an arrow. Seek out Bishop Cirillo or Father Casale. Let one of them know that a wicked murderer has been taken up and might be possessed of devils.' Amy frowned. No one could do anything for themselves. Servant or not, she wanted just a moment with Jack to convince him to escape.

'And me?'

'You come with me. You know too much of this matter. You might look upon the creature with me. Put it to him yourself that you believe him to be but a feinting trickster.' Moretti snapped his fingers and began striding away. Jack looked after him and then, apparently satisfied with what he saw, he leant down, grabbed Amy, and kissed her hard on the mouth, his tongue forcing its way between her teeth. With one hand she reached up to keep her cap on. As he released her, he mouthed 'sorry', whether for the impulsive, post-survival kiss or the fact that he was again running away, she did not know.

When they had gone, she kicked the piles of dust about the chamber. Whoever was set to sweep it all up before the cardinals processed into the chapel later, it wouldn't be her. Or Jack. She stuck her head into the Sistine Chapel, more out of curiosity about seeing somewhere Jack had been than anything else. She frowned. Far too gaudy a mingle-mangle of hues – garish, even. Her hand flew to her stomach, as if to protect the baby from the onslaught of colour and outlandish taste.

Leaving the doors open, she hurried away to seek the bishop.

***

Jack held up a long bar from the broken bedframe – one of the pieces that stretched from head to foot, and which had iron hooks on either side to fix it to each. 'Will this do?' Pietro had gone, released by Moretti's men, and he had left the cell in as much a bare and neglected mess as he had found it.

'Yes. Good.'

Moretti had been brought a thick metal collar which fastened and unfastened at the middle, opening and locking on hinges. Once it was round the semi-conscious prisoner's neck, he took a length of rope and slid it underneath, tying it in a tight knot. The other end he tied to one of the wooden bar's metal hooks. With another rope, he bound the man's hands tightly and tied the other end to the other hook. By these means, the old man could not fight to free his hands without choking himself, nor reach to free his neck-rope from its hook. It was a neat, if cruel, setup.

'Will he die?' Jack eyed the greyness of the prisoner's face warily. His eyes fluttered open and closed, but he still seemed eager to speak.

'Not if the apothecary can … do something for him.'

As if summoned, Bianchi appeared in the doorway. 'You sent for me?'

'This creature has been wounded. Here.' Moretti gestured towards his own armpit. 'I have seen worse. It is not a killing wound. We would have him speak.'

A clinical interest seemed to overtake the apothecary as he leant down. 'You have shot him.' He looked up with a smile. 'Alas, you did not pierce his slanderous tongue.'

'He has much to answer for. Can he be mended?'

'You want a surgeon, captain, to stitch closed the wound properly. I can do but a poor job of it.' He sucked in his cheeks. 'Though … yes, I think he deserves no better. Then the best I can do is put an ointment on it and bandage it. First I need to get a look at it.'

'Do so.'

Jack and Moretti stood back whilst the apothecary tore the man's sleeves to bits. The silence seemed awkward, unnatural. Smiling, Jack said, 'he said he was a devil.' From the other two men's reactions, he knew he had made an error. Looking at Moretti in appeal, he added, 'I mean, he did say that, didn't he, captain?'

The apothecary had jerked away from him, and stood with his back to the wall. 'What is this of devilry?'

'The devil has come upon me now, Bianchi!' Everyone jerked at the sudden croak from the old man.

'You told him my name? I didn't tell him!'

'I see with the demon's far sight. I know your name, your failed record of study, the truth about our captain, all. A better educated man would have seen me for what I am when first he examined me but you … you could not take a degree even in Bologna.' The sudden burst of speech seemed to exhaust him, and his voice broke up in spluttering coughs. Afterwards, he turned his head and vomited out a thin stream of green-studded vomit. A noxious, musky odour immediately claimed the room. Moretti seized on the sudden burst of lucidity.

'Tell me now is there a plot still laid, you dog? A treason against the new holy father?'

'Ah.' A rasping cough. 'It was all but jesting and mummery. As a poor carpenter fooled ignorant gulls some time ago in Nazareth. And does still, the cunning fellow. I remember him well, the misbegotten bastard whose whore of a mother was the mother of all gullery herself.'

All mouths fell open, each listener crossing himself.

But the prisoner said no more.

Jack considered the old man's words, his jaw setting. Blasphemy aside, he rejected them. Three men were not dead for simple trickery. Now, more than ever, he felt that the almost voluntary giving up of himself was part of some plan – some design to fool Moretti, to fool all of them, into thinking that they had been chasing nothing. To think, his mind added, that it was all over now, and that the Vatican was safe.

'The bishop has been sent for,' said Moretti, squeezing the bridge of his nose. 'He must be told of this … this foulness. These mad speeches.'

'But … but I have touched him. I've touched his blood. You did not say it might be cursed.'

'I do not know, sir, that it is.'

'The bishop will,' said Jack.

'You give this serving whelp fair license,' snapped Bianchi. Jack closed his mouth. It was clear that the man's sudden fear and nervousness sought an outlet, someone to shout at.

'You might stay with us until the bishop comes. And hear whether the mad knave spoke truth or sought to frighten us.'

***

The ruddy little Bishop Cirillo and the graceful Father Casale, senior clerics both, were locked in the most tiresome, circuitous argument Amy had ever heard. She stood aside, ignored, having delivered the message that their opinion was sought on the matter of a mad killer who had given himself up and was claiming possession.

At first they had argued over whether such a thing was possible in so holy a place at so auspicious a time. Cirillo was for; Casale against. That progressed to which of the pair was the unworthiest to tackle such a terrible investigation. Cirillo was deeply unworthy; Casale was unworthier. Both, apparently, felt that unworthiness and humility were the surest possible qualifications for exorcists. When they ultimately began disputing whether or not incense and holy water might be needed or prayer alone could cast out devils – Casale was a partisan of the extra help, Casale confident in words – Amy gave a discreet cough. Casale looked at her in irritation, apparently only remembering her presence, and bowed his head. A final, private consultation took place. Afterwards, the priest raised his chin. 'Very well, Bernardino.' He turned and looked down his long nose at Amy. 'I shall instruct the better sort of servitor to sweep up the filth that this creature has strewn around the Sala Regia.' Then he turned on his heel and glided away.

Amy found herself leading the bishop, scarcely taller than herself, bounding from the episcopal chambers hard by the Raphael hallway and towards the dormitories.

'What do you make of this?' he squeaked as they stepped into daylight.

'Me, father?' She cursed inwardly. She did not want to speak too much to him. Something about having a man so close to her in height made her feel vulnerable – it was as though he might more readily read femininity in her features. 'I'm ignorant.'

'Ignorance is not blindness, child. Did you see the devil in the man or mere trickery?'

'I don't know.'

'Yet it is a sure thing he has murdered a clerk, a guard, and a poor labourer.'

'He was a baker, father. But yes.'

'Yes,' repeated the bishop. He paused to fix the collar of his white robes. Determination hardened his copper-coin nose. 'And murder is always a mark of devilry, is it not?'

'Always?' Alarm clutched at her throat. She had killed before. So had Jack. There had been a satisfaction in doing it, in ridding the world of a threat, that she had refused to look upon. Knowing she should feign the stupidity of a bumpkin, she said, 'but if the men are bad – not that those poor folks were bad – but if they had been. You can – a man can kill bad men. For safety's sake. Like a prince's hangman kills thieves and murderers.'

'All murder is the devil's work. All punishment for the devil's work is the Lord's justice,' said Cirillo. His voice was low and sincere. Yet the words made little sense to Amy. She pushed them out of her mind as they entered the foul-smelling dormitory block. She gestured towards the cell that had held Pietro, and the bishop crossed himself before entering.

19

Jack saw Amy linger in the doorway, hesitant, as the little bishop strode in, his round features sharpened with concentration. He gave the prone prisoner one hard look and then turned his attention to the apothecary. 'Mr Bianchi. Is the man hurt?'

'But a little. I have patched his arm. Yet he has voided himself of this filth. Ugh, the smell.'

'And he has spoken,' put in Moretti, 'the foulest speeches I have ever heard. He blasphemed the sacred persons of Jesus Christ and the Virgin.'

Cirillo drew in his cheeks and then exhaled before speaking. 'Do not speak with him. Stop your ears to him.'

'Should we leave you?' asked the captain. 'Close you in with him? He is well tethered.'

'Indeed not. If he is possessed by a devil, then the door must remain open to all who wish to see the miracle of his release. This practice is not a secret, it is not a hidden shame. It is part of our great community of souls. I pray I am unworthy enough to let the Holy Spirit work through me.' Jack shifted his weight. Part of him was curious, part afraid to see what kind of tests and rituals the old man had in his armoury. 'Do we know the name of this afflicted creature?'

Moretti bowed his head a fraction. 'Alas, no, father. He is nameless still. We do not know where he came from nor why he came. Nor how, even, he came to be here. I regret we could not break conclave to cast about Rome for intelligence of him.'

The old man began to roll to his side. He glared at the bishop warily, before hissing. And then, to Jack's horror, he laughed. 'You sent this old man to battle the eternal one caged in this fading vessel? Do you not yet understand – I am in the air you breathe. I am everywhere.'

Cirillo ignored the outburst. When the prisoner began chanting Latin in a falsetto, the bishop simply raised his voice to speak over him. 'It is a regret indeed. We might know him to be surely possessed if he manifested a manner much altered from his usual custom. You note he is singing in Latin?' At that, the singing stopped abruptly. The prisoner belched. 'If it is a tongue not known to him in his natural state, that should be a sign. Has he revealed knowledge that he should not have?'

'Yes!' burst Bianchi. 'He knows … things … uses them to mock.'

'I see,' said Cirillo, nodding. 'He appears to me a lame creature. Old. Deformed. Yet three men are dead by those broken hands.' Moretti nodded in assent. Jack looked at the floor. Still he did not believe that the old man was the killer, nor that it had been the old man who cast the flaming robe into the basilica vault. But he could not interrupt a bishop, and nor did he know whether possessed men – if he was possessed – worked with others. That was the special knowledge of divines. 'It is not unknown that a devil, when it has taken a body for its own, will overcome bodily infirmity. The possessed man, though he is old and weak, might lift and hurl great rocks, might wield heavy weapons. In their great hatred they will blaspheme and detest all holy men, all sacred things.'

'That he has done,' said Moretti.

'Help me, father,' said the old man. All eyes shifted downwards. The voice was not the sophisticated railing of his previous conversation, but that of a sad, tired old man. Tears began to flow. 'I am hurt. It hurts. I would to God I were dead.' And then he grinned. Jack shivered. If he was not possessed, he was a good actor.

'Melancholy often falls on the possessed man,' said Cirillo. 'You say he has vomited.' He wrinkled his nose. 'Has he brought forth anything strange? Knives? Glass?'

'No,' said Bianchi. 'Just this foulness.' He gestured at the green-flecked slime which stained the floor.

Bishop Cirillo stood for some time, saying nothing. Then he turned his attention on the stricken prisoner. Their gazes met, but neither spoke. Again, time ticked away, the only sound in the room laboured breathing.

'Devils lie in the air,' said the bishop at last. 'Waiting to deceive us. They live on lies and tricks. They live only to ruin souls. I am satisfied that a devil has overtaken this poor wretch. The deaths alone assure me, the sacrilege, the poor men slain in this holy place. Proof enough of devil's work. He aims, I should think, to trouble this great day. To cast a long shadow over the holiest of our rituals. It is to the greater glory of God that we do this thing. I thank Him that in His wisdom He has seen that I should fast and spend many weeks in prayer as the conclave approached. I only pray it was part of the great design that I should have done so so as to be ready for this unseen task. I will begin.'

***

Amy brought what she was ordered to find: a censer, olive oil, holy water, and a crucifix. It was only when she returned to the to bishop that she realised she had forgotten the incense. Cirillo did not seem to mind. Gone was the tentative little white-robed figure: in his place was a crusader. Jack, Moretti, and Bianchi were lined up against the far wall of the tiny room, as though eager to melt into it.

'I am just sick, it is a pain in the hands,' pleaded the old man, his weak and confused voice returning. 'Where am I? Please, father.'

Cirillo ignored him and knelt, kissing the crucifix. In high, clear Italian, he said, 'in the name of the Father, and the Son, and the Holy Spirit. Amen. Our help is in the name of the Lord. He made heaven and earth. Now and forever.' He tilted his head back and began reciting the Lord's Prayer. Moretti joined in, and then Bianchi, followed by Jack and then Amy. When they had finished, the bishop held the cross aloft.

'Protect, O Lord, this servant of yours who hopes in You. Here is the cross of our Lord Jesus Christ. Flee the enemy forces, for Christ pursues you.'

It might have been her imagination, but Amy felt the air grow thicker, the smell fouler. As though to prove it, the old man vomited again, but managed only a thin trickle. She put one hand to her face, the other to her stomach. Whatever was happening, she feared what it might mean for the child to be in the presence of a struggle between good and evil.

Images of the morality plays she had seen in the north of England danced through her mind: the masquerading of northern folk as angels and devils, the good vanquishing the evil in the end. She knew that Jack had seen them too – and afterwards witnessed the drunken players disporting themselves, shattering the illusion. If this were an illusion, it was a good one. But those plays had been made for people like them – made to make them think that good would always win. This was different. The man on the floor was no drunken villager in a mask; he was rotten, soulless. And the man fighting him with words and holy relics was transformed from a tubby little prelate to a soldier of God.

Yes, she did believe. Seeing made her a believer. And she willed that belief to hurt the man she felt certain had killed her friend through devilry.

Cirillo was repeating his prayer. 'By this sign of the cross, may God send away every evil being. May they not injure the mind, and may every ghost disappear. Oh, good cross, worthy cross, way of virtue, way of true salvation. Cross, strength of men, that leads us to the Lord.'

As he chanted, the man on the floor began writhing and twisting, before going rigid. The board limited his movements, but his back and legs were free; he could gyrate, swivel, and kick out weakly. And he did. His tongue lolled. And then his eyes opened, gleaming with spite. 'What shit. Do you believe that? It is a piece of wood held by a puffed-up old fool. Is this the best you have? Is this what you use to keep men in awe? Is this your sacred, stinking mystery? Ha! For this you burn, and you torture, and you stifle art. I would say Jesus wept, but that young trickster has been rotting in the ground for some time now.'

'Accursed devil,' continued the bishop, unfazed, 'damned and reprobate creature, great seducer of souls, you who with evils promise wondrous things, this will be the end for you. They will no longer call you Lord, but you will be defeated and derided everywhere you are. Praise to you, O Christ.' He rose to his feet, standing over the prisoner, whose wary look returned.

'Now I shall begin the true ritual,' said Cirillo, wiping his brow with a cloth. Amy started, only realising how transfixed she had been by the strange scene. Her hands were still positioned over her mouth and belly. The bishop did not turn from his prey, but said loudly, 'I shall have need of that incense.'

Without a word, she fled to fetch it.

***

Jack stood, awe-struck, as the bishop began on a course of Latin prayers. The prisoner alternated between laughing, mocking him, insulting him, and sitting in sullen silence. Sometimes he sang in Latin, forcing Cirillo to raise his voice. Time seemed to be standing still in the rising heat of the cell.

A similar feeling to that he had experienced when first entering the Sistine Chapel came upon him. It was brought about by the change in the bishop, the sudden leaping fire that brought unwavering authority to his voice, to his eyes. It was difficult to reconcile the politicking of the cardinals with the light of faith that seemed to have come into the smelly, ugly little cell. Jack did not understand possession, nor need to, to see that Cirillo did, and that that understanding went beyond politics and worldliness. Faith wasn't in the election of a new pope. It kindled within people – an inner sort of light that could glow out in the voice and through the eyes when drawn on. And which, he thought, watching the scene unfold, could counter and overwhelm the darkness of evil.

'You cannot defeat me, preacher,' hissed the old man. 'You cannot expel me. My work is in the motion of the spheres. You cannot run. You cannot leave this place. I move amongst you. I move through you.' He attempted a smile through clenched teeth. 'You see what you have done? You have killed him. Look at the blood.' Though they had been warned to ignore his ranting, the three spectators looked down to where redness had begun to seep through the strips of torn sleeve Bianchi had wrapped around the arrow wound.

Cirillo broke off his prayers. 'See to the poor body.'

'I … I … I have nothing with me,' said the quivering apothecary. Shaking hands had flown to his ear flaps, as though to drown out the noise. But he stepped forward. 'I'll have to go and fetch some things.'

'No. I would have you here to watch him. It is right that a man of some learning in physic is present.'

Jack stepped forward. 'I'll go. Just tell me what to get.'

'I'm going too,' said Moretti. Jack turned to him. Though the room was poorly lit even at the height of the afternoon, the captain looked deathly pale.

Bianchi protested, only to be silenced by the newly energised bishop. 'Tell them what they need,' he snapped. 'And bring it hence quickly. The greatest harm the devil can cause is to the stricken soul's body, not to us. Christ is with us. Always. You must not argue amongst yourselves.'

'I like to see it,' offered the prisoner, grinning. 'The idiot battles of frightened, proud men. It is small wonder you are so easy to take. You see how foul you are?' At that, he broke wind. 'Disgusting, bestial creatures. If you are the image of God, what does that say about God?'

'The smell,' said Bianchi, closing his eyes for a second and covering his nose. 'Where is the little brat with that incense? I can fetch my own – the stuff that chases away foul plague airs and cleans the chest.'

'He will come,' said Cirillo, his voice tranquil. 'What do we need?'

The apothecary frowned. 'Bandages,' he snapped. 'Fresh. And a needle and thread, I suppose, though I warn you I'm no surgeon. And there's an ointment on my coffer for the stopping of running blood. A small, stoppered vial, brown in colour. Touch nothing else. Take nothing. And by God,' he said, apparently noticing the sickly hue of the captain, 'see that you eat nothing. There are things I keep that are a danger to men who do not know them.'

Jack and Moretti followed Amy's path towards the servants' quarters and cut through a swath of servants only stopped from requesting news of what was going on by the captain's harried expression. They slid into the apothecary's closet. 'Should be locked,' mumbled Moretti. 'Dangerous stuff in an apothecary's closet, as the man said. Anyone might come and go from here when he is … in that dread place.' Jack said nothing. The thought that poison might again be a possibility – some stolen medicine turned to it – would have to wait.

A jumble of items met them. Glass instruments, innumerable

vials, weights and measures, and roughly chopped herbs fought for attention on every available surface. The needle and thread were the first things Jack found. 'Where would bandages be?' he asked mildly.

'What news?'

Moretti and Jack turned, the latter nearly sending a rough shelf of metal beakers tumbling. Amy, a box in her arms, had stuck her head in the door. Moretti, who had jumped at the intrusion too, hissed, 'haven't you learned to knock in service?'

'Sorry, captain. I saw you come in. Dunno what they'll use for the mass later if we burn this all up to chase out devils. Do you think that's all real, what we saw? What's going on now, what news?'

'The creature's sick,' said Jack, shaking his head. She was excited – too excited. It was her custom to race through speech when she got like that. But this wasn't the time to indulge her. 'We just have to find bandages and something to stop up blood. A vial. Quickly.' She came in and began looking around.

'Did that goat say on a coffer or in a coffer,' Moretti grumbled, throwing open the first box he found and thrusting his face in. He sniffed. 'Nothing but more of what you have, and nothing on top.' Amy peering over his shoulder, turned her head. 'What colour of vial?'

'Brown,' said Jack.

'Is that it?' she asked, pointing her nose. On a chest next to the one Moretti had been bothering was a little glass bottle about the size of a fist. Brown.'

'You have a good eye,' said Moretti. 'Jack, you couldn't have chosen a better brother.' Both froze, but the captain said nothing more. Instead, he grasped the vial.

'Here are bandages. I think,' said Jack, peering at a small spool of linen. 'They'll do anyway, won't they?'

'Yes. We must get back.'

A sudden noise stayed their departure.

'What was that?' asked Amy. Moretti put a finger to his lips. 'Here, it's coming from outside. There's a physic garden out there. Giuseppe told me. Before,' she added, 'that devil murdered him.'

Moretti nodded to Jack, and the two set down their items. They flanked a low wooden door in the rear of the small chamber, the captain holding up a hand to keep Amy back. Without speaking, he held up a finger. Two. Three.

He flung open the door and the two fell out into the light.

It took a moment for Jack's eyes to readjust. The little garden was square was, as he knew, bordered by high sandstone walls. A confusion of bushes and hedges, dotted with reds and browns, obscured a full view. Moretti began stomping around them, a hand on his sword hilt. Jack followed.

A murmur of surprise, which swiftly graduated into a cry, burst over the greenery. It was followed by the crunch of gravel. 'After him!' The pair began pushing hedges aside. Ahead, a gate scraped open. 'Don't let him get away!' Moretti shouted. And then he was off.

Jack followed, amazed by the sudden burst of speed from the captain.

Through the gate lay the rear of the kitchen block, and farther east the guardhouses. Moretti was off, and Jack had the brief impression of a small, buff-coloured back zig zagging between buildings. He jogged after, momentarily stumbling at the sight of a group of senior servants emptying dustpans and wringing out sodden cloths by a waste ditch. The fleeing man had startled them; he had to weave his way around, boots flying.

As he reached the guardhouses, a sudden pain in his side flared up. He paused, head turning from side to side, and caught his breath. Moretti had disappeared after the mystery figure. 'Where are they?'

He wheeled. 'Jesus, Amy!' Her name came out in a pant, but he had wit enough to keep it low. The other servants were gathering together, making tentative moves towards them.

'Where are they?'

'I don't–'

A shrill scream stabbed into the air. Birds took off from somewhere, sending white bodies and a shower of protests upwards. Amy grabbed at his arm and together they half-ran towards the source.

Stumbling through the eastern buildings, they found Moretti

with his sword held to the throat of a man whose back was to the city wall.

Heart fluttering, Jack realised it was Pietro.

20

Blood ran.

Jack closed his eyes, opening them again only at the sound of Pietro's hysterical voice.

'Please, I meant no harm, sir, please. Don't kill me, don't lock me up, let me go. There – him, there, he was part of the group of us that raided the old pope's rooms, roughed up the clerk, why didn't you take him?' The raving Pietro, his eyes wild and staring, raised a shaking finger to Amy. Then he looked again at the point of the sword, which had drawn the spot of blood now trickling down his white neck.

Moretti slowly removed the sword, bringing forth a stream of semi-articulate thanks. Jack had positioned himself in front of Amy, but she moved around him and walked up to the young servant, who remained pinned to the wall by fear. He watched as she put a restraining hand on Moretti's arm and stood toe to toe with the panting man. 'Did you kill my friend? You told me you were a spy.'

'No, no, I spoke true, I never killed anyone.'

Amy wrinkled her nose and took a step back. 'It's true, captain. He's been spying for Cardinal Granvelle's man. Taking news to ambassadors outside the gates. About the conclave, the new pope, all of that.'

'That's all, that's all!'

'Why were you in the physic garden?' asked Moretti. 'Why did you run?'

'I was hiding only. I thought there might be food there.'

'There's food enough in the kitchen,' said Jack. His voice came reluctantly; he had to summon it up from the pit of his gut and it sounded strangulated in his ears. Pietro had been – was – his friend. He didn't want to get involved. But Amy had ensured he would be. 'I believe you, though.'

'I … I didn't want to be locked up again,' said Pietro. Tears came into his eyes. 'You put me in that cell all morning.'

'You were suspected of great evil,' snapped Moretti. 'And you let a short time in a cell unman you?' He spat at the ground. A loud murmuring drew his attention, but before turning he put his left forearm to Pietro's chest, the sword in his right pointed at the ground. 'What the devil are you about?' he shouted, as a group of servants began swelling from between the buildings behind them.

'Just finished sweeping the Regia, captain, sir,' said one of them, a spare, middle-aged man with a humble bearing and sharp eyes.

'And?'

'And we've to make ready for the passage of the cardinals. When the bells ring, they'll be taking their walk, sir, to the chapel. Soon, sir.'

'Then be about it, sweep, attend your work!'

'Yes, sir.' The servant gave one last look at the group before turning and whispering something to his fellows. They melted away – probably, Jack thought, just out of sight. Moretti returned his attention to his captive.

'And so you sought to steal food from the garden.'

'I would have left money,' said the weeping Pietro. 'I have money, I'd have left it. As payment. I wanted to hide until … until the conclave was over. I want to go home. I'm sorry.'

Jack looked at the ground. A damp patch on his friend's breeches showed how sorry he was. However cocky Pietro had been – however smart-mouthed he must have been when he led Amy and the others on their daring raid – he had lost it now. The threat of a hangman might do that to anyone. Even stealing could still see him dancing a foot above the ground.

'Wretch,' growled Moretti. 'Coward.'

'Yes, sir.' The servant's voice had lost all sense of pleading. Even the fear seemed to have flattened. 'I'm that. I'm sorry. Man,' he said, turning to Jack before looking down again, 'I'm sorry. I just thought … if there was any blame for selling tales with that old priest … you'd get it, you know? That's what he said, you so thick with his master, you'd get the blame. I'm sorry.'

'I ought to have you taken up as a thief, warded, hanged,' said Moretti, cutting him short.

'Please.' He looked up, and, to Jack's surprise, there was something like dignity in his face. 'I'm … scared. I've made mistakes, I made a mistake coming here, saying I'd carry messages, telling everyone I'd make money. I'm not eighteen yet. I'm a fool.'

Surprisingly, the captain did not issue any further threats or insults. Instead, his red eyes softened. He returned his sword to its sheath in a swift movement, the scabbard barely tapping his leg. 'Go from my sight, son. Stay out of it.'

Pietro began to walk away without looking at any of them.

'Was that wise?' asked Amy. 'I don't reckon him a murderer but … was that wise?'

'He cannot leave the city. None of us can. Whatever strangeness walks within these walls, it walks with us. I … Ugh.' His right hand shot out to the wall and he stumbled forward.

'Captain?' Jack put out a steadying hand but wasn't quite sure of touching him.

'I am unhurt,' he said. 'My head again. My eyes.'

'Have you eaten?' asked Amy. Jack winced. She had forgotten her manly growl. Thankfully, Moretti seemed too weakened to notice.

'We must return. That young fool has wasted our time.'

'Do you need assistance, Captain Moretti?' A brusque new voice. Jack recognised it as the sergeant, Hasler, who had been with Amy outside the Sistine Chapel. He strode towards them from amid the jumble of buildings, his sword drawn. 'I heard reports of screaming.' He took the scene in with a glance, speculative eyes lingering on Jack and Amy.

'That was some time ago, sergeant. A young thief, no trouble. I have attended the matter my … myself.' Again, Moretti seemed to sway on the spot. Hasler noticed. No sympathy touched his expression, but something like triumph brought out the tip of his tongue.

'I see. Captain.' He clicked his heels.

'Halt, sergeant. I understand the cardinals are preparing to make their way to the chapel. The conclave will be broken up.'

'That's the common tongue.'

'Then we must be ready. I wish men stationed along the route. They will progress in all pomp from the dormitories and out to the Raphael. Up through the entrance yard and so through the Regias. I would have every inch of that route covered. Men on roofs looking over the San Damaso, well-armed with bows. Any man who stirs to meddle with the procession … I wish shot dead.'

'Dead, sir.' Hasler seemed to be fighting a smile as he saluted. Before leaving, he said, in what seemed to be mock innocence, 'shall we have your little lad there, the one who likes the weight of a bow, up on the roof with us?'

'No, sergeant. See to it.'

When he had gone, Jack said, very quietly. 'So, does that mean you think there's still a danger?'

'No, it does not. It means that this place is as well served and … protected …' he took a deep breath, 'as if Commander von Brunegg himself were not ill disposed.'

Together, they retraced their steps towards the garden and through the apothecary's room, gathering up the things they had dumped before their flight.

***

'Reprobate, murderer, son of sedition, I command you …' Latin. 'Again, I exorcise you.' The cross raised. Latin. 'Oh iniquitous devil, ancient serpent, I command you.' 'I order all of you, unclean spirits, who have come out of this body, in the name of the most Holy Trinity, no longer to have any power to show yourselves to this servant of God. May you no longer be able to offend or injure him in body and soul.' The prisoner sang, spat, grew silent, yipped like a dog, wept.

They had given the bishop his items, fighting through a small gaggle of curious servants who had crowded the doorway, curiosity and terror stamped on their faces. The whole pack of spectators had scurried out of the building as Moretti had led Jack and Amy in. Bianchi had then patched the old man up, and the room was thick with the sweet, acrid scent of incense. Quickly it blanketed and smothered the back-of-the-throat sickroom reek.

Cirillo knelt, making the sign of the cross on the prisoner's forehead. Sweat, Amy noticed, beaded the bishop's own, but his voice was stronger than ever despite its uninterrupted use. She bowed her head, wondering how long the exorcism would go on for. It seemed to have no end, to be cyclical, the same prayers, the same Latin words. Jack, at her side, was not watching. Instead, he seemed to be preoccupied with Moretti. If they weren't under the damned captain's gaze – if Jack didn't seem so pathetically enamoured of him – they could have been in hiding by now. Rather than remaining hidden through the conclave, keeping their heads down and working, they had somehow contrived to become known to the captain of the guard. It was absurd. But, she supposed, as the prayers penetrated her mind again, far less absurd than some of what had gone on.

'Captain!'

Amy started. It was Jack, an arm out to Moretti, who had collapsed against a wall and was sliding down it. Both were shrouded in the sickly smog.

'What ails him?' Bianchi was on his knees beside him before Amy could ask the same question. 'You touched nothing in my chamber, you ate nothing?'

'Mmph,' said Moretti.

'Boy, sit him up.'

'Did you eat something, captain?' Jack helped Moretti to a sitting position. Whilst all this was going on, Cirillo kept up the low rumble of prayer. The prisoner, mercifully, had fallen into total silence.

'I …' began the captain. A thin trickle of blood ran from his nose to his upper lip. 'My head again. I ate nothing. My head is worse than before.'

'Then you are not poisoned.' Bianchi leant in close. 'Oh God.' He turned his head towards the bishop. 'Can the devils leap from man to man, father?' Cirillo ignored him, continuing his prayer. Bianchi gave himself a shake. 'When did you last eat something, captain?'

Amy smiled in triumph. That had been her question exactly. It was clear, to her if no one else, that Moretti had been going without food or sleep since the conclave opened the previous day. If he was in a state of collapse now, his final reserves of energy drained by chasing Pietro and standing in a fume-choked cell, he had no one but himself to blame. Now he would have to part from Jack.

'A bite … of cheese … Haven't … had time … to eat.'

'No. Nor to sleep.' Bianchi sucked on his teeth. 'Well you can't avoid it now.'

'Shall I help carry him, sir?' asked Jack. 'Fetch men to help me?'

'You will not,' hissed Moretti, strength returning to his voice. His features hardened, authority breaking through illness. Throwing away the arms that were thrust out to aid him, he used the wall to propel himself up. To no one in particular, it seemed, he said, 'Sergeant Hasler. He is in charge. He will like that. Too much. I will retire now. Leave me.'

He stumbled from the room, crashing through the incense smoke like a departing devil.

***

The devil had gone, indeed. The fire had gone out of Cirillo with it. The bishop was bone-white, shaking, and begging for water, which a servant who had been peeking in fetched immediately. To Jack's amazement, the exorcism seemed to have breathed life and power into the exorcist before robbing him of it, leaving him like a deflated bladder used for sports.

The prisoner, however, had not fared half as well as that. He had been transformed into a confused, inarticulate old man. This time it seemed not to be an act: it stuck. His jaw was slack, ribbons of drool trailing down over mottled purple lips that had been partly bitten through.

'By Your holy power,' said Cirillo, in a far weaker voice, 'the devil has been confused, flagellated, and expelled from this creature, whom you have designed to redeem through your only begotten son. We give thanks to all the saints, the angels, and men, for, thanks to the power of God, through our hands the infernal dragon has been defeated.'

He turned and gave an exhausted smile to the room. A chorus of 'Amen' went up.

'Might I be released now?' asked Bianchi. 'If he is free of the dragon then he must need sleep. He has not disturbed those new bandages.'

'Yes, yes, go, do. And give thanks to God that it is over. In another time, in another place, it might have taken days. Weeks. God is here, within these walls.' When the apothecary had gone, Cirillo asked, 'where is Captain Moretti?'

'He took ill, father,' said Jack.

'Oh. Oh dear. Poor man. You are his servant, are you not?'

'I suppose so, yes. Father.'

'Release this man from his bondage.'

'What?' snapped Amy. Then, when she saw the bishop's indignant look, a muted, 'would the captain want that?'

'The man is no murderer. It was the devil's work. He is free of that vile burden.'

'But ... but shouldn't we just leave him as he is?' asked Jack. 'Three men are still dead.'

'By the hands of a creature now returned to the darkness. Kindly free him, boy.' His tone hardened. 'Now. He is an old and frail creature but a servant of God nonetheless. He is hardly likely to go anywhere. And the city remains sealed.' As if to support him, bells began ringing out from somewhere in the Vatican. 'Ah, but we move closer to our new pontiff. Our work today has truly pleased God.' Jack felt Cirillo's expectant eyes on him. Biting his tongue, he stepped over to the prisoner and untied the rope which bound his hands to the wooden plank. Then freed and unclasped the metal collar.

'What do I do with this, father?'

Cirillo was already gathering his things, apparently eager to follow the summons of the bells. 'Oh, I cannot say. That is a thing of punishment.'

A sudden grunt from the old man sent Jack juddering across the floor on his backside, the coil of metal held up like a weapon. 'Hungry,' said the prisoner thickly. More saliva gushed. 'Like cake.' His eyes had no glint of malevolence. They were glazed and flat.

'You might bring him something soft, boy.' Cirillo started to leave.

'What about my friend?' The sharpness in Amy's tone drew Jack's attention from the invalid, who now lay totally prone on the floor. Turning, he saw she had moved to block the bishop's exit. His heart froze.

'I beg your pardon, lad?'

'The man that was killed, Giuseppe. And the other two. Still need justice, don't they? A hanging, or something.'

'Justice,' said the bishop, clearly unaccustomed to being challenged by a youth, 'has been done. Even now the true and damned killer is suffering all the torments of hell.'

'Doesn't look like it. Looks like he's just lying there like the village idiot waiting for his pie to cool.'

'Someone get this ignorant child out of my way,' said Cirillo, floundering.

'Come on, brother,' said Jack, struggling to keep his voice level.

'Yes, mind your place, lad. Listen to your brother.' With his round nose in the air, the bishop left the cell. When he had gone, Jack stood and went to Amy. He peeped over her shoulder to make sure they were alone. The bells, whatever they signified, seemed to have sent everyone running to their duties.

'I spoke out, I'm sorry, I couldn't help it,' she said, holding up her hands.

'Are you well? The baby?'

'Yes.'

His arms encircled her. 'Thank God,' he said, kissing her.

'But I don't like it. Freeing him like that. How stupid can you get?'

'What harm is it though if … if the evil is gone from him?' Jack could not bring himself to say the word 'devil' in case it somehow invited the presence back.

'You believe all that?'

'Don't you?'

'I don't know.' She shrugged. 'But … I don't know, I feel like it isn't over yet. Like somehow as if we've been watching a play, a kind of interlude.'

'The … the exorcism, do you mean?' He said the word quickly, disliking it.

'I don't know,' was all she managed again. 'Something isn't right. Phew,' she added in English. 'What a fug.' The smoke had cleared, leaving the old undertone of muskiness. 'Let's get

207

out of here.'

Jack followed her gaze to the man on the floor. Snores erupted from him in phlegmatic blasts. Then he looked at the metal collar in his hand. 'I better get this to Moretti.'

'What? Throw it away in a ditch. Come on, let's hide.'

'I can't ... I have to ... the captain's been good to me.'

'Ha! Like an old Roman master was good to his slaves. He's been working you.'

'Still, I ... I'll just give him this and tell him what happened. See if he's well.'

'He'll be sleeping, eating.' Amy's voice shifted from pleading to exasperation. 'Christ, Jack he's not some friendly fa- uncle or something. Just stay away from him. The conclave's nearly over now. If something's going to happen it won't want for us. We can hide somewhere.'

Jack ran a hand through his hair before tossing his head. 'You find somewhere for us. Now. I'll meet you in the San Damaso in ... in a quarter of an hour.' He made to kiss her again, but she pulled away.

'Fine.'

Before he could say anything more, she stomped off, straightening her cap, without a backward look. Jack did turn, to give one last look at the slumbering old man. Whether he was truly the murderer – or the devil was, working through him – or whether he was part of a conspiracy of plotters, he had no idea. Yet Amy's words lingered. Something they had seen had been for show. But what?

And why?

And, most of all, what was a show intended to distract them from?

Lacking answers, he followed Amy's passage out of the dormitory. Outside, servants rushed to and fro, rakes and brooms and baskets of rushes held pell-mell. Guards, too, were conferring, holding up their arms to judge angles. He ignored them all and made for the guardhouse in the eastern reaches of the city.

It took him a few minutes to find the main building. Moretti, he knew, must be in the two-storey one – the one outside which flags bearing the Swiss Guards' insignia fluttered on slanting poles. It was unlocked and he entered, finding the wooden staircase and creeping up. Amy had blathered something about someone being kept up here. Perhaps, he thought, that was why he had come. He shook away the thought. If there was still some danger, Captain Moretti was nothing to do with it. What reason could he have for risking his like and his job to harm the men and city he was paid to protect?

Jack put his hand out and took the metal handle, lifting gently and pushing. The door was unlocked. He took a deep breath and stepped inside, the metal collar still gripped in his other hand.

The room was half-shuttered, but enough light poured in. Rugs were dotted about the floorboards and tapestries blushed with colour. He spied the captain seated at a table on the far side of the room.

He raised his hand in greeting and stepped inside, crossing halfway. Even as his mouth opened, he realised that it wasn't Moretti. The figure noticed the intrusion at the same time, and let out a guttural moan, turning. Jack gasped when he saw the profile. Hastily, the man threw a hood over his head. A black one.

'Stay where you are.'

Jack wheeled, his mouth still agape.

Standing in his shirtsleeves, his uniform cast aside, Moretti was holding his sword up. Its point lay inches from Jack's throat.

He closed his eyes. How, he wondered, fighting the urges to laugh and cry, could he have got it all so wrong?

21

'Captain?'

'Silence. You cannot help but intrude, can you? You busy, foolish youth.'

'Who is that?'

Jack did not turn back to the figure at the table, but he could hear something like thick, heavy sobbing. Moretti stood, his reddened eyes blazing with fury, his sword quivering. 'Hold your tongue. I ought to open you up, damn you, from throat to belly.'

Jack wet his lips. 'You were behind all this. You.' He very nearly said 'Amy was right', but something told him to protect her even now.

'What?' Moretti screwed his eyes, not quite closing them, as anger and confusion wrestled. 'What are you speaking of, you fool?'

'Argh!'

Jack jumped back, not sure where the angered roar had come from. Everything seemed to happen at once: the cry, accompanied by a sudden whirl of buff-coloured material, and Moretti falling towards him; he only narrowly missed being pierced by the captain's sword as it clattered to the floor. Moretti went down like a sack of flour under the weight of the sudden assault from behind.

'Amy!' Her name passed his lips before he could stop himself. Did Italians use the name? He began shouting, hoping to bury it in more words. He needn't have bothered. Amy had launched herself into the room, a little ball of fury, and clamped herself to Moretti's back. Jack stood, irresolute, unable to remember the false name he'd given her.

'Get the other one,' panted Amy, straddling the fallen captain. 'Don't let him get away.'

'No!' Moretti bucked, throwing her. 'No! No!'

'Stop him, Jack!'

Amy was thrown in a heap as Moretti dragged himself up. He did not reach for the sword, yet the movement forced Jack into action. He leapt across the floor, intent on gathering up his wife.

'I told you,' she said, breathing heavily. 'I told you don't trust him. He's a lying shit. There, there's the thing in black he was with. I told you.'

Jack helped her to her feet before turning to Moretti. The captain was shielding the robed figure, which was rocking backwards and forwards in a frenzy, battering hands against its hidden ears and moaning. 'Get out, both of you. Or I will have you both locked up.'

'What is this? Who is that?' Jack tried to stand in front of Amy.

'It's the murderer. It's a plot. They're all in on it. Conspiracy! Sneaking around in the dark like that. They killed Giuseppe,' she said, pushing him aside. Triumph, Jack noticed, had made her bold. But if she were right, he had no intention of robbing her of satisfaction.

'Shut your mouth, you stupid girl,' said Moretti.

Jack felt cold hands crawl up his back as he and Amy froze. For a few seconds, the only sounds were the inarticulate cries from the strange figure. 'You … you knew?' To his surprise, Moretti gave a ghastly, humourless smile.

'Do you think I am blind, boy? Lover or sister?'

'… Amy's my wife.'

'Ah.'

'Don't change the subject,' snapped Amy. 'You see a lot, captain. Well, so do we. You've been hiding that … that plotter. Murderer. You've been behind this all along. Still are, I reckon. Threatening the old pope and the new one. Here,' she added, turning to Jack, her voice rising to its excited pitch, 'I reckon he's had you all searching the wrong places. For the wrong thing. Because he knows what's planned, because he planned it.' She looked again at Moretti. 'What is it, a gun? Does your man there plan to shoot the new pope?'

'Jack,' said Moretti, quite calmly. He started at the sound of his name. 'Would you take charge of your mad wife. She raves like a lunatic.'

'Lunatic hell,' shouted Amy, shaking off Jack's hand. 'We can see him, you can't hide him away any longer. Ho, there! Ho!' She leant forward and starting waving her hand. She did, indeed, look mad. The suddenness of the attack on Moretti had unbalanced her.

'How did you find me?' he asked her in English.

'Followed you. I told you I didn't trust him. And I were right!'

'Would you cease your savage tongues,' Moretti said, putting a hand on the shaking shoulder of his guest. 'You are upsetting my son.'

As one, Jack and Amy turned to him. 'Your son?'

'Yes.' He sighed and rubbed at his eyes. 'This is my boy.'

'Liar! You don't hide your boy away, you don't take your boy out in the dark. Why would your son even be here?'

Moretti leant over the figure again. Seconds stretched into minutes as he made soothing sounds. The rocking stopped, and the muttering. Eventually, he pulled back the hood. 'I won't have my boy made a figure of fun. Or fear. Not by a ranting woman in boy's weeds, not by anyone.'

Jack's eyebrows rose; Amy put a hand to her throat.

The man in black was no man. The body was that of a boy, about twelve or thirteen but thick-boned. The face, however, was a tortured mass of scarred flesh, one eye gone and the other, untouched, narrow and slitted. He looked at them.

'What happened?' Jack whispered.

'I did it,' said Moretti. 'It is my fault. My error.'

'Does … is he supposed to be here?' asked Amy.

'What would you have me do with my boy? Leave him to be mocked and spat at outside whilst I am locked in here?'

'But … do people know?'

'The commander knows. My men know. The prelates, no. They might think it an unholy thing to have … him here.'

'I don't understand,' said Jack, tossing his head. He meant it. If Moretti were merely protecting his son, was he free of the taint of conspiracy?

'Well, it seems the pair of you know my secret, as I know yours. I suppose that makes us conspirators of a kind. Come. Sit.'

Awkwardly, Jack and Amy joined him at the table, sitting on boxes and stools. Jack tried not to look at the boy's burnt face, nor to pay attention to the distracting noises he kept making.

Amy, however, sat next to him. 'What's your name?' No response.

'His name is Girolamo.'

'What age are you, Girolamo?' This time he held up a hand. Jack was struck by how young it looked. The head might have belonged to someone of any age. Soft brown curls sparsely populated the crown, standing in unruly tufts.

'He is twelve.'

'You're a big boy for twelve,' Amy smiled, touching his hand. He didn't pull away.

'What is all this, captain?' asked Jack, tearing his eyes away. 'Why this … this secrecy?'

'If I tell you, I trust you will stop your wife's wild accusations? You will finally leave me to rest?' Jack said nothing, but felt a grin pull at the side of his mouth. Taking it as encouragement, Moretti gave another long, despairing sigh. 'I suppose it is my penance that I must rehearse my shame over and over. So be it.

'Girolamo was born … slow of wit. His mother, God rest her soul, went to God after his birth.'

'Like mine,' said Jack, quickly closing his mouth.

'It was a difficult birth. There was trouble bringing him. Not his fault, of course. God's will to leave me short of a wife and the poor imp motherless. I saw it as my duty to do what she would have wanted. To protect him, to teach him what I could.' The words circled in Jack's mind. There, he thought, was a true father.

'And then what?' Amy asked. She had removed her cap and started playing with Girolamo, holding it as though she were going to give it to him then snatching it away. It seemed to please the boy, bringing rumbling laughter from his chest. Moretti smiled before continuing.

'That is what I did. I could see he was not … as other boys. His eyes, his tongue seemed duller. He did not speak when he should. I was told there was no hope for him – to put him away in some monastery where he might be taught the basics of service and worked like a dumb beast. That … I could not do. So I kept him with me. And the years passed. No one bothered us. Ah, people might laugh at him in the street, throw things. He understood. I could see that. His wits might have been scattered but he could understand what he saw. In time he could speak, too, although his tongue gave him trouble. I put a stop to anyone troubling him, though. I suppose … perhaps I was over hard in my parenting. I grew fearful of ever leaving him alone.' Amy, Jack noticed, stopped playing and turned solemn features towards Moretti. 'And then came Lepanto.

'I did not have to go. Off to battle the Turk. Off to fight the infidel for God's glory. Only the best of the guard went – the golden company, we called ourselves. I told myself I could show my boy foreign climes, the wild seas, the glory of war. Vanity,' he sniffed. 'I took him, only eleven. I thought I could not leave him in Rome to endure taunts. I never left him. And the others came to look on him as a kind of … talisman. I heard one say that an idiot brought good fortune. And I struck him for that. Yet … yes, I suppose I was proud that others welcomed my boy somewhere.

'And so we went off to the great sea battle. I will not detail it. Ships are no place for any boys, no matter their wits. There is cursing, crowds. There is powder. Fire. I was careless. I let him get too close to a gun on deck. The damned thing backfired, exploded, its powder scattering in flame. You can see what happened. My fault, taking a poor innocent to such a thing. My error.'

Amy, Jack saw, had a tear running down her cheek. She raised a hand and touched Girolamo's face. 'I think you're very handsome,' she said. 'I think you'll break lots of ladies' hearts when you're full grown. Every girl loves a soldier.'

'We're sorry, captain,' said Jack.

'But you see how it looked?' Amy added. 'I saw you walking out at night with someone in black, a hood – and with all that's been happening. You see how it looked?'

'He's not my prisoner,' snapped Moretti. 'He might take the air when … when he can. He went out wandering. I had to find him. He might …' he hung his head. 'Have frightened the ignorant if they saw his poor face.'

'Do you like walking out?' she asked Girolamo.

'Farm … farm … farm.' He began gesticulating.

'He said that last night.'

'It's English,' Amy said. 'You speak English, do you?'

'He does not. Foul tongue.'

'La fattoria,' said Amy, putting a finger to his scarred chin. 'La fattoria.' Smiling at Jack, she said, 'our boy here wants to be a farmer, not a soldier.'

'Farm!'

'There's still danger,' said Jack, reaching into his tunic and removing the letters Amy had found. Her easy way with the burned boy was shaming him. Still he could not quite look him in the eye. 'These, written to the old pope.' Frowning, Moretti took them and squinted. 'I told you about them before. I didn't say we took them.'

'Yes. I remember. I see. The devil, this drawing, suggests that our old friend in the cell was the author.'

'The bishop has freed him,' said Jack, turning the metal collar still clutched in his hand.

'What? A foolish thing. Ah, but he cannot go anywhere. If he attempts anything he will be shot from above. Let me see.' He looked down at the papers again. Such a judgement,' he quoted, 'that none shall take your throne. The Last Judgement. We saw that enacted with the bodies of those unfortunates. And this here, this threat – a great blow. Well there is no powder. It seems these letters were written to threaten and distract.'

'You think there's nothing in them?'

'I did not say that.' He read again. 'When death comes to the Vatican, they shall not see its approach.' Bells began chiming again, and, close as they were to the city walls, the sound of excited cheering reached them too. The beginning of the end, Jack thought. Girolamo began clapping.

'Guns,' he said. 'He might have a friend, a conspirator, who has a gun.'

'Then I trust my men to see him. The conclave is ending and they are stationed all about. If there is some other, some madman with a gun, he shall accomplish nothing.'

'What do we do then?' Jack pressed. 'We can't just … do nothing.'

'You are here in service. You might turn your hands to serving. My uniform needs laundered. You might see to it that it is cleaned, dried, and returned to me.' He stood, crossed the room, picked up the bundle and tossed it to Jack, who sniffed at it.

'Hey. I –'

The sound of Amy's stool scraping across the floorboards broke in. She had been reading the letters again. His train of thought was lost. 'Oh. Oh shit.'

'Not in front of my boy, Mrs Jack,' said Moretti.

'What is it?' She looked at him, her eyes wild.

'Nothing. Stay here. I … I need to pee. Stay!' She pushed herself up. 'You stay good, Girolamo.'

'Farm!' he insisted.

On that, she darted from the room.

'Your wife,' said Moretti drily, 'is a strange woman. And I hope a pretty one when not dressed in such a manner.'

'She's beautiful. But … what was that?'

'Women,' Moretti shrugged. 'I have memories enough. Now, I should like my uniform ready for when I wake. I will not sleep long. I just … I have had such trouble in my head. Better now that I am free of that dread cell.'

'Mm.' Jack gathered the uniform in his arms. Again, that smell. 'Captain, did the old man get his sick on you?'

'What? No.'

'Right. Right. I'll go. I'll get this laundered. And I'll see about getting you something to fix those headaches.'

'Yes, yes, just go. And keep … this matter quiet. My boy.'

'Yes, sir.'

Jack gave Girolamo a smile, but kept his gaze fixed on managing the bundle in his arms. He left the room, keeping his step measured until he reached the stairs. Once the door was closed securely behind him, he flew. The captain's uniform went unceremoniously into a corner before he left the guardhouse.

22

Bells clamoured in Amy's head, seeming to come from everywhere as she ran between the abandoned guardhouses. Shadows were lengthening in the spring evening. Abruptly the bells ceased, just as she rounded a corner and passed into the San Damaso. Servants were ranked in rows. She half-tripped and began elbowing her way through.

'Watch it!'

'Brat!'

'Hey, where's the fire?'

She did not have time to exchange quips nor to swear.

She knew what the weapon was, who it was intended for, and what destruction it would wreak.

Abruptly the bells ceased. In their place a choir of angelic voices began singing a haunting Te Deum. Shit, she thought. It was all beginning. Out of the passageway that led to the dormitory courtyard a flock of boys appeared, robed in white. Heralds of the new papacy.

Amy edged her way through the crowd like a struggling swimmer. She crossed the fringes of the San Damaso, her head bent, and got behind the singers, flinging herself along the passage. Her heart was battering her chest and her stomach began to ache. There was no time to think what that meant.

In the courtyard the cardinals were beginning their procession, ordered in twos, each wearing round red hats. At their head was a stocky man and beside him a stately one with a serious, set face. The little one, she guessed, must be the camerlengo. The other had to be the new pope. Four guards stood around them, each holding an ornately carved gilt pole supporting a red canopy fringed in gold. She scanned the cardinals but could not see what she was looking for. She prayed it had not gone on ahead. If it had, the men might be walking into a trap. Worse, they would stream into their deaths, walk off a cliff.

Amy hugged the walls and jogged towards the doorway of the main block from which they spilled. As she passed the building that had become a cell block, something whistled over her head, landing a foot in front of her. She jerked to a halt. An arrow. She spun, looking up, arms across her belly, head spinning. Someone shot at me, she thought. The idea seemed to come from far away.

High up on the red roof was Sergeant Hasler, down on one knee, his bow poised. His left side was bathed in light from the retreating sun. Amy shook herself out of her stupor and held up her palms. Desperately, she tried to mime innocence, to indicate the cardinals. She considered shouting, and settled instead for mouthing, 'Moretti sent me', unsure if he could see her. He raised a hand, whether in acknowledgement or apology she didn't know, but she turned away and leapt over the arrow. No more followed.

The procession of cardinals was underway, the chain of men swaying rhythmically as they marched in step, red-robed soldiers of God. Amy scanned them, looking for the weapon that spelled their destruction. She could not see it. It must be at the rear, carried behind. Or, at least, she hoped it must be.

She stood on tiptoes against a wall, waiting for the column to pass through. When the last cardinals had exited their dormitory, she spotted the tall priest, Casale, and Bishop Cirillo flanking the doorway, a serving boy between them. The lad was holding something. Her heart bounced into her throat. As they moved to join the rear of the procession, she threw herself in front of them.

'What is this?' snapped Casale, sneering down.

'You!' said Cirillo, fluttering his hands. 'What news? This lad was present for part of the miracle, Alessandro.'

Amy's words tumbled over one another. 'The chest, that chest, don't open it!' She reached out to snatch at the coffer held by the servant. He drew it to his chest. 'It's a plot!'

'Has the lad run mad, Bernardino? When the devil fled did it take this boy?'

'What?' Cirillo asked. 'Oh, oh dear.' His hands rose to his cheeks in a fussy little gesture.

'Listen to me!' Amy threw her head back, took a deep breath, and willed sense into her words. 'It's a plot. There's been a plot to kill the cardinals. That box is … it's the instrument.'

'It is mere incense,' sniffed Casale. She turned to Cirillo, who looked the easier to convince. 'Please, father. Please listen. Captain Moretti sent me,' she lied. Then, hoping to anchor it with the truth, she added, 'it was put into the storeroom not long since. It … it was brought in but poisoned first. By the devil acting in that old man.'

The servant looked down, gasping, and held the box out. Frowning, Casale snatched it and made to open it. Amy slapped at his hand. 'How dare you touch me!'

'Don't open it! Don't breathe its fumes. It'll … I don't know what it'll do, but when it's burnt it'll poison all who breathe it.' Amy tried to force reason into her features. 'If it's taken to the chapel, if it's burned in the mass, all the cardinals will die. All of them.'

'Can it be true?' Cirillo asked.

'Yes – yes, it's true! We used the good stuff, father, with the old man.' She gestured behind her towards the other dormitory building. 'And someone put that in its place. It has no scent. No,' she shouted again at Casale, 'don't open it!'

'We cannot take the chance, Alessandro,' said the bishop. 'Boy,' he added, looking to the servant, 'find more incense. I do not care where from but do it now and do it quickly.' The lad took to his feet, clearly eager to be away from the mysterious chest.

'How do you know this, whelp?' asked Casale. Amy could see that he, too, was holding the box away from himself. 'How does Captain Moretti know?'

Amy opened her mouth but Cirillo cut her off. 'We can discuss that later.' He nodded towards the passageway that led out to the Raphael hallway. The last of the cardinals was out of sight. 'Come, we must be in attendance. And we must have good incense. We might keep this with us to be examined afterwards.'

'Make sure the new stuff has a smell,' Amy called as they hurried off. 'Don't burn it if it doesn't have the right strong smell.' If they heard her, they gave no signal. She watched until they were gone. The sound of the distant singing grew fainter and fainter.

Left alone in the courtyard, she put her hands to her forehead and wiped away perspiration. She looked again to the rooftops but could see only the backs of the snipers. Clearly they had turned to survey potential enemies harassing the procession from the San Damaso.

She had done it. She had prevented a mass murder of every cardinal in the Vatican. The conclave was now all but over. Once the mass was sung the new pope would be announced. She and Jack could leave the place, leave Italy, return to England, and have their baby.

Amy began walking along the fringe of the courtyard, slapping her hand along the walls of the cell block, letting her heart slow. As she passed the doorway, a shadow moved. Before she could turn to it, something slid round her throat. She tried to cry out. No good.

'Shut your mouth, you little fool.' The angry hiss bored into her ear like a hot needle.

The only thing that stopped her fighting was the nip of the arrowhead as it pressed into her throat.

***

'I need something that'll help the captain sleep, doctor,' said Jack.

Bianchi was seated on a chair in his chamber, his knuckles whitening on the sides. 'I am no doctor, lad. Yet I think I can help. What the fellow needs is a proper meal.'

'Yes.'

Jack watched as the apothecary bustled about, lifting vials and examining them, replacing them and tutting. 'He said that there was something outside. In your physic garden.'

'What?'

'I said I'd look.' Without waiting for a response, Jack opened the door and crouched through it, his hair brushing the lintel. He stepped out and began moving through the hedgerows.

He stopped at one. Sniffed. Yes, the musky odour rose, wrinkling his nostrils. He touched the leaves. The same ones that had stuck to Moretti's uniform during their mad dash, infecting it with their stench. The same little green flecks that had studded the prisoner's drooling vomit. 'Phew,' he said.

'These surely do stink.'

'What the devil do you mean, boy?' Bianchi had followed him out. Jack didn't turn to him. Instead, he bent down, leaving his back exposed.

'It's strange, I think I know this smell. These leaves. Yeah, the mustiness.'

'It is called rue.'

'Rue. I know. I remember – it's the same rotten reek that came up out of that old man's vomit. A remedy for swollen hands, maybe.' He tensed, his head low, waiting, listening for the light crunch of footsteps. 'It's almost like you'd been helping the man. Giving him medicine.'

There was one last chance for Bianchi. He might, Jack had supposed, have given plausible reasons – perhaps the treatment was given out by all mediciners, nothing to do with him. But no denial came. Instead, Jack felt the apothecary's presence rear up behind him. He tried not to flinch as the man's hand snaked around his neck.

He had a momentary glimpse of the thin, surgical blade poised to slash his throat.

Bianchi struck, swiping left to right.

The blade bounced.

Seizing the apothecary's grunt of confusion, Jack sprang to his heels and pivoted, pushing the older man hard in the chest. Stunned, confused, Bianchi fell into a potted bush. His knife fell and Jack kicked it away. It slid across the ground, hitting the wall with a ting.

He had been right.

Anger flooded him – the kind of venomous fury he often tried to bury. He let it come. Grabbing Bianchi by his furred tippet and doublet, he lifted him off his feet. Where the sudden strength came from, he had no idea. He walked, holding him, to the wall and held him against it. 'You bastard,' he growled. 'You were going to kill them all. You killed those men, you were going to kill me. What, were you going to strip me bare-arsed and do me up as Michelangelo's fucking David?!'

Bianchi's eyes were wide, but he recovered and began scrabbling. 'What is this? Why do you not bleed?'

Jack almost smiled. The metal collar that had been used to restrain the prisoner was snug around his neck, chafing and sore. But it had worked. He cracked the back of Bianchi's head against the wall. 'Unhhh' The man's hat fell off, revealing a purpled, swollen ear. Someone had hit him recently, cracking the side of his head.

'Bastard!'

The apothecary began making gasping noises. Jack realised, with horror, that he had begun strangling him. He relaxed the pressure.

'It's too late,' Bianchi hissed. 'The procession has begun. They all die.'

'No. I've stopped it. You lost.' It was a lie, but he hoped – he prayed – that Amy had worked something out.

'You lie!'

'Fuck you!' Jack said, before returning to Italian. 'You killed them all, the guard, the two men.'

'They saw too much. Damned Agosti, I told him not to come into this place.'

'But he did, didn't he? And only you and the guard you killed were ever alone with him. And what – he hid out here whilst you worked out how to try and make good on his presence? Well it was all for nothing. You're undone, you … you fuck! You didn't get everyone who saw something, did you?'

'What?'

'You were seen.' Jack drew out the Italian word for apothecary. 'Farmacista. Farm, farm, farm.'

Bianchi's head lolled. As Jack followed it, it sprung up, catching his chin. The surprise threw him. He released his grip entirely. In a blur, the apothecary sank to the ground, scrabbling. Jack, his anger blinding him, began to kick. He caught Bianchi in the ribs and felt something break. The sound spurred him on to more. Again. Again. He stomped on the man's back, hoping it would snap too.

And then the mad rush of fury abated. The apothecary lay still. Jack put his hand on the wall and began gulping the herby air of the garden. 'You bastard,' he said again, but weakly. 'Your plot's failed. No one dies now but you.'

He began to move, but before he could, the fallen Bianchi's hand shot out and grabbed his ankle. 'What?' he said dumbly, as it was wrenched from under him. Greenery and sandstone shot up around him.

As his vision steadied, he saw his enemy's black-clad arm rise in the air. 'Oh, shit,' he said. A metal collar wouldn't save him now. The blade, recovered, arced downward. At first it felt like a punch. The pain then narrowed, sharpened. And he knew he had been stabbed.

23

The old man led Amy out into the San Damaso, the pair of them hugging the wall of the passageway. His wretched, swollen hand frightened her as much as what he held in it. The arrow, which remained pressed against the side of her windpipe, could too easily slip in that uncertain fist.

'Where are you taking me?'

'Be silent.'

'You weren't ever possessed at all, were you? That was all cheap trickery.'

'I said be silent.' His voice was, again, faintly mocking. Yet she sensed in it a restrained fury. His plan, he knew, had failed. She had been either the cause or the instrument. That would hardly go in her favour. But he was keeping her alive. He must, then, mean to escape, to use her as a hostage if one were needed.

'All trickery,' she repeated.

'You stupid peasant,' he snarled. 'There are no angels and no devils. They live only in men's fevered imaginings. A man might use one to excuse his cruelty and the other his fears. And switch the pair at will. Yet it is so easy to gull the superstitious. You see, I hope, how false your faith is that an old man can make a fool of a bishop.'

'You're the cruel one. Murderer. You killed my friend.'

'I did not. Alas, some fools who saw too much in the night had to die to accomplish a greater design. Yet you have spoiled that, haven't you, you and your stumbling captain.'

'Yes, yes, it's over,' she said. They had entered the sprawling San Damaso, but the huge crowd of servants was gone. She cursed silently. Of course they had. The whole pack of them, probably every man in the place, would be jostling for position as close to the Sistine Chapel as possible. Each one would want to be the first to welcome the new pope, to snatch up pieces of the carpets laid out for him to step on when he left. And every guard, too, would be ranged in the Sala Regia. 'So,' she said, scared to swallow in case the swell of her throat encouraged the arrowhead, 'you can let me go. You can go. Just go. Before the guards find you.'

'Oh, I intend to go. A lost battle is no lost war. Yet I am not so foolish as to go alone. Journeys are so much pleasanter with company.'

'Then take that apothecary, take Bianchi. If he hadn't sent us for bandages, I wouldn't have noticed the stuff in his room had no smell. And sniffing it made the captain much worse. Made him faint, made his nose bleed.'

'Oh. So it was you, was it? It was your sharp eyes and sharper nose that caused our enterprise to fail? That will make our eventual parting much the sweeter.'

Amy closed her mouth, biting on her loose tongue, glad only that he didn't appear to recognise her as the one who had shot him.

She had to get free, had to find some moment of weakness. She refused to remain either a hostage or, worse, become a victim of this aged lunatic. Nor would she let Jack's baby die in her womb at the madman's hand.

He marched her eastwards, in amongst the guardhouses. Here, she thought, she could scream if she dared. The commander was in one of the outbuildings, and Moretti and Girolamo in another. Tears of frustration burst at the corners of her eyes. She was close to salvation, close to help, and yet unable to get it.

The old man stopped moving and she jerked to a halt with him. They were standing in front of the oddly shaped building, attached to the wall, that she had spotted that morning – the thin, tall one with a wooden door hidden by potted cypresses. 'The secret escape of the popes,' he said. She said nothing. 'Did you not know of it? Clement VII used it flee the Vatican whilst his Swiss Guard were slaughtered on the steps of the old basilica. A very human response for a man touched by the divine, no? It is said he lifted his robes and ran, ran, ran, piss dribbling down his leg in fear. Open it.'

'What?'

Roughly jerking her, he grunted as he kicked at the cypresses' pots. They did not move; they barely scraped the gravel. Apparently realising the futility, he manoeuvred her behind them. She tried the ancient handle. Turning it did nothing. 'It's locked.'

'Sharp lad.'

Hoping to surprise him, she said, 'I'm no lad. I'm a woman.' Rather than startling him, giving her an opening to escape, he laughed.

'A whore smuggled in to satisfy the carnal lusts of the red robes?'

'No. I joined my husband.'

'You need not think to shock me, girl. Of the hundred or so men in there I should guess at least a dozen are women with shorn locks. Whores, mistresses, all hoping to satisfy for coin.' Amy felt tears sting again.

'Kick it,' he growled. She delivered a weak kick at the base of the door. Nothing. 'Harder, you little fool. You break a door at the middle, where the bolt slides home. You should be well learned in breaking into places you ought not to be. You had better hope you are, girl. If you cannot, you are of no use to me.'

The arrowhead held only an inch from her neck and her captor's putrid breath hot at her side, Amy put her hands behind her to grip one of the trees. They sank into its leaves, finding purchase on the thin trunk. With all her might, she kicked with one leg, aiming her boot at the centre of the door. Nothing but a slight wobble. Again. Again. Again, she kicked, cursing.

The crunch of splintering wood cracked through the guardhouses.

The ancient door fell inwards, the locking mechanism shattered.

'Good girl,' he said, as bells began to peal again. 'Now climb.'

***

Jack tensed for another blow, a killing one. It never came. Bianchi kept the knife upraised, but he lacked the strength for a prolonged fight. Instead, he struggled to a crawling position, one arm held to his ribcage. He rasped in shallow breaths, his head swivelling from side to side.

Jack screwed his face, trying to blot out the pain. His vision swam. Yet he dared not fully close his eyes, for fear he might not open them again. Judging by the sounds, the apothecary seemed to be trying to hobble away. Chancing a full look, he saw the older man scrabbling in the undergrowth, pulling something out of it. A bundle of black material, not unlike the black robes Girolamo wore. He tore savagely at them before tying them tight around his body and dragging himself up, using the wall as a support. Aiming for the gate. As pain radiated up through his body, Jack tried to sit. He had watched a man bleed to death from a blow to the thigh once before. It had been quick – there had been more blood. His hand pressed against his wounded right leg, he used the left to get to a sitting position.

He could not let Bianchi escape.

Yelping as a sudden burst of pain shot through him, he got to his feet, his weight entirely pressing down on his left leg. He followed the apothecary's passage.

The gate stood open and he took stuttering steps towards it. Once through, he squinted into the jumble of buildings. Daylight was in fast retreat, spring reluctant to be generous. He heard Bianchi before he saw him; he was still clutching his wounded side, as though trying to hold his battered body together. He was heading for the San Damaso. Jack followed.

Almost immediately he stopped, his mind reeling, as a cracking sound rent the air somewhere behind them – from the direction of the guardhouses. At first it sounded like a gunshot, but it was difficult to discern over the rush of blood in his ears. It came again, and again. Bianchi had turned too. The apothecary spotted him and began moving more quickly as bells started singing through the air.

The two men continued their sluggish chase. It was not long before Jack realised what Bianchi was doing. His goal was the main entrance of the Vatican. It might be opened at any moment, allowing him safe passage out.

Let him go, whispered a little voice born of pain. Let him go. The plot has failed.

He pressed on. Taking halting steps, he started to grow used to the bursts of agony. First a step on the left, then, through gritted teeth, dragging the right. He moved along the Raphael hallway after crossing the San Damaso, conscious that he was leaving spots of blood on the polished floor. Someone would have to clean that up, he thought, before realising that his

227

thinking, too, was getting groggy. He gnawed on the inside of his cheek to clear his head.

He turned left when he reached the entrance courtyard which he had been sweeping when Cardinal Granvelle first arrived. Turning left again, his back to the Paolina, he rested his hand on a sandstone wall. The urge swept over him to put his face against the cool stone, just for a moment. He ignored it.

Ahead, he could see Bianchi. The apothecary had somehow made it all the way across the black-and-white tiles. He was locked in animated conversation with a Swiss Guard who stood sentry at the great door to the city. He could hear nothing of what they were saying. The bells, the cheers from behind him, all were rushing in. His heart sinking, he saw the guard shrug and shake his head. He looked like a colourful little figure in a play. The apothecary turned and looked towards him, but at such a distance he could not read the man's expression. Triumph, he supposed, as the guard began unlocking the door.

It was over.

And then something extraordinary happened. As the guard struggled to haul open the great wooden gate, he seemed to lose control of it. The thing burst wide, as though pushed by a tremendous hand, its keeper suddenly struggling against it. Bianchi jerked back, a marionette figure, as a seething mass of humanity poured in, cheering, men and women falling over one another.

Jack watched as Bianchi tried to struggle away from the sudden, unthinking avalanche of the faithful. It was no use. He could not hobble as quickly as they could run. First he was pushed, then he was trampled, then he was buried.

The guard, wiping his brow, managed to stem the flow only by cursing and yelling. Another colourful body had joined him in wrestling the door shut. Still, dozens of people had swept into the courtyard, all racing past Jack and towards the Scala Regia. In their wake, Bianchi lay crushed and bleeding. No one bothered to turn back to attend the fallen body until the gate was closed and locked again. Then, Jack saw, the first guard jogged over, leant down, and crossed himself.

He smiled.

***

The passageway seemed unending. It rose high above the city. 'Where are we going?' asked Amy.

'This leads, I believe, to the Castel Sant'Angelo.' The old man's breath was coming in laboured gasps. Though she knew he had rested – he had, after all, been given a cell and must have had somewhere to hide all night – she didn't know if he had eaten anything. Besides, he was old and he had been wounded in the shoulder. Their pace since reaching the upper, enclosed walkway had been noticeably slow.

As they tramped along, a breeze began blowing towards them, carrying twilight on its cold breath. Ahead, the passage lightened; as they moved closer, the ceiling gave way to a sky the colour of rose quartz. The walls, too, shortened, becoming crenelated battlements. The sounds of the city became clearer.

But there was another sound too. Stamping boots. Shouts. It was hard to know whether it came from ahead or behind, but it caused her captor to pause. She sensed the arrow waver away from her as he turned, seeking the source.

And she sprang.

Arching her leg, Amy aimed the heel of her boot between the man's legs and with her right hand she drove a thumb into his bandages. She felt him wince, heard him grunt, and saw the arrow slip from his hand. As he staggered backwards, she threw herself down, grabbing the weapon – which was better than nothing – and scuttling ahead.

'Stop where you are.' Moretti's voice came from behind them. Looking like a dead thing himself, the captain advanced, his sword drawn. The old man looked at him and then at Amy. She placed her feet wide apart and held up the arrow.

'I'll kill you,' she said, meaning it. 'I've shot you before. I'll finish you.'

'It seems my revels are ended,' he said, his voice without inflection. He moved, and both Amy and Moretti tensed. But his steps were slow and deliberate. He climbed heavily up onto a crenel, groaning gutturally as he flexed his wounded shoulder, and looked over. 'Ah,' he said looking down at his gnarled hands. 'My own error has brought me to this. I ought to have stayed away and all might have been well. To quote one old Roman, what an artist dies in me. Captain, dear lady, I bid you farewell.'

And he stepped over the edge.

Amy leapt towards the wall and peeped over. As she did so, a collective gasp from the crowds below rose to greet her. It was followed by screams. Sensing Moretti beside her, she turned but said nothing. Together, they looked down into the shade of the elevated passage's walls. It was not a huge drop, but it was enough. The figure of the old man was lying in a widening pool of blood. In a circle around him a crowd had formed. People were looking up, some shouting, some waving.

'Who was he?' asked Amy.

Moretti shrugged, sheathed his sword, and offered her his shirt-sleeved arm. 'I neither know nor care at present. I need my bed.' She took it, and together they began the long walk back to the Vatican, the sound of bells and celebration growing louder with each step.

24

'His name was Agosti. Marcello Agosti. He was not hard to find,' said Moretti. He was seated at the head of a table not in the guardhouse, which had been reclaimed by its commander, but in his own house in Rome. Jack was seated next to him, his thigh tightly bandaged, whilst at the other side of the table Amy was spooning honey into Girolamo's mouth. Every so often pain flared in his leg, but the physicians who had tended the cardinals had seen him. They could not say if he would have a permanent limp, but certainly that he would not lose the leg.

The conclave had broken up. Ugo Boncompagni was the new pope, having been crowned as Gregory XIII, and both the Vatican and Rome had become the centre of an enormous Italian festival of thanksgiving and frivolity. It was, it seemed to Jack, more akin to a king's coronation than a religious festival, and it had been going on for over a week.

'Agosti,' said Jack. It did not fit the strange old man. But, he supposed, he had no idea what might do better.

'A failed artist,' said Moretti, leaning back in his chair. He nodded thanks as a serving woman brought in trenchers of food but continued to speak as they began eating. 'Turned away by every princely house of the Church he sought patronage from. It must have bred in him a great hatred. He was lodging in the city before the conclave. Found easily enough. He did not even trouble to use a false name.'

'No need.' Amy dug her spoon in again as she spoke. 'Why would he if he thought the plot would succeed?' Jack grinned. The body had been displayed and a reward offered in the search for his identity in the week after the conclave.

'How he came to know Bianchi we have no idea. Perhaps the foul apothecary treated him. Yet he was another failure, it seems. Dreamed of being a physician. Turned away from the universities at Bologna, Siena, Turin. More, most likely.'

'Crushed to death,' said Amy. 'I hope it hurt.'

'He was not alone. When those gates were opened after the *accessus*, four more were pressed to death in the crowd. People are warned. They do not listen. But yes, two failures. Agosti, would you believe, wished to paint only the land – scenes of hills and valleys. It is said he refused to paint men, still less to flatter them. And he could never paint again, not with those withering hands. No amount of rue in any decoction would relieve them.

'Bianchi, he had fond and ugly ideas about the movement of blood within the body and wished to overturn the current teaching by cutting live men. No men of reason would employ such creatures as those in either university or religious house. Though they, I little doubt, saw this as the tyrannous Church out to get them. How is the soup?'

'Very good, sir,' said Jack. He was still digesting the information. 'So they were sore at the Church for their own failings?'

'Some men are,' shrugged Moretti.

'Some men can't stand failure,' added Amy. Jack looked at her. The boy's clothes were gone. She had found a hairpiece somewhere in the city and it was attached somehow to the back of her neck, like a knotted bun. She had insisted on it – it was the only way she could appear in public as a woman without having people shun her as lice-ridden. Over the top of her head, covering the cropped section of her own hair, was a gauzy headdress in the Italian style. She had never looked more beautiful, he thought, her cheeks so rosy. He reached across the table and took her free hand.

Moretti smirked before speaking again. 'Some men, indeed, cannot make their way in the world and wish to see it all broken.'

'Where did they get the poison from? Poisoned incense … did they make it?'

'We do not know. Commander von Brunegg thought they were acting on orders from the French,' he said, giving a short, curt laugh. 'If the plot had succeeded, the French cardinals who did not attend the conclave would almost be the only ones left. As the Church crumbled, they might leap onto the throne of St Peter and snatch the papal tiara before it hit the ground. I have convinced him otherwise.'

'How is the commander?' asked Amy.

'Much recovered, without that devil Bianchi feeding him foul potions.'

'You don't mean he poisoned him?'

Moretti shrugged. 'The commander had an upset stomach after we dined together. Bianchi then saw to him and it got worse and worse. I suspect – cannot prove, of course – but suspect that the mad apothecary grasped the opportunity. Not intending to kill the commander, perhaps, but to keep him out of the way. I suppose he imagined the plot might proceed more smoothly if only a distracted captain like me were in charge of security.'

'He said the old man – Agosti – wasn't meant to be there,' said Jack. 'I've been thinking on that. Their whole plot was so … it seemed so …' His Italian fled him. He settled for gestures of exasperation as he said, in English, 'haphazard'. Switching back, he added, 'so much down to chance. To sudden distractions.'

'Yes. When Agosti was found to be there when he should not have been, he gave himself up. Then engineered that they should meet. Bianchi must have been furious. It was a quite simple plan, and none would have suspected a thing if Agosti had not thrust himself into it, made himself a part of it. Just like an artist.'

'And then … I suppose Bianchi promised to get him out of the cell.'

'Or,' Moretti held up a finger, 'wished to speak further with him and did not want anyone knowing of it.'

'So he killed the guard and then … and then …'

'And then they let matters unfold. That is when the distraction began. Making us think there was poison when there was none, and then powder when there was none, and maybe even a gun when they had none. Perhaps they hoped we would find nothing and think the whole thing trickery – at the last we should be content to let matters proceed, never knowing what threat truly lurked. All was ad hoc.'

'Like that robe,' said Jack.

'Hm. Yes. Bianchi knew we were going under the basilica. He was right there inspecting the bodies before we went down.

The robe he must have found during the night and intended for some other purpose. Perhaps to make us think one particular cardinal was threatened. Yet it found better use to make us further suspect a great fire was intended.' He stroked his beard. 'That young fool Pietro was in luck. The pair must have seen him throw away the robe. If he had seen them watching him, he might have had his throat opened too. It makes me think they never intended to kill anyone. Yet Pavesi and ... what was the baker called?'

'Giuseppe,' said Amy.

'Yes. They must have witnessed the two together. They had to be silenced. And so that was worked into the plot. Messy, ugly, but necessary.'

'He'd have killed me too!' Amy snapped. 'I ran, I fought. He'd have killed me too for being out in the night.' She turned, her excited expression giving way to softness as she looked at Girolamo. 'Giro here, he's the real hero. Farm, farm, farm.'

Jack smiled, looking the boy in the face. 'That's the truth. I realised what you were saying when I smelled the herbs that stuck to your dad's uniform. That's when I knew you meant you'd seen Bianchi. You were warning us. Good boy, Giro.' The lad rocked in his seat, and Amy put a hand on his shoulder.

'You did well yourselves,' said Moretti. 'You, Mrs Cole, especially, saved the lives of fifty cardinals. Saved the faith.'

'I ... I didn't really do anything. I just ... when you said that Bianchi had incense in that box, I was right by you. Didn't smell anything. It *looked* like the stuff I'd smelt in the storeroom, but it didn't smell like it. I didn't think anything of it until I saw how quickly you got sick. Weak. And then when I looked at those letters again, the threats of blowing. And I remembered the old devil said something about being in the air we breathed. It was a guess.'

'A damned good one.'

'I only knew for sure when I saw the little serving lad with the priests was carrying the same box. What happened to it anyway?'

'It will be examined,' said Moretti, evidently not liking that subject.

'Devil,' said Jack, softly.

'What's that?' This was Moretti again, who paused with a piece of oil-soaked bread halfway to this mouth.

'All that … stuff with the exorcism. It was all false. Agosti tricked the bishop. Fooled us all.'

'Hm. Yet,' began the captain, looking ruminatively at the bread before putting it down. 'I have been thinking on that myself. And I wonder…'

'It's not good for the faith,' said Jack. 'Makes it all look false. Foolish. A fantasy.'

'Does it? Agosti might or might not have been possessed by some devil or other.' Jack looked at him. Moretti was still staring down at the table, as though not really seeing it. Eventually he met Jack's gaze. 'Something causes men to do evil. We might say he was disappointed in his life, that he bore a grudge. And we might be right. But at some point, I think, the vessel of man fills with a taint of wickedness that turns a grudge into action. Into evil. I think the devil is as good a name for that … whatever it is … as anything else.'

'But the exorcism didn't work,' Jack persisted.

'Did it not?'

'Go on,' Amy prompted. Jack could feel her gaze on him. He knew she had no interest in religion. For the briefest second, he had the impression that she was willing Moretti to make him feel better because he did. And he loved her for it all the more.

The captain cleared his throat. 'It might be that exorcisms are not for the possessed, not for the wicked, at all. They are for us. A test of our faith.'

'How do you mean?'

'I saw the bishop as you did. He became like another man. Altogether changed. There was something alight within him. And I confess I found myself willing his prayers to work. I believed in it all. I could see the magic, the … the metamorphosis. Whatever Agosti was, I saw faith work miracles in that room. Even in my own mind, I believed. Perhaps,' he added, a little self-consciously, 'that is what such rituals do. They affirm our faith.'

'Perhaps,' said Jack. He felt he had half understood.

'And perhaps Agosti was an empty vessel from which the devil – or the evil – could not be driven. When he abjured all religion and welcomed blasphemy, he lost any soul he had had. I cannot say. I am a simple soldier, not a divine. And you two simple servants. But welcome any time at my table.' He raised his cup. 'To us, and to the new Holy Father. To Gregory XIII!'

'To Gregory XIII' they repeated, raising their own. Girolamo banged the table in excitement.

'Will he be a good pope?' asked Amy.

'There are only good popes.' Moretti gave another smile. 'And they all need stout protection. Well, he should have an interest in your nation. They say the French dowager wishes her son wed to Elizabeth. And the other queen in England, the charming Mary of Scotland – perhaps the new Holy Father will give her support beyond the spiritual. The last, God rest him, was said to have aided her little after she married a heretic. What we need now is a militant pope, a pope who will fight the Turk as well as heresy.' His voice had turned commanding. Amy, however, had frozen and made a face at the mention of Mary Queen of Scots, as she always did. Moretti, to his credit, seemed to realise it, and swiftly changed the subject. 'What is next for you both – will you find work in the city?'

Jack felt Amy's eyes on him. Moretti seemed to sense tension. He coughed. 'If you would be good enough to excuse me.' He started to rise. 'No, please, stay. Eat. I will put Girolamo to bed. Come, son.'

As they left the table, Amy stood and kissed each on the cheek. To Jack's surprise, Moretti blushed. 'Mr Cole, you have a beautiful wife,' he said, before taking his son by the hand and exiting quickly.

When they were alone, Jack said, 'that was good. A good dinner. Good people. It was like being part of a family.'

'Yes,' said Amy. She nudged her chair close to his. 'But they're not our family, Jack. We're our family. She moved his hand to her stomacher. And it's time to find us a home.'

He leant in and kissed her.

EPILOGUE

<u>Paris, August 1572</u>

They had a long wait. Seated on a rough wooden bench outside Francis Walsingham's office, Jack sitting on his hands and Amy's clasped over her swollen stomach, they watched as men filed in and out, their faces grim. The Paris they had returned to was in uproar, gangs roaming the streets, shouting and swearing at one another. It made a queer sort preparation for the feast day that would fall the next day. The news cast about was that some Protestant leader or other had been shot, the bullet blowing off his finger. Amy had begun crying at the news, not, she said, because she cared – but because it was clear that there would never be any escape from the terror that seemed to be swallowing up the whole world. Scotland, she had said, Italy, France – there was no such thing as safety. It would be a relief to return to the ordinary troubles of England – if Walsingham would let them. They had agreed on how to present themselves on the long journey from Italy.

More footsteps. Jack was surprised to see a tiny face dominated by enormous eyes appear at the head of the stairs: a girl of about five, dressed and corseted like a miniature lady. She regarded them solemnly, saying nothing. Jack nudged Amy, who emerged from her doze, before crossing his eyes and sticking out his tongue. He regretted it instantly. The little girl did not laugh but somehow managed to look disapproving.

'Mistress Frances,' hissed a shrill voice. A stout governess in a white cap hove into view as she clattered up the staircase. The woman looked at Jack and Amy, clearly measuring up their importance. Taking in their cheap, weather- and mud-battered clothing, she frowned and spoke again to the child. 'I've told you time and again, don't be bothering your pa's … your pa. Come, child. Now.' She began descending. The child started to follow, pausing only briefly to turn, stare directly at Jack, and stick out her little pink tongue.

At that moment the door to Walsingham's chamber opened. 'About bloody time,' said Amy, not troubling to lower her voice as Jack helped her to her feet. A dull throb echoed in his leg and they leant upon one another. As they hobbled into the room, Jack saw that it was not Walsingham who admitted them, but a boy of his own height, fair-haired and very young looking. The lad's chin was held high. 'Mr Walsingham,' he said, his voice weighted with affected solemnity, 'will see you.'

They entered.

Walsingham's study was an oasis of order in the brash and rocking sea of Paris. Its master, however, looked greyer than Jack had ever seen him. He did not, at first, invite them to sit, until he caught sight of Amy's belly. Then he pursed his lips and relented. Yet still he said nothing, the only sound in the room a ticking clock. It was getting late. Eventually, the boy in the room gave a discreet cough. The secretary looked at him with just a trace of irritation. 'My guest,' he said at last, 'Sir Philip Sidney. Member of Parliament for Shrewsbury.' The boy's chest exploded outwards as he assumed a military stance against a bookcase covered in neatly arranged volumes.

'Good day, Sir Philip,' smiled Jack. Sidney did not respond.

'It has been,' said Walsingham, letting the coldness of his voice chill the room, 'some time since you creatures troubled me last. And in that long space you have delivered me no news. In fact, I had imagined you both dead. Am I to understand that this sudden appearance means you want something, or have you come to inform against the madman who shot the admiral?'

In fact, Jack and Amy had run out on him. But, thought Jack, that was not something he was likely to admit in front of a guest. He looked at Amy, who gave the briefest of nods, before he continued. 'We have news now, Mr Walsingham.'

'Of Admiral Coligny's attacker?'

'No, sir. Of the papal election in May. The conclave.'

'What?' Walsingham's mask slipped and allowed the briefest glimpse of confusion and interest. 'That was some months ago. The world knows whom the false priests chose as their bishop. Your news is stale.'

'Yes, sir. But we were there – we were in service. We saw terrible things. Things,' he added, 'that won't be in any reports.' Walsingham's tongue darted over his thin lips.

'Sir Philip, would you be so good as to take a pen and paper?' The boy did so, scraping a chair over to the desk and sitting, pen poised. 'No, dear boy, do not lean over it so – sit upright, lest your humours fall down to your forehead. That way lies strain of the eyes.' Sidney reddened, but resumed his rigid stance as he began to write. Briefly, Jack wondered at the relationship between the unlikely pair. Then he realised he didn't care. 'Now, Cole. Tell me all that has passed. Omit nothing.'

Jack poured out the story, only pausing when Amy reminded him of certain points or when Walsingham stopped him and requested clarification. Throughout, he emphasised the foreignness of the players, what a bewildering world it all was to his and Amy's simple English eyes. Two things seemed to dominate the secretary's interest: what was said about England and its queen upstairs, and the nature of the poison downstairs.

'The whole papist rabble should have been left to kill one another,' said Sidney, apparently animated by all the talk of soldiers and death.

'Now, Sir Philip,' said Walsingham, condescension heavy, 'I should like to see the tyranny of Rome ended as much as you. But never this way. Such a monstrous enterprise would have made martyrs of the slain cardinals. It would have raised the world in arms. Those of our true faith would have the blame. By my truth, we should have similar plots aimed at our queen and her council if this madness had succeeded.'

'Yes, Mr Walsingham,' said an abashed Sidney, his head lowering. 'It would have been dishonourable to let such a thing happen. I misspoke. It is for the people to see the errors of Rome and rise against it as one. It is not for madmen to make mischief.' He glanced over at the elder man.

'Well said.'

Hoping to take advantage of the talk of seeing errors, Jack added, staring at the polished desk, 'I saw that in choosing a … a bishop of Rome … the cardinals there served an earthly master rather than God. Or a Holy Spirit.'

'I might have said this to you,' said Walsingham. He grimaced. 'I ever knew the Catholic rabble to be corrupt and venal. But all this foolish deceit – and now they aim at our friends in this city.' Spots of colour rose in his pallid features and fire raged at the edges of his voice. Jack had never seen Walsingham so animated about the faith. Something seemed to be hardening in him. 'And the filthy papists claim this Holy Spirit acts through their actions. Superstitious fools.'

Jack thought that they might have been right in that - at any rate as right as Walsingham, who believed God had chosen a barren old woman to rule England. Whatever he said to the spymaster, whatever doubts had risen in his mind about the Roman religion and its leaders, he still trusted Walsingham's stark faith even less. The Catholics, at least, had the value of antiquity, however worldly the men who governed the Church now. The Church of Rome had lasted. If what was unfolding on the streets of Paris was any indication, the new religion might not. 'I understand,' frowned Walsingham, 'the new bishop of Rome has a bastard son. There is a whelp will find his way in this world paved with riches and reward.' Jack did not add that the son, about whom much of Europe was talking, had been born before the pope had even become a priest. It would not do to mention that now.

He swallowed, feeling his heart begin to speed. 'And so ... so now we're thinking right about the faith, Mr Walsingham, we'd like ...' he swallowed again, 'to go back to England. If you can get us there.'

Walsingham exchanged a look with Sidney. 'Times are unsettled,' he said. 'You cannot have failed to notice. Why should I give you aid?'

'But we've told you all this,' said Amy. Jack tried to silence her with a look. 'That poison, we've told you all about it. Now you can be sure to write back and – and tell the queen's men to be careful of such stuff. Her Majesty Queen Elizabeth must be safe from it, mustn't she?' Jack fought a smirk. She knew, as Jack did, where the old man's weak spot lay.

'This woman,' said Sidney, setting down his pen, 'is with child.' All eyes turned to him. 'Mr Walsingham, it would not stand on our honour to refuse such a creature. With your leave, I should vote to release them back into England.'

'Bless you, sir. I confess I'd like our child to be born a good

English one.' She turned doe eyes on him. 'I'd like that ever so much.'

The closest thing to amusement Jack had yet seen crossed Walsingham's wan face. It faded as quickly as it had appeared. 'You have a stout heart, dear boy. I was minded to do so myself. Write the appropriate letters, would you?' Sidney did not smile but began furiously writing on a fresh sheet of paper. Walsingham turned, now shark-like, to them. 'I will admit to you both, I have my doubts. Yet I would rather you were in England and well protected than cast abroad and friendless.'

The threat was clear. They could return to England, but they would be watched, spied on, followed. Possibly it would be for the rest of their lives – or at least for the rest of Walsingham's.

The door behind them banged open. A messenger entered, his hair and eyes wild. He carried on him the smells of the street – horse muck, sweat, and trouble. 'Mr Walsingham!' He looked around the room. 'Danger. A great tumult is rising.'

Walsingham stood, as Sidney slid the papers across the desk. 'Go out, would you?' He took the pen from his young guest's hand and added his signature to the paper, before writing something else along the top. 'A ship – out of Harfleur. It is well trusted. Its crewmen are my friends. They have good eyes and ears. Now get you gone. I should get out of the town,' he added with something approaching a pained smile, 'tonight. Before St Bartholomew's Day devours the place in revelry on the morrow.'

They were all but pushed out of the room as Walsingham and Sidney began pummelling the messenger with questions. Leaving Walsingham's house, Jack and Amy clasped hands and began making their way through the congested streets of Paris, oblivious to the cries and screams that began erupting around them. They were traitors to England no longer. They were going home.

AUTHOR'S NOTE

The papal conclave which elected Pope Gregory XIII following the death of Pius V was an extremely short one, lasting only from May 12th to May 13th. As shown in the novel, Cardinal Granvelle, Viceroy of Naples and a creature of Philip II of Spain (once married to 'Bloody' Mary Tudor) entered almost as the gates of the Vatican were locked. His sudden arrival put paid to the hopes of Cardinal Farnese – allegedly, he produced a letter blocking Farnese's candidacy 'this time'. I relied on a number of sources for the politics of the 1572 conclave, including Frederic J. Baumgartner's *Behind Locked Doors: A History of the Papal Elections* (2003: Palgrave Macmillan). This was especially useful in providing an insight into the workings of conclaves in the period, particularly with regard to the numbers of staff and servants allowed each cardinal. To my surprise and delight, contemporary complaints focused on how leaky conclaves were despite rules on secrecy, with servants taking bets and voting intentions scrawled in chalk on the underside of meal trays taken in and out of the cardinals' quarters. Even whilst the cardinals remained immured, people were coming and going with meals, news, and gossip – and those outside the city were invariably well up-to-date with the progress of the runners and riders. Crucial also was Michael Walsh's *The Conclave: A Sometimes Secret and Occasionally Bloody History of Papal Elections* (2003: Canterbury Press). For information on the papal household, Deborah L. Krohn's *Food and Knowledge in Renaissance Italy* (2015: Routledge) was a great help. One interesting figure I did not include in the story was Monsignor Cornelio Firmano, the papal master of ceremonies, whose diaries exist in manuscript in the Vatican library. I split the role he would have had between the real-life figures of Bishop Bernardino Cirillo and Pius V's *maestro di camera*, Alessandro Casale, reckoning that a surfeit of priests (papal households and officers numbered dozens) would have been tedious. For the same reason I minimised the role of Cardinal Cornaro, who officiated as camerlengo.

A number of factors influenced the election, not least of which was 1571's Battle of Lepanto, in which papal forces had won a victory over the Turkish fleet. Captain Moretti and his son are fictional, but a small company of the pontifical Swiss Guard fought aboard the flagship of the fleet during the battle. For information on the smallest army in the world, see Eamon Duffy's *Saints and Sinners: A History of the Popes* (2002: Yale University Press) and Robert Royal's *The Pope's Army: 500 Years of the Papal Swiss Guard* (2006: Crossroad). Joost von Brunegg was, indeed, the commander of the Swiss Guard. I have found no record of what he did during the conclave but should add that having him chained to a privy with a dodgy stomach throughout is pure fiction.

The geographical layout of the Vatican in 1572 was impossible to reconstruct with absolute accuracy, due to the constant state of construction and reconstruction that went on throughout the sixteenth and seventeenth centuries. Indeed, the beautiful circular plaza which stands today, as well as the basilica with its splendid frontage and dome, were not yet built, and many of the interiors we might be familiar with today were either incomplete or have been moved. I have sought to present the Holy See as it might have looked halfway between sketches from 1509 and the 1580s, conscious, of course, that each new papacy brought more building and rebuilding. I can only apologise for any errors in geography. Interestingly, a painted image does survive in the *Codex Maggi*, depicting a stylised view of Pius V's conclave. It is notable especially for showing the uniform of the Swiss Guard as it was in the period. For information on the Vatican throughout the ages, I would recommend Sonia Gallico's *Vatican* (1999: ATS Italia) and Ellen Schulz's *The Vatican Collections: The Papacy and Art* (1982: Harry N. Abrams). I also enjoyed and made use of Benjamin Blech and Roy Doliner's provocative *The Sistine Secrets: Unlocking the Codes in Michelangelo's Defiant Masterpiece* (2008: JR Books). Their discussion of The Last Judgement is particularly interesting. The Sistine Chapel was, upon its initial construction, the site of conclaves, but as the number of cardinals taking part swelled in the sixteenth century, it was no longer able to provide sleeping spaces for them all.

Dormitory buildings were constructed in front of the chapel and Sala Regia, though these have long since vanished. I have attempted to place them where they would have stood, but their layout and interiors are products of imagination. Likewise, I could find no record of how the cardinals moved from these dormitories to the chapel; it is possible that they went directly through a door from their cell block and into the Sala Regia. However, I found the idea of a procession along the longer route provided greater spectacle more in keeping with the occasion.

No exorcism took place in the Vatican during the 1572 conclave, but exorcisms did, in fact, take place with regularity throughout the Renaissance. I am hugely indebted to Gaetano Praxia's *The Devil's Scourge: Exorcism During the Italian Renaissance* (2002: Weiser Books). This fascinating must-read is a translation, with introduction and commentary, of famed sixteenth-century exorcist Girolamo Menghi's guide to assessing potential victims of possession and then, just as interestingly, how to go about exorcising them. I confess that I picked and chose words and prayers from the seven different rituals provided in the text according to which I found the most appealing. Of course, all books which feature the procedure (or ritual, or practice) owe much to the late William Peter Blatty's blockbuster novel *The Exorcist* (1971: Harper & Row). However, I would encourage anyone who hasn't to check out his follow-up novel, *Legion* (1983: Simon and Schuster), which follows the progress of the original novel's Lieutenant Kinderman (memorably played by Lee J. Cobb in the 1972 movie) as he attempts to solve a series of murders linked to the original exorcism of Regan MacNeil. It is one of the scariest books I've ever read (and reread and reread). I am probably too cynical about the whole notion of demonic possession. Blatty is not, and his books are all the more terrifying and thought-provoking for it.

There were also no plots to assassinate the college of cardinals during the real conclave – or at least none that have been recorded. Poisoned incense, however, did exist – as I learnt from Eleanor Herman's *The Royal Art of Poison* (2018: Prelude Books). Murderous monks allegedly concocted it, although there is no record of it ever being put to use (one wonders where it was intended for use and on whom!). It was certainly known to early modern dramatists: Thomas Middleton employed it in the tragedy *Women Beware Women*.

In terms of real-life bloodshed, Jack and Amy leave Walsingham as the infamous St Bartholomew's Day Massacre, which began late on the eve of the feast day, is about to unfold. Walsingham and a young Sir Philip Sidney (a Protestant hero and poet of considerable skill, whose sonnet sequence *Astrophil and Stella* I had to torture students with for years) were indeed present in town during the outbreak of hideous violence. Excited to fever pitch by the shooting and subsequent murder of Huguenot leader Admiral Coligny, Catholics began murdering Protestants across the city in a hideous orgy of indiscriminate violence. Walsingham and Sidney provided shelter at the former's home, which functioned as the English embassy, for those who sought refuge from the horror. The best biography of Sidney is Katherine Duncan-Jones' *Sir Philip Sidney* (1994: Oxford University Press). Accounts of the massacre can be found in Arlette Jouanna's *The Saint Bartholomew's Day Massacre: The Mysteries of a Crime of State* (2016: Manchester University Press) and Barbara B. Diefendorf's *The St. Bartholomew's Day Massacre: A Brief History with Documents* (2008: St Martin's Press). Whether Jack and Amy Cole survived the slaughter, which stains Paris' tumultuous history, I don't know. I hope they do.

If you enjoyed this bloody twenty-fours spent in the Vatican, please let me know on Twitter @ScrutinEye or on Instagram: steven.veerapen.3

*

Printed in Great Britain
by Amazon

69328291R00151